THE ROOM
BY THE LAKE

EMMA DIBDIN grew up in Oxford
and now lives in New York. She is a
writer and journalist whose work has
appeared in *Esquire*, *Marie Claire*,
Harper's Bazaar, *Cosmopolitan*
and *Total Film*. Her father was the
bestselling crime writer Michael
Dibdin. This is her first novel.

THE
ROOM
BY
THE
LAKE

EMMA DIBDIN

HEAD
of ZEUS

First published in 2017 by Head of Zeus, Ltd.

9 7 5 3 1 2 4 6 8

A catalogue record for this book is available from
the British Library.

ISBN (HB): 9781786694027
ISBN (XTPB): 9781786694034
ISBN (E): 9781786694010

Typeset by Adrian McLaughlin

Printed and bound in Great Britain by
CPI Group (UK) Ltd, Croydon CR0 4YY

Head of Zeus Ltd
First Floor East
5–8 Hardwick Street
London EC1R 4RG

WWW.HEADOFZEUS.COM

For my parents, *sine qua non*.

CHAPTER ONE

New York, new start, New York, new start, I repeat to myself like a slogan as the 1 train screeches hard around a bend. It's not rush hour but the subway is still full, horizontal sardines packed together from Penn Station onwards, and I wonder whether anyone on board can tell that I have no destination. Here for the ride.

I stay on until the very last stop, watching the carriage grow gradually empty, and at Van Cortlandt Park I cross over the platform and wait for a train back downtown. A roundtrip, one end of the line to the other. And why not? The subway is soothing, the 123 line in particular because it has electronic screens listing when the next train is coming, and I like my environment to be predictable. Maybe tomorrow I'll tackle the 2 train, all the way from the Bronx down to the farthest reaches of Brooklyn, its distance mind-boggling even when scaled down to fit onto an MTA map. The subway is cheap, after all, and I'm broke.

The platform is deserted, and it strikes me I'm a very long way from anywhere. This is the Bronx, unchartered territory for a tourist, and though my surroundings look leafy and harmless maybe going to the end of the line was a bad idea. Maybe something will happen to me here.

I know that in thinking this I'm only echoing my cab driver from JFK, who whiled away the drive with ominous nuggets like 'girl like you should watch your back in the city' and 'whatever you do, don't go east of Prospect Park' and 'nothing good happens past a hundred and tenth'. Right before he forced me to write down his number and told me to call him if I got lonely.

Nothing happens to me in the Bronx. Nothing happens to me on the train back downtown, and when I finally emerge at South Ferry I feel deflated, robbed of the false purpose that roundtrip gave me.

I need a job. After putting it off for as long as I could, this morning I finally sat down cross-legged on my hotel quilt and counted my remaining cash, crumpled dollar bills laid out corner-to-corner like a bleak mosaic. Adding up the cash with the figure on the ATM receipt, I have enough to get me through another two weeks, if I eat only two meals a day and don't run up any more $60 tabs in moments of ostentatious desperation. I spent last night in a sparse midtown bar, the kind of place that seems sleek and empty even at its most crowded, feeling like this was the thing to do as a single girl alone in New York. Getting steadily more drunk, half-hoping that one of the sharp-suited Wall Street types would make a move, half-terrified of the same.

If one of them did buy me a drink and take me back to

a high-rise apartment that feels closer to cloud than ground, the kind that envelops you in space and silence, I could stay the night and maybe stay forever, and my memory of home would fade like the street noise below, just faint enough to be soothing.

But nobody approached me, and I wandered back to my no-frills solo-traveller-friendly hotel at the very tip of downtown Manhattan, and watched *Good Will Hunting* on Netflix until I fell into five hours of twitchy sleep.

And now I have a stack of CVs and a head full of caffeine, and I'm trying to get a job against the odds. I have thought none of this through.

'You Australian?' the barista asks. She's chubby in that uniquely wholesome, self-confident American way, the kind of girl who could say 'There's just more of me to love,' with a straight face. She wears a name badge that tells me she's Marcie.

'English,' I answer. People always guess Australian. My accent morphs involuntarily when I'm in America, probably betraying my desperation to belong.

'Cool. We're actually not hiring right now, they just made cutbacks.'

'Oh. Sorry.'

'Yeah,' Marcie shrugs. 'But I'm still here, so.'

'You think anywhere nearby's likely to be hiring?'

'You might have better luck in Brooklyn, I feel like there's more new places opening up over there. Bed-Stuy, Crown Heights maybe? Around here's pretty static.'

I nod, trying to look unfazed. This is the fourth variation on the same conversation I've had this morning.

'I can take a copy of your résumé anyway, keep it on file if you want?'

'That'd be great.'

We both know this is not the kind of place where anything is kept on file. I order a flat white because it seems like what you order here, and slide my CV across the counter like the afterthought it already is.

'You live out here?' It takes me a second to realize she's talking to me, her back turned as she wrestles espresso from a gleaming, steaming machine.

'No, I live in London, I'm just here for the summer. Staying with family,' I lie.

'I'd love to go to London someday.'

'You should, it's an amazing city.'

I have a sudden impulse to invite her to stay with me, back home. Life feels like it's simple for this girl, not because she's stupid but because she has an inherent confidence in her own worth, a belief that the world has enough in it for her. But I no longer have a home, in London or anywhere else. Just a house where my dad lives, for however much longer he lives.

'Have you always lived in New York?' I ask.

'No, I'm from North Carolina. I moved out here for college, and after I dropped out I just stuck around. I'm a total city girl now, can't imagine living back there.'

I watch her create a perfect leaf shape in the foam atop my coffee, her mouth screwed over to one side in concentration.

'So what family do you have out here?'

'My dad. He remarried and moved here a few years back,' I say, almost without thinking. Why not? This could be true.

'I come out here most summers. He lives in Tribeca. He's a photographer, so he's got a studio space downstairs and then the flat upstairs.'

'Is it weird? Seeing him with his new wife?'

This is the kind of intimate question that just doesn't get asked after four minutes of small talk back home. I'm enjoying it.

'It was tricky at first, you know, adjusting to him having this whole other life. But we're pretty close, so now I just try to be grateful that I get to spend time with him.'

She nods, but there's another customer behind me waiting to be served, and the moment is gone.

I spend the afternoon wandering the streets of Manhattan with false purpose, ballet flats slap-slapping the pavement with every step in a rhythm that's almost soothing. Trendy Tribeca is not what I expected, dusty and flat and choked with scaffolding, faded graffiti on construction boards, dark restaurants with papered-up windows promising a brunch they clearly haven't served in a while. One bar is offering a Happy Hour, which looks like grounds for false advertising. It's a pretty bleak scene, all in all.

I've always been sensitive to aesthetics, as my mum charitably put it. The right kind of ugly building or barren suburban street can leave me almost nauseous, and as a child I refused to look directly at one house at the end of our street for this reason. Number 11, a squat bungalow, its facade brown cottage cheese, its dark windows gaping like a malevolent stare. Melodramatic, but I was only seven. What's my excuse now?

I walk until West Broadway turns into Fifth Avenue – not

into Broadway, I was startled to realize on my second day. The buildings grow taller, shabby-chic giving way to gloss and chain stores after the brief leafy respite of Washington Square, and though I've never been here before it's all familiar. Instead of feeling smothered by the vertical pressure of granite and glass on either side, I feel safe, enveloped by infrastructure and thick city air.

I pause to check my reflection against an impossibly bright glass building, and it's less of a disappointment than I expect. When I first arrived in the city the humidity was unbearable, my hair in a permanent state of frizzy revolt, but now it hangs calmly at my shoulders and I can pass for put-together. Even my skin seems improved, though this may be a trick of the tinted window. I should not have worn tights with this dress – they look wrong in the sunlight, too opaque, but bare legs are a struggle for me. Though I have not been overweight in years, thanks to some borderline-disordered eating I coaxed myself into before university, I still suspect that somehow people can tell when they look at me, at my legs in particular. She's faking it, I imagine them thinking, as though my thinness is newly acquired and therefore discountable, as easily lost as it was gained. *Nouveau thin.*

In Times Square I stop, underwhelmed. I should have come here at night, as my *Time Out* guidebook suggested. It's Piccadilly Circus on steroids, all metal and negative space and people swarming to look at nothing. There's a building that says 'New York Police Dept', positively shouts it in neon pink and blue, and I have to look very, very hard at it to work out whether it's a police station or the entrance to a Broadway show. Things are weird here.

I keep walking up Seventh Avenue, past banks and bodegas and theatres that look sad and bleached-out by day, until I hit Central Park. After hours of walking on a grid, the less regimented angles of the park are almost alarming, and I wander in a daze that's not so much wide-eyed wonder as wide-eyed panic. For a second, my mental defences fail, and I'm overcome by the question of what the hell I'm doing here, in this city where I know nobody and nobody knows me. Getting the tube to Heathrow and spontaneously flying to New York is beyond out of character. But standing in the tube station on Saturday night, salt tracks drying on my cheeks and passport stuffed hastily into my pocket, running this far felt suddenly obvious.

I pass families, dog-walkers, runners, and distract myself by coming up with a backstory for each of them, none of them happy. This woman is a seasoned runner with ongoing food issues: she used to compulsively over-eat and now she runs 10ks and lifts weights and counts out her grams of daily protein to feed the same craving for control.

That man offered to dog-sit for his pretty neighbour, the one he's always hoped he might have a shot with, but he actually hates animals, which is why he looks so uncomfortable with the leash. The corgis seem to resent him too, yapping and straining against their collars as he tries to drag them back onto the footpath.

This woman got pregnant by accident: she kept it because she was in her thirties and it seemed like time, but she has never longed for a child and now will always wonder how her life would have been different had she aborted.

My internal monologue is getting bleaker by the minute,

so I stand on the terrace beside the Bethesda Fountain and watch the water instead of the people, and try not to think about anything.

New York, new start, yes, but why New York? On the tube to Heathrow I'd had a romantic notion of looking up at the departures board and picking a place at random, but this was the only destination I ever really had in mind. I've never been here before. No one in my family has been here before, as far as I know. My concept of New York is a charismatic jigsaw made up from fragments of pop culture and my own imagination. I could have gone to Paris or Florence or Berlin, where the language barrier would at least have given me an excuse to isolate myself. I could have gone to Budapest, where my mum spent what she always called the best three years of her life. I could have run anywhere in Europe, except that none of it was far away enough.

There's rage in the streets here, a general thrum of aggression powering the city through its never-sleeping existence. Earlier I saw a cab drive straight through a red light, side-swiping a cyclist who smashed his palm hard against the driver's side window, hitting the car again as it drove on past him, screaming '*Are you fucking serious?*' Nobody around me gave the scene a second look. I assume I'll get used to sights like this, just as the constant car horns have become like white noise.

The roads and pavements are all wide, the grid system laid out in vast, greedy swathes of right angles, and I'm reminded of colouring books and how I never, ever went outside the lines. How I cried after Natalie Bickers elbowed me while I was colouring in a tree once, my crayon zigzagging into the white and ruining the picture. I've been dreaming of kindergarten a lot this week.

Coming to New York for a new start on a visa waiver might be the stupidest, because I know perfectly well that I can't get a job here, can't even stay for more than three months. When the border official at JFK asked how long I planned to stay in the US, I told him my flight home leaves on 10th August, a flight I booked with no intention of taking. For once in my life, I'm refusing to think things through too much.

'You've had a tough couple of years,' the university counsellor told me, a box of tissues placed pointedly on the table between us. I should be crying, the subtext says. The fact that I'm not is suspect, maybe monstrous.

'Sure.' I'd promised myself I wouldn't be snappy, not with this one, but it was better than the alternative of not speaking at all. 'Could be worse.'

'The death of a parent is one of the most profound losses a person can suffer. At your age, all the more so.'

'High up on the stressful life event scale, yeah. Can I ask something?'

'Of course, Caitlin.'

'What would you say to someone who's not only mourning the death of a parent, but sort of mourning the fact that the wrong parent died?'

She didn't flinch, but I liked to think I blindsided her at least for a second. I knew I should feel disloyal to my dad, and horrified by the idea of my mum looking down from wherever and hearing me say it, but all I felt in that moment was satisfaction, like I'd finally grasped something I hadn't dared to reach for before.

It's the same satisfaction I feel now at the thought that maybe, just maybe, my dad will have sobered up for long enough to wonder where I am. Maybe even tried to call. What happens when you call a phone that has been thrown into the canal? Does it go straight to voicemail? Can the network tell when a SIM card is waterlogged?

I'd left a voicemail with my aunt Chloe and another with my best friend Sophie: clipped, utilitarian messages designed solely as insurance. I'm fine, I'm going away, don't try to contact me and don't report me as missing. I don't want to give him a reason to turn this into a police procedural.

I just want to stay. In this lonely five days in New York I've been as low and high as I ever have, miserable and exhilarated, drunk on freedom and fear and the city's collective, propulsive desire for *more*. In these streets where anger hums in the air, where cars keep driving straight towards you as you cross on a corner, where there's no real expectation that you're safe. Here, I can imagine dying, or else living forever.

CHAPTER TWO

As soon as I walk into the house that Friday night, my last night in London, I know I should leave.

I'll never know exactly what it was about the hallway – the piles of post on the sideboard, neglected for months, the jumble of boots and trainers by the door making a mockery of the shoe rack, the way mundane objects felt overgrown – that gave me pause. Nausea in the pit of my stomach, buried like a bullet. The faint sound of opera reaches me, muffled by walls and a door ajar, and I lean hard against the front door as it closes behind me.

'Hello? Dad?'

He's sitting in his armchair, *The New Grove Dictionary of Opera* open on his lap, and he looks so familiar and comforting and appropriate that something young in me wants to run to him. Curl up at his side and let him read to me about a favourite aria or a composer's biography, not because I have any interest in opera but because he does, and because I will remember this moment as something true. The knot in my stomach dares to loosen, until I see the glass. Stashed clumsily behind the leg of the side table, empty, because he drained it in a hurry.

We'd had a real afternoon together earlier in the week, a walk around Hampstead Heath, starting at the south-west entrance and skirting the edge of Parliament Hill, passing the ponds as the ground sloped gently upwards.

'I really feel different about it this time, darling,' he'd said to me as we passed the model boating pond, heading up towards Hampstead Gate and the dense, soothing forestry beyond. 'When I think about drinking now, it just feels like some kind of nightmare. What the hell was I thinking, you know?'

I held onto these words like salt and threw them hard over my shoulder, and dared not to worry about him for an entire day afterwards.

Back in the living room, my voice is high and thin as I ask, 'What are you drinking?'

'Nothing.'

Almost worse than the lying itself is how bad he is at it. I need to brace for a fight but I'm just too tired, the weight of nausea in my stomach anchoring me in place. I want to join him in his denial, but I can't do that either, not this time.

'What are you drinking?'

'I just said, darling, nothing.'

'Yes you are. Dad, I can see the glass, okay?'

He looks slowly down at it, back at me, and I can see the lie failing to form, the wheels turning so slowly. It had made him so dull, the drinking, his once-sharp mind blunted.

'You're not fooling anyone.'

'How dare you?' he snaps, and suddenly he's not slow any more. A live wire has been sparked and his eyes are wild, and he's so far away from me now.

'Dad—'

'You don't speak to me that way,' he says. 'You've always been disrespectful. I didn't realize it for so long, but with everything happening with your mother, I just saw what I wanted to in you.'

It shouldn't sting any more, this whiplash shift. My nails are pressing hard into my palms.

'I'm stating facts, Dad.'

'Stating facts? Well, yeah, you've always been good at that, good brain. Pity about your spine.'

'What's that even supposed to mean?'

'Don't pretend you don't know, you little creep.'

I mentally recite the Google results I had spent whole evenings poring over, trying to remember all of the statistics about relapse and withdrawal. All that comes back to me are the facts about long-term liver damage, the early symptoms of cirrhosis, and how death has been hanging over this house for such a long time.

'You know what the doctor told you,' I manage, my throat closing up. He stares at me, eyes less wild now than cold, all affect gone.

I'm halfway up the stairs before I know what I'm doing, and in my room I throw clothes into my battered suitcase, grabbing toiletries with a rat-a-tat list of essentials ringing in my head. Toothbrush. Razor. Passport. Leave. Leave. Leave.

I look around the room and don't feel anything, not even

as I look at the childhood teddy bears I used to love so much. All I want is out, and I have just enough resolve left to get me there. As I'm locking my case with steady hands I think I hear him in the doorway and turn, fists tight again. But he's passed my door, going to his study, a room that has not earned its name in months.

And a minute later, I'm back out in the night air, gasping because I've been holding my breath for minutes on end, or maybe that house is just airless. And when I reach the canal almost an hour later, I throw my phone in with such force I think my body may follow.

I'm back at the coffee shop.

'Hey!' Marcie says, either startled or pleased, and I force myself not to over-analyse. 'You came back!'

'Yeah,' I grin, trying to seem anything but desperate and dark. 'Just did a massive loop of Central Park and kind of ended up where I started.'

'Did you see the fountain?'

'Yeah! So beautiful.'

'They filmed *Gossip Girl* there,' she says proudly. 'That scene in the first season where Blair forgives Serena, and it's raining, that's right there. Have you seen it?'

I nod. *Gossip Girl* and its glossy lunacy has played a substantial role in my image of New York as a place where even pain holds glamorous possibility.

'I went to watch them shoot sometimes. It wasn't a closed set or anything, they used to shoot all over town and you could just watch. Ed Westwick looked right at me one time.'

I nod and smile enthusiastically, because I'm so hoping that this anecdote means we're bonding. She seems like the kind of person who likes to be listened to and doesn't need much in return. Maybe we can get a drink this evening, and I can remind myself what it's like to converse.

'Well, I'm taking off,' Marcie chirps, half to me and half to her disinterested bearded manager. 'Meeting some friends over in Meatpacking.'

'Have fun! What's Meatpacking?'

'It's downtown, right on the highway near the Village. Lots of bars, but it's kind of a clubby vibe, if that's your thing.'

'Cool. Cool.'

'Do you go out a lot in London?'

'Yeah, I love it. The east is great, Shoreditch and Dalston, and there's a few places I like in Kensington, near where I grew up.'

I don't even sound like myself. I have no concept of what the nightlife is or isn't like in Kensington. I hate Shoreditch. But I'm enjoying being this subtly obnoxious person, a trust fund baby with Daddy in Tribeca and Mummy in a Holland Park mansion.

'Is it super expensive there?'

'Oh yeah. I don't know how it compares to New York, but it's pricey.'

'I'm totally still adjusting to Manhattan prices. When I moved out here I thought Brooklyn was, like, the affordable alternative, but even in fucking Crown Heights my rent is bananas. I'm Marcie, by the way. Maybe see you back in here sometime?'

'I'm sure you will!' I'm much too perky, over-compensating for how betrayed I feel. I thought we had a thing going here, Marcie. But of course we didn't, because Marcie doesn't know me and Marcie has plenty of friends already, and doesn't need to invite socially awkward English randoms to gatecrash ladies' night.

For a while after she leaves I genuinely consider following her, tracking her through hot, hazy streets like a John le Carré antihero, ending up at the same trendy club and effortlessly chirping 'Oh my God, Marcie! So random. What can I say, you inspired me to check out Meatpacking!' Desperate at best, stalker at worst.

I do not follow Marcie. But I do get on the subway and stay on it until it terminates early at 14th Street due to construction, and when I emerge everything feels different. The streets here are quieter, slower, most of them narrow, some of them cobbled, none of them numbered. Their names are actual names – Jane, Horatio – and I'm so disoriented I think maybe I have left New York altogether.

I end up in a bar where a sports game is playing on every screen, five or six or seven identical versions blaring down from every angle. I ask somebody what game this is, and he laughs at me not unkindly and says baseball, sweetheart, the great American sport. He's middle-aged and wearing it badly, forehead sweaty, stomach creeping over the top of his too-tight belt, eyes unfocused. But he keeps talking to me and I keep responding, though really I'm just watching him talk.

The room looks strange around me, threatening in some quiet throbbing way, and I can feel my heartbeat pulsing against my eardrum. It's so loud. Someone pushes past me, and the man is looking expectantly at me like he wants a response, but when he leans in I recoil, spinning and walking and colliding with other bodies.

Finally I reach the bar, its glossy wood stable beneath my hand, and the air is getting thicker. I wonder vaguely whether there is dry ice in this place, because there's a kind of fog in the air, thin, not exactly hiding my surroundings but screening them.

'Do...' I start, trying to get the bartender's attention. But she hasn't noticed anything. Of course. There is nothing.

The room still looms, and when a gaggle of young women descend around us wearing identical college shirts – all of them like Marcie, chunky, effusive, so alive, so sure – it takes everything in me not to flinch. This evening now feels like something I'm watching on TV, a gathering that should never have included me and will play out without my participation. I've somehow become part of this group at the bar, and though I want to be polite I feel jarred every time one of them looks at me. Just leave the fog. Let it lie.

Their voices get louder, or the room around us gets quieter, and either way it's unbearable. I can see myself from above now like an aerial photograph and it's clear that I'm restless and need quiet. I watch myself looking around the room, eyes darting around for an escape route through the glossy film that's coating everything. Why can't these idiots see it? Why aren't they shutting up? Something is wrong.

I cannot stay here any longer. It's been hours.

I make a mumbled excuse and slide gracelessly out of my seat, shooting the women a smile that can only look insane,

Norman Bates at the end of *Psycho* weird, and leave. The fog lifts, but the air outside is thick and balmy and it's still very, very light.

'Excuse me,' I see myself ask a middle-aged woman in a headscarf. 'Do you have the time?'

'It's a quarter after seven.'

I was in that bar for less than half an hour. This feels impossible.

Back in my hotel, I watch the daylight disappear through a tiny gap between brick walls, and feel the memories of the evening slip away like sand. I can find no purchase on them. The whole day could not have happened, the moments falling away from me, and if I were dissolving I would never know it. Am I here?

CHAPTER THREE

Then I meet him, at a Fourth of July potluck full of strangers. The overly friendly cashier at Trader Joe's invites me, as she bags up the groceries I can't really afford. Her name is Jennifer, and this is the fourth time she's served me here, which apparently qualifies me for invitations. She seems worried when I tell her I'm here alone, hands me a flyer for an 'Independence Day Potluck!'

'You should come!' she yells. 'It's just a whole bunch of people from my building, sort of like a block party, everybody brings something. Super casual.'

The thought fills me with dread, but what's my alternative?

'That's so sweet of you,' I beam back, feeling fraudulent. 'I'd love to come along, I haven't really met many people here.'

'How long are you in town for?'

'I'm not sure yet. I've got some family in Connecticut I'd like to go and visit,' I lie. Again. I abandoned the Daddy-in-Tribeca story after Marcie.

So I take the flyer, half-planning on throwing it in the recycling bin outside the store.

And three days later, I wake up terrified in my hotel bed and stand in front of the window for ten beats, counting slowly back until my heart stops pounding so fast in my ears. Forcing myself to breathe deeply into my diaphragm, thinking of nothing but the physical reality of things around me, and the present moment. And that evening, I put on the one party outfit I brought with me, a deep green scoop-neck dress that stops just short of my knees, the ten-denier tights that don't ruin my silhouette with a tiny ring of muffin top, the kitten heels that make me feel long-legged and reckless.

And here I am at a potluck in Hell's Kitchen (only in New York would this be the name of a desirable neighbourhood), drinking a stranger's cheap chilled Merlot (why is chilling red wine an acceptable thing here?) and trying to look like I'm waiting for somebody. It's moments like this that make me regret leaving my phone behind – without the option of pretend-texting, or checking my non-existent Twitter feed, it's a lot harder to avoid looking like a loner.

I look around the apartment – a shoebox with lofty aspir- ations in the literal sense, one wall given over to 'exposed brickwork' that appears fake even to my untrained eye. People are jammed at awkward right angles into corners, scrunched down into murmuring huddles that seem impenetrable. This was a bad idea.

Jennifer the intense cashier bounds up to me, just as I'm starting to consider slipping out as unnoticed as I'd come in.

'You came!'

'Yeah, of course!' I parrot in my best good-time-girl

voice. 'Here, these are my contribution to the celebration of Independence.'

I've brought patriotically iced red velvet cupcakes from a bakery in SoHo, a desperate impulse purchase that set me back an obscene $42, and made me wish more than anything that I had a kitchen here to bake in. But Jennifer is in raptures over them, marvelling at each tiny perfectly formed icing flag, and I hear myself squealing along with her and wonder when I became such a good liar.

'Here's hoping we'll actually be able to see some of the fireworks,' she sighs, setting the cupcakes down beside a morose tray of devilled eggs. 'I'm so annoyed, I thought they were meant to be alternating each year, but they're on the goddamn east side again so I'm not sure what kind of view we're gonna get from the roof.'

We both get a refill of wine, and my head's finally starting to feel pleasantly fuzzy, a kind of warmth spreading upwards through my legs. And it's then that he appears.

Good-looking in a completely American way, bronzed and blondish and broad, miles from the willowy-sallow boys whose affections I'd half-heartedly craved at Oxford. I stare at him over the rim of my glass for several beats longer than I should, and he looks back and smiles and okay, this is a moment that is happening.

'So, how long have you lived here?' I ask, turning towards Jennifer, and as I half-listen to the response I'm thinking only about my own face, how it looks at this angle, what is he seeing when he looks at me?

Maybe he's seeing right through me. Maybe he sees somebody who's been called 'so mature for your age' her entire life and has never felt younger or more afraid. There's a thickness in my throat, and I swallow down the rest of my wine, hard.

'I'm just gonna investigate the drinks table,' I smile, tilting myself past Jennifer, entirely conscious that I'm crossing his path. And I wait.

'May I not recommend the pre-mixed Mojito?' comes his voice, and I know it's his voice somehow without turning around.

'Oh, but I'd just decided I could really go for a Bacardi Silver!' I say, turning with a playful smile.

'I mean, don't let me stop you, but… let me stop you. It's not good.'

'You've tried it?'

'I brought it,' he grimaces. 'Sorry about that. It seemed summery, but I think it's mostly corn syrup.'

'You know what would be really slick is if you whipped out a cocktail shaker and the ingredients for a fresh Mojito right now. Just, like, you had them with you the whole time.'

'Right. Saving them for the good people.'

He smiles at me.

'I don't really drink much,' he says then, 'hence the horrible beverage choice. But I hear you can't go wrong with a gin and tonic.'

'Actually, since we're making confessions,' I start, riding a brief wave of bravado, 'I don't really want another drink. I just came over here because I was hoping you'd talk to me.'

Bold. Brazen, even. I can be this girl for a while.

'Wow. Well, I'm glad you did.'

My eyes feel wheel-wide in my head as I gaze at him,

grinning, and he holds out a hand saying, 'I'm Jake.' When I take it he doesn't shake but squeezes, and doesn't let go.

And neither do I.

He opens a beer for me using a Swiss Army knife he carries on him, and we melt into a corner together, the space around us now feeling just the right size. The room is emptying gradually, people heading up to the roof to watch the fireworks now that dusk is settling, but instead I watch his eyes as he talks about summer in New York and how he never understood why people fled from the heat because, for him, the city felt most natural when it was sweltering, hazy with pent-up energy, and how his parents used to bring him to Manhattan every July to see Broadway shows and watch the Nicks play.

I watch the tiny crinkles around the far point of his eye as he smiles, the angle of his jaw, and marvel.

'Anyway,' he interjects midway through his own sentence, 'sorry. I'm talking about myself a lot. I do that when I'm nervous.'

I've never seen anybody look less nervous.

'What's weird is that I've been wanting to ask you about yourself since I first saw you. That is a British accent, right?'

'Indeed.'

'So, are you studying in New York? Or on vacation?'

He waits expectantly, and I'm already formulating the lie in my head but the words will not come.

'Is it okay if we stay on you for a while?' I ask finally, heart in my throat. 'It's... I'm sort of complicated. I might need a PowerPoint presentation to explain myself to you.'

I'm right on the brink of breaking character and telling

him everything. What's the worst that could happen? He'll turn away, not understanding, not wanting to understand, and politely make an excuse and this whole encounter will play like a daydream in my memory.

My fist is clenched against the floor, anticipating the blow. But he just nods and says, 'You'll have to fill me in another day,' and starts telling me a self-deprecating story about his botched attempt to build a table out of driftwood for his family's house upstate, and I've never heard anything more soothing.

As he's talking, I slip a hand into his hair before I lose my newfound nerve, and his hand rests in the arch of my waist like an anchor.

He doesn't kiss me with urgency so much as curiosity, his lips light against mine without a hint of tongue and this is nothing like I have ever been kissed before. I've been kissed only in nightclubs, the handful of times I'd galvanized myself to join in with the cycle of drink-dance-vomit-repeat at university, and the experiences had varied from sloppy to inoffensive to genuinely unpleasant. Tongues and teeth clashing, men who momentarily tried to devour me before we parted ways forever, our time in one another's orbit typically less than an hour. I never went home with anyone.

Kissing him makes me understand, for the first time, why anyone would voluntarily do it sober. And as I weave my way home later that night, after scribbling my hotel name and room number on a piece of paper that Jake had scrunched in his fist and held to his chest with his eyes locked on me, the world feels safe and somehow limitless.

When I wake up the next morning, I don't open my eyes

immediately. The wan morning sun presses on my eyelids, pouring in through the open blinds, but I pretend it's not there. Staving off the inevitable. I want to put off the crushing self-doubt and anxiety for as long as possible, the hours I'll spend telling myself it doesn't matter if he calls or not, because I'm fine on my own. And without a cellphone, I have no way of knowing he's called unless I stay here, literally waiting by the phone like the teenage daughter from a 1950s soap. No.

I shower decisively, if such a thing is possible, dress and apply my makeup, telling myself all the things I can do today that aren't pining. I sketch out a route in pencil on the now well-worn map in the back of my *Time Out* guide to New York, checking the opening times for the Frick and the Met and the zoo. It's about time I see some tourist attractions.

I waver on my feet for a few minutes, watching the silent phone smirk at me. Then in a moment of bravado I grab my bag and leave, half-jogging to the creaky lift that always takes at least four minutes to arrive. I spend those four minutes trying hard not to listen for a phone ringing.

Once I'm out, things are better. I'm realizing that what I enjoy most in New York is walking the streets. I know that I've been neglecting the obvious tourist attractions during my time here, and yet even if I do visit the High Line and the Statue of Liberty soon I'm sure my strongest memories of the city will simply be buildings, wide pavements, the thrum of certainty all around me. Sightseeing feels beside the point.

After I get off the subway at 86th Street I'm tempted just to keep walking, up the east side of Central Park into the triple-numbered streets my overly cautious cab driver warned me to avoid. But I do go into the Met, walk up those grand front steps and exchange $8 for a little plastic token and walk in a random direction after a cursory look at the museum map, because I have no idea what I want to see.

I end up in the American Wing, looking at portraits of presidents and late colonial furniture, wishing I were the kind of person who found solace in art. Impressionism always works best for me – shapes and blurs, a feeling more than an image – or surrealism, Dalí's clocks, images that are deliberately wrong. Anything too much like life, too much like people, and I'm bored.

If this were a film, I might conveniently happen upon a portrait of some senator who bore an uncanny resemblance to Jake, and it would be the final straw, the moment when I finally spun on my heel and raced back down the steps, hellbent on reunion. But none of the men in these portraits look anything like him, and I realize I'm struggling to remember his face. I've never been good with faces. It takes me a long time to mentally file away someone's features, two or three meetings at least, but I thought he would be different. How can I not remember that face?

There's still a deep ache in my chest and I have to sit with the weight of it, because I need to see him again. The possibility of it not happening is overwhelming. I can see that future so clearly, the one in which I stay in this museum until dark, buy a mediocre sandwich for dinner, go back to my empty hotel room where the phone has not rung and I will wake up tomorrow and he will be a memory. With no immediacy, he'll fade, and I'll forget that I ever had him.

'Jake,' I murmur, as if saying his name will keep him solid.

My heart's beating hard in my ears. I try to breathe, try to reason my way out of this. I don't have his number, but I can get it. I can go back to Jennifer's apartment, or find her at Trader Joe's, and I can ask her. She'll think it's cute. Or desperate. I just want to see him again.

Love has been so foreign to me for so long. I've seen love at first sight on screen a hundred times, read heartfelt descriptions of infatuation in novels, listened to hours of Taylor Swift on repeat, but romance has always resonated with me on the level of science fiction. Intriguing in abstract, but nothing to do with my reality. Now I have butterflies, and my stomach feels at once tight and unwound.

I force myself round more of the collections, and Egyptian Art is my saviour for an hour or two. I stand in front of one scarab beetle for so long I must look insane, too calmed by the shade of blue to move, trying to focus on the colour and shape and nothing else.

My friend Sophie told me this, once, trying to persuade me to think less. 'It's not about thinking of nothing,' she explained, hands resting cool on mine. 'It's just focusing on something external, so you can sort of quiet down the noise.' The noise has been getting louder and louder here, and I miss Sophie, so much. Her tip is working.

When I do finally take the subway back downtown, it's not as bad as I expect, probably because I've built this moment up with such melodramatic force. I will be okay. I won't see him again, and in time the ache will fade, and it won't matter that I can't remember his face. And when I reach the lobby, it's his voice I hear first. As the door squeaks open it's unmistakable, echoing though I can't yet see the reception desk.

'Could I leave a message, then?'
I round the corner, heart in my throat.
'Jake?'
And he turns around, and smiles that wide toothy smile,
and I've never felt safer.

CHAPTER FOUR

I feel drunk. We're sitting on a bench in Washington Square Park in the warm dusk, the traffic blurring into white noise around us. He's holding my hand in his, his thumb stroking circles onto my knuckle.

'I kept expecting to see you in the city today. I was at the Met, trying to distract myself, and kept thinking I'd see you around the next corner.'

'Me showing up at your hotel kind of killed the irony.'

'That's not really what ironic means.'

He doesn't look up, keeps his eyes on our entwined hands.

'If we'd run into each other in the street, that wouldn't be ironic. It'd be a coincidence, but irony would be like if… let's say I left the hotel to try and get your number from Jennifer, and while I was gone you came to try and find me at the hotel. And we missed each other and never met again. That'd be ironic.'

'Hm. Irony's kind of a downer.'

'Sorry.' I have no idea why I felt the need to say any of this.

'You need to relax.'

'I do. This is helping, though.'

'Is that why you came to New York? To relax?'

'It's not really known for being a relaxing city, is it? I've never been that great at relaxing.'

'You gotta learn to breathe. Here, put one hand on your stomach, and take a deep breath in.'

Feeling my own stomach is not among the list of activities that relaxes me. At least I haven't eaten much today.

'When you inhale, your stomach should expand right out. Then exhale, you should feel it shrink back down. Like blowing up a balloon and letting the air back out, blowing it up, letting it out.'

I do this, feel the air expand and retract, and it works, gradually, a warmth settling in place of the raw nerves.

'Better?' he asks, after a time, and I answer yes in an exhale of warm air.

We end up in a diner just before midnight, and suddenly there is structure. This is a date. I've been on exactly two dates in my life before this, and both were excruciating disappointments. The desperate small talk, the mechanical process of where-shall-we-meet and what-do-you-study, the judgement, the anxiety, the terrifying lack of control.

'That's the fun part,' my sort-of friend Isabelle said once, with a glint in her eye. 'That back-and-forth, not knowing what he's thinking, not knowing what it's going to turn into…'

I wish I were the kind of person who found uncertainty

thrilling. My life to date would have been a lot more interesting for it. I might have gone outside the lines more.

'You guys know what you want?' our waitress asks, dark crescents under her eyes showing through concealer.

'Could I get the chicken Caesar salad, no croutons?'

Jake looks at me, eyebrows raised.

'What?' I ask defensively.

'That's not what you order in a diner at midnight. Come on.'

'I like salad!'

'Can I get the cheeseburger, chilli fries and a chocolate malt?' he says, and I want that more than anything, and he knows it.

'Actually, I'll have the same,' I tell the waitress.

'Now we're talking.'

'I'm not really one of those dressing-on-the-side types of girls. Usually.' I'm not. I ordered it on autopilot, the part of my brain that cares about looking restrained and feminine winning over the part of my brain that is starving.

'You like to eat?'

'Love it. Cooking's the thing I miss most about home.'

'Where's home?'

'London. Highgate, to be specific.'

He rolls the two syllables around his tongue a couple of times, High-gate.

'I've been away at university for the last few years, though.'

'Where did you study?'

'Oxford,' I say, with a wince I can never hide, bracing for judgement.

'Wow. Now I'm intimidated. College dropout over here.'

'You're not missing much,' and I regret this as soon as I

say it. As if my education were nothing. Easy to be ungrateful when it's handed to you. 'How long were you there?'

'A year. I went home for the summer, and ended up enlisting.'

'Oh, wow.'

'Five years of service, two tours in Afghanistan. I'm on inactive reserve duty now, till next year.'

'What does that mean?'

'They can call me back whenever they want. But it's not likely I'll be deployed again.'

'And you were actually… were you fighting?'

'Yeah, I was infantry.'

I have the overwhelming urge to ask him more, but there's a rigidness to his shoulders that keeps me silent.

'Would you be okay with going back?' is what I ask instead. 'If you're called?'

'I'd serve again. But that's probably not going to happen.'

'What made you want to enlist?'

'I'll make you a deal. For every piece of info about my military days, you trade me something about yourself. No more of this one-sided shit.'

His tone is light but his eyes are earnest. And he's right.

'You're on. Here, we'll make this the ketchup bottle of truth,' and I slide the bottle across to him. 'Whoever has it has to speak. So. What made you want to enlist?'

'Boredom. My turn.'

He pushes the bottle back across to me.

'No, that was not the deal. One-word answers don't count.'

'Never agreed on that. So. What brings you to New York?'

I narrow my eyes at him.

'Upheaval.'

'Upheaval?'

'Yup.'

'All right, maybe one-word answers shouldn't count.'

'See? We'll come out of this knowing less than ever about each other. So… what made you want to enlist?'

My mind is already working overtime as he pauses, threading a straw through the gap between his index and middle fingers and twisting it into a knot.

'Mostly for college. My folks didn't really have the money to pay for me, but they didn't want to admit it and I didn't get it until I was already there.'

His hand pauses on the table, straw now bent back on itself and wound around three fingers, and everything about him is large without actually taking up much space. He drums out a rhythm against the wood and something within me responds, a twinge around my pelvis. He's not especially muscular but he is solid, grounded, and I think again of the buildings enveloping us on every side.

'What brings you to New York?' he asks again.

'My mum died.'

After so long unspoken, the words slip out like nothing.

'That's not the only thing – I mean, it was almost a year ago. But that was the first thing that happened. And it started this chain of events, at home, which came to a head last month. I'd never been here before, and that made it appealing.'

'I'm sorry.'

'It's okay.'

Gently, he pulls the ketchup bottle out of the vice grip I didn't know I had it in.

'So, do you have another question for me?' he prompts.

'Do you live with family?'

'No. I did, when I first came back. But after you've gotten used to that kind of structure, all your days divided for you, every hour accounted for, it's tough to readjust. There's things you can't explain. They didn't get why I enlisted to begin with, and afterward they still didn't. We weren't really speaking the same language. And my little sister was just going off to college, so it felt like a good time to check out.'

Our malt shakes have arrived, a metal tumbler of leftovers delivered alongside each frosty glass, and I down a third of mine almost without pausing for breath, too hungry to care how this looks.

'So do you have a place in New York? In Jennifer's building?'

'I'm just staying there for a few weeks, my uncle owns an apartment there. And don't think I haven't noticed you're three questions deep right now,' he says, sliding the ketchup bottle so hard back across the table I barely catch it.

'I think that's what they call misplaced aggression, soldier. It's not my fault my questions were so good you didn't notice them coming. What's the military term for that, like, covert fire, when you don't even know you're being fired on till it's too late?'

'That would be an ambush.'

'No, that's when you lie in wait and then launch a surprise attack. This was more like sniper fire. Subtle, deadly. But go on.'

'You said your mom dying was the first thing. What was the last?'

'My dad and I had a fight. He drinks.'

I feel like I'm in a parallel reality. I've spent so much of my life trying to package the facts about my parents, feeling pride every time I described them in a way that sounded normal, all subterfuge and shame. And now I'm telling the absolute truth to an absolute stranger, and he isn't flinching. Maybe I've been alone for too long, but I don't want to hide anything from him.

'Next question?' I ask. 'I owe you two more.'

'I'll let you off the hook after that one. Your turn.'

'Okay. Well, good, because I should have asked this way before now. Why did you come to my hotel tonight?'

'Because I wanted to see you again. And you didn't pick up when I called.'

'I was out! I realized the huge flaw in giving you my hotel phone number – no voicemail. But coming all the way to my hotel, that is commitment.'

'You didn't give me a lot of choice. Is that a British thing, giving out a landline number and then not being near your landline?'

'No, just a me thing. I wasn't deliberately playing hard to get. I did briefly consider staying in all day.'

'Only briefly? Come on, throw me a bone.'

'Oh God, okay, I seriously contemplated it. I was at the Met all afternoon just thinking "What if I never get to speak to him again because I left my room and came here to look at late colonial furniture from the White House?"'

'Late colonial furniture? That's weak,' he says through laughter. 'That's really weak. If you're gonna try and get your mind off me, you need to shoot for something a little more stimulating.'

'Yeah, the furniture did not do a great job of distracting me. The Egyptian Art, though, thank God for those sarcophagi. By the time I was finished there I was barely even thinking about you at all.'

'Oh, really?'

'Really. Had to rack my brain to even remember who you were when I saw you in the lobby.'

His eyes crinkling at the edges, he grips my hand and tugs me just slightly towards him, our knees meeting underneath the table. We're too far apart to kiss but our gazes lock and there's something coursing through me, close to adrenalin but rawer and warmer. I have to crush down the urge to cross the table and push myself into him; the distance between us feeling suddenly cruel.

'Here you go,' comes the waitress's voice, and I pull back before he does. 'Two cheeseburgers, two sides of chilli fries. Can I get you guys any more sauces?'

Jake asks for mayo, and I focus hard on my burger, which tastes a lot better than I suspect it should.

'You know, we've kind of inverted the traditional rules of dating here,' I say.

'How's that?'

'You're meant to start with small talk, the basics, the stuff nobody really cares about but everybody has to pretend to. We just dived right in at the deep end.'

'Do you date a lot?' he asks, licking a stray dab of mustard from his knuckle.

'No, actually.'

'So do you think we should back it up a few steps?'

'Well, I don't know. I hate small talk, but at the same

time I'm English, so it's sort of hardwired into me. I've been crushing down the urge to talk about the weather all evening.'

'It was a really nice day, right?'

'It was! Okay, small talk. What's your favourite colour?'

'Does anybody really ask that on dates? This is like in Spanish class when they teach you useful phrases that aren't actually useful, like "My name is Caitlin. My favourite colour is red."'

'Blue, actually. You still haven't told me yours.'

'I guess mine would be red.'

'Okay, do you have any advance on favourite colour? What's your idea of good dating small talk?'

'My dating game's a little rusty,' he admits. 'If you'd told me talking about your favourite colour on dates is normal, I'd have believed you.'

'How rusty?'

'That's for me to know and you to figure out. So why do you think people do small talk on dates?'

'Well, it's safe. It's harder to scare someone away when you're talking about the weather, or public transport, or what subject you're studying. Or your job, I suppose, since we're in the real world now.'

And this strikes me as very funny the moment it's out of my mouth, because nothing about this feels like the real world. Not this street, not this diner, not this warm-eyed perfect stranger. Not me.

After we finish eating, I tell him I want to go to Central Park. It feels like the thing to do, at night in New York; we're hand in hand and all I can picture is strolling along the mall in the moonlight, a real-life movie moment.

'Central Park is not really a place you want to be this late at night.'

Of course. The reality check. We are walking up Eighth Avenue past a row of boarded-up stores and rubbish bags piled high, the air thick with the smell of something that might be urine.

'I don't know why I'm always…'

'What?'

'It's like I'm sort of trying to direct my own life. Like a film. I've got these images in my head of what adult life should look like, if I just play my cards right. And the more I actually look at them, the more I realize they're all just scenes I've seen in movies or TV shows.'

He's silent for a long time.

'Did that make any sense whatsoever?' I ask, finally.

'It did. I think everyone has unrealistic expectations of life.'

'Me more than most. Growing up, pop culture saved my life,' I shrug, then sing the same sentence to the tune of 'Last Night a DJ Saved My Life'.

'Really?'

'Really.'

We've stopped in silent accord, something about this moment too charged to walk on through.

'What saved yours?'

His arms enclose mine, his fingertips five hot pressure points against my elbows.

'Enough questions,' he murmurs into my ear, and the vibration reverberates deep inside me.

CHAPTER FIVE

'I want you to meet my family,' he says on our fifth day together, his arm slung loose around my waist on the ferry back from Staten Island. The latest in a series of underwhelming tourist attractions. The weather is foggy, and the ferry's outdoor deck was closed, so we stood inside and saw the Statue of Liberty through smear-covered plastic.

And I stop, and stare at him.

'Are you serious?'

'Dead serious. I think they'd like you.'

'Didn't you say they live upstate?'

'Yeah but it's not far, a couple of hours from here. It's real quiet, there's a lake, great hiking, fishing, if you're into that. It'd be a total change of pace from the city.'

'You know, a lot of horror movies have begun with this basic premise. Guy meets girl, guy invites girl back to his remote wood cabin…'

'Not a cabin. It's a real house, with doors that lock. It's beautiful up there.'

'And that's exactly what the cute serial killer in the film would say.'

I'm extra-spiky, working hard to hide when all I really want to do is say yes, of course. I've never come anywhere close to meeting a boy's family before, and this boy is asking with his muscular chest pressed against my back, fingers intertwined over my abdomen.

'I think you're avoiding the question.'

I lean back into him.

'You were saying you craved space,' he pushes. 'There's nothing but space upstate. You'd love it. And if you don't, the city's only a two-hour drive away.'

'Okay.'

'Okay?'

'Yeah. Take me upstate.'

And that's that.

He hasn't tried to sleep with me. We've been sharing a bed for four nights in his apartment, where the city noise is so much closer and louder than in my hotel, the drapes too thin to shut out the street lights' glow, and yet every night I've fallen asleep easily, to the sound of horns and revving engines and the shouts of drunken men with something to prove.

Jake doesn't sleep well. He warned me of this on our first night and it's true, because every night too I've fallen asleep listening to the sound of his distinctly wakeful breathing. The one time I awoke during the night and he was asleep, it looked more like drowning: his eyelids twitching rapidly, his left hand braced against the mattress as though trying to keep himself anchored.

On our last night in the city, I'm more awake than normal. I drift off to sleep almost instantly but come back to myself with a jolting inhale, flailing against imaginary gravity.

Jake is silent beside me, too quiet, and even the street noise now feels too far away. The fog is descending again, enough to make the room around me feel distant, and I have to press my hand hard against the wall and focus on the feeling of it with my eyes closed.

Once I feel grounded in my own body again, I pull a chair up to the window and listen to my heartbeat gradually slow, watching the traffic. The prospect of leaving the city feels ludicrous. I can't remember my life without traffic and the enclosure of tall buildings, don't want to remember. New York has cradled me in its busy embrace and now I'm pulling away so fast, and I can feel the city looking at me in reproach.

Don't be ridiculous. The city is indifferent.

We spend the next day killing time in jagged portions, trying to savour our last day in New York, but it's hard to enjoy much of anything when it all feels so final. Jake takes me to the Empire State Building ('You've gotta do it, it's a tourist non-negotiable'), and it feels mostly like a theme park ride. We wait a long time for an elevator that will take us all the way up to the very top, crammed in alongside other tourists like battery chickens, someone's overheated child whimpering in protest on behalf of us all.

When I've pictured the top of the Empire State Building, it's like a clock tower in a medieval city, and you can see for miles in every direction. But there's wire mesh raised higher than my head, vivisecting the view so that it looks small and sad. If I had my phone with me, I could place it against one of the gaps and zoom in just so, until the skyline is unrestricted, and take a better picture of this moment than the view I actually saw.

'You all right?' Jake asks in the elevator back down, and I nod and smile, wishing the heaviness in my chest would lift.

Jake's friend lends us his car to drive upstate. He arrives at the apartment early in dress shirt and pressed trousers, his hair white-blonde and meticulously gelled, and I'm conscious of my scuffed ballet flats and slightly shrunken dress, although he's clearly the one who's overdressed for the occasion.

'Kris, with a K,' he introduces himself as he shakes my hand with gusto, greeting Jake with a one-armed hug that is not returned. 'So you're going up to the lake house?'

'Yeah,' Jake nods, his hand on the small of my back. 'Just gonna give her the tour.'

There's something tense in the space between them, Kris's stance half-slanted like he's awaiting a fight.

'You'll have a great time,' he says, addressing me. 'Make sure you hike the lakeside loop, amazing views when you get to the top.'

I busy myself with unlocking my suitcase and pretending to re-pack a few items, sensing a conversation to be had without me. The two of them look like negative images of each other: Jake controlled, contained, every movement he makes deliberate, Kris pulsing with repressed energy, his gait twitchy.

'Don't let him lead you astray,' he says finally to me, as Jake opens the passenger door for me. I smile widely and don't acknowledge how strange this is as a parting shot.

'How do you two know each other?' I ask as we drive away, straight into rush hour traffic.

'Army.'

Something in the way Jake's gripping the wheel tells me not to press the subject.

I'm disappointed to find out the drive will take barely two hours – in my head, driving from anywhere to anywhere else in the US is an epic undertaking, requiring overnight stays at seedy-yet-atmospheric motels along the way. He promises me the scenic route. But after the view from the Washington Bridge recedes, the motorway stretches out blank and bleak ahead of us, suburban houses dotted dutifully at its edges, and I feel dread. This is flat land, no variation, nothing but road for miles in any direction. What on earth am I doing?

'Is there a way back from where we're going? Other than by car?'

'Let me guess – you don't drive.'

I can't work out whether he's mocking me.

'No. I never had much reason to learn. Nobody drives in London, and in Oxford I just cycled everywhere. Ever since I've been old enough to care, there's been public transport.'

'I guess there was public transport where I grew up, but nobody really took the time to find out. If you don't drive you're basically dead.'

'Yikes. That's comforting.'

He grins, reaching over to squeeze my leg.

'Already planning your escape route?'

'Have you heard of the final girl?'

'What?'

'The final girl. It's this device in horror movies, where a group of people gets picked off one by one by the serial killer, or the monster or whatever, until there's just one girl left alive. Everybody else dies but she survives, and gets out, and tells the story.'

'Like in *Alien*?'

'Yeah, Ripley in *Alien*, and it happens in *Nightmare on Elm Street*, *Halloween*... there are others I'm forgetting. The girl in *Carrie*, who has the grave nightmare right at the end.'

'That movie messed me up.'

'Me too. She survives because she's kind to Carrie – the final girl's usually like that. She's innocent, in contrast to her hedonistic friends who do drugs and have sex and die for their sins.'

He smiles at me, raises an eyebrow. 'Well, the closest town to where we're going is Forestburgh, but I don't know what the transport's like. There's buses back to New York from Monticello for sure.'

I make a mental note of Monticello, though this whole conversation has put me back at ease and the landscape is opening up around us as we drive, the foliage getting denser. The scenery Jake promised. As sun dapples through the narrow gaps in leaves, I wind down my window and extend my arm sideways into the air, fingers splayed against the forward motion.

From the corner of my eye I can see him looking over at me, but I can't make out his expression without turning. To do that would be to break the moment, so instead I fill in the gaps for myself. He's looking at me thinking I'm unlike any girl he's ever met before, and maybe thinking that he doesn't want to let me go now he's found me.

I breathe in deep all the way to my diaphragm, and let the city go.

It takes a long time before I lay eyes on the house.

A few miles after we pass the sign for Forestburgh Jake turns the wheel sharply, and for one jarring moment I think he's driving the car straight into the undergrowth. But there is a road, half-overgrown and barely wide enough to drive down, so that branches whip hard against the windows as we move forward.

After perhaps ten minutes of this, the path starts to widen, the trees ahead opening into a clearing, and as we turn again I see a flash of white through the leaves up ahead. The clutching branches fall away, clattering loudly like a parting shot against the back window right as the house comes fully into view, incongruously bright white in the sun.

'Wow.'

It's substantially bigger than I'd imagined. The log cabin in my mind's eye fades like a half-remembered dream, as Jake pulls up alongside a grassy slope. This is a wooden mansion, slanting slats in place of bricks and mortar, three storeys high and lifted off the ground by a raised porch and lattice beneath, so that as we approach the house looks like it's levitating.

One side of the house is almost obscured by trees, and I imagine the view from those rooms must be like being inside a canopy. Before us lies a vast lawn, sloping gently upwards towards the house with picnic tables and what looks like a large barbecue grill at its base.

'The lake is just about a quarter mile down that way,' Jake says, 'through that kind of H-shaped gap in the trees. We're pretty much surrounded by forest here, two hundred acres of it is private.'

'I know land is cheaper out here and everything,' I start, gazing up, 'but as summer homes go, this is… wow.'

'It's been in the family for a hundred years. Just sits here empty half the time. My dad's always talking about renting it out online, but he's kind of a technophobe.'

'You'd make a killing on it. You could hold weddings here.'

I ascend the stairs tentatively, irrationally scared I'm going to fall between the slats into the four-foot crawlspace beneath. Being this high up and still on the ground floor is foreign.

'Just wait out here for a second. I'm not sure what state the inside of the place is in, I don't want to scare you off.'

'Sure,' I murmur, only half-listening. I'm imagining being in those woods, just walking and walking and walking until I can see nothing but trees in any direction, enveloped again. And yet I don't have any urge to cross the lawn and make this a reality, yet. One step at a time.

In the wooden porch swing I close my eyes, and listen to the perfect near silence. Last night's patchy sleep has finally caught up with me and I feel half-drugged, content to lie perfectly still and doze while Jake disappears inside. When I open my eyes fully, the sun is turning the dimming sky rusty, and there are tiny goosebumps on my arms. I close them again just as I feel the air shift in front of me, pretend not to know he's there.

His lips press against mine, and I can't hold back a smile.

'Cheesy.'

'And you loved it.'

I take his hand and let him pull me to my feet.

'Is there somewhere I can go and have a shower?'

'Right upstairs, second on the left. I'll put your bags in the bedroom.'

The strength and heat of the shower makes me realize just how weak the water pressure was at Jake's sublet, and I stay under for a long, long time. I put on a sundress, because that feels like the kind of thing you wear at a house like this, and brush out my hair into a glossy dripping sheet against my neck, and venture out into the rest of the house to explore.

The bedroom is cosy but sparse, its simple furniture bathed in early evening sunlight, a bay window looking out onto the sprawling lawn and the woods beyond. I feel oddly like I'm intruding before I've even made it past the threshold. The corridor is long, five closed doors on either side, a narrow table holding a vase of fake flowers at the far end and I can see a turning there too, leading to more doors.

The first handle I try turns uselessly from side to side; the door is locked. And without even trying the rest, I know they will all be the same. This place has the feeling of being more preserved than lived in.

The smell of something rich – tomato, beef, cumin – calls me into the kitchen, my mouth watering. Jake has cooked. There's a very slight fog in the air again, as I watch him shredding Romaine lettuce into a chequered bowl. The black squares seem to stand out from the white like solidly three-dimensional cubes, and focusing on them I feel dizzy, and distant. Am I here?

After dinner we're dancing around the kitchen in the light of the refrigerator door, his fingers pressed warm against the small of my back, and I still feel as though I'm watching this moment from above.

None of this feels like a part of my life. It's like I've willed him into existence, this all-American boy with doe eyes and sandy hair and an impossibly wide smile.

'What, even, are you?' I mumble against his shoulder, not really expecting him to hear me.

'What?'

'Nothing. I'm just... nothing.'

We dance to the sound of silence, and for once I'm not unnerved by the feeling of unreality settling around me, the fog gathering behind my eyelids.

CHAPTER SIX

'Haven't you been watering these?'
My mum is hovering over a vase of wilting flowers,
their petals brown and crinkled at the edges.

'Oh, God. I forgot.'

There were so many flowers after the funeral, choking the
air. Dad and I had made a kind of silent game out of finding
new receptacles to put them in and surfaces to put them on,
finally placing them like a conga line around the skirting
boards of our house.

'Darling,' Mum says reproachfully, 'you've got to take
some responsibility for things.'

'That's not fair. All I do is take responsibility for things.'

I cast around for my dad. He should be here. He's always
here, in the living room, sitting in his armchair with the red-
and-blue checked pattern, but the chair isn't here and this
isn't quite our living room.

'Why are you out of bed?'

'I'm fine, darling.'

'No, you need to rest.'

The French window is covered up by slabs of cardboard, taped in place. That's why the room is so dark.

'We can't let them hear us,' she says by way of explanation, her lips barely moving.

'No one's listening, Mum.'

There's a lump in my throat, and there never has been any sense in trying to reason with her. They've told me this so many times, solemn-eyed Dr Stamford and the nurse who wears too much apricot-coloured blusher. They both told me, don't try to challenge her reality. It could make things worse.

Her face darkens. And there's fear in my chest now, a kind of ambient noise rising. The flowers are twigs, and the smell of rotting fills the air; the worst smell I've ever known is that of rotting flowers.

'Mum?'

I reach out for her, but she's leaving, muttering to herself in the darkness.

'Mum, wait—'

My cheeks are wet and I'm trying to breathe past the lump in my throat. It's completely dark, now.

'Caitlin?'

Completely dark. When I begin to make out shapes, they are strange. This isn't our living room, not at all.

'Hey.'

I jerk away from his touch, just as my mind slips into focus. Jake. I'm hundreds of miles from that living room, and my mum has been dead for hundreds of days.

'Are you okay?'

He puts a hand on my back, and I make an effort not to stiffen. I'm half out of bed, one foot against cold wood, and I let it centre me as he rubs a circle against my shoulder blades.

'Fine. Yeah, I'm fine.'

'Bad dream?'

My cheeks are cold, salty, and I nod, though that doesn't really sum it up. I'd been wondering, without really letting myself wonder, whether last night would be the night we finally slept together. And we didn't, and now this is the furthest possible thing from a sexy middle-of-the-night moment.

'What was it about?'

'Nothing specific.'

His chin rests against my hair.

'My mum. I haven't really dreamed about her at all, since. I used to, before. But when she died, it was like she completely stopped existing, even in my subconscious. She was just gone.'

This felt so cruel to me. We'd known for a long time that her death was coming, but my brain's denial of her afterwards was a blow I hadn't anticipated. 'I'll always be with you,' she had told me in one of her few lucid moments, and I'd clung on to the belief that this was true, if only in the most abstract sense.

But she was demonstrably not with me, not in the aftermath when my dad wandered the house like a ghost and I answered the phone and the door to a seemingly endless procession of well-wishers. And not months later, when I was back at university and sure that the time must have come, my initial grief having given way to a dimmer underlying hollowness.

Surely now, I would see her again. And dreams being what they are, she would be well, I could make her healthy and sane and whole again in my subconscious.

But nothing. Ever. I Googled 'how to control dreams' and 'can you make yourself dream of someone' and 'lucid dreaming' until I was certain that I was ready. When that failed, I worried I was spending too much of my waking time thinking about her, so I deliberately kept my mind on other things all day, sure that this was the answer. I spent so many endless nights trying to conjure her and she was gone gone gone.

'So maybe it's a good thing you dreamed about her.'

'Maybe. Sorry I woke you.'

'You didn't.'

I watch the rectangle of silver and black on the floor before us, moonlight shifting around the silhouettes of branches. The moisture in my eyes blurs the outlines into one, and Jake wipes each falling tear from my cheek with his thumb.

Eventually, he tugs me gently back down to the mattress and lies warm against my back. I focus on mirroring the shape of his body, holding on tight to his hand, and name London streets in alphabetical order in my head until I sleep.

I wake up tired, my eyes scratchy-dry and a headache building at the base of my skull. Jake is still asleep, and I push myself out of bed before I have time to second guess the impulse. My desire to be outside is suddenly overwhelming, as is the memory of dense greenery and endless space when we arrived. How did I resist exploring yesterday?

I dress as quietly as I can, half an eye on Jake as I pull on the first clothes that come to hand. I'm sick of living out of a suitcase, and in theory I could unpack. But if I stop and really buy into this reality, the last week with Jake, and the three before that without him, I'm afraid something about it will be over. I'll realize I'm living out a dissociative fantasy, and everything that's happened will fall away and become a memory. An anecdote. That time I played at being reckless.

Downstairs, I make a pot of coffee from the rolled-up bag I find in the fridge door, and leave Jake a note propped up against the coffee pot ('Gone for a walk ☺'). This seems like the kind of thing you do when you're in a couple, and maybe he'll worry if he finds me gone. I like the idea of him worrying for me.

The air outside is crisp as I walk towards the forest, taking mental note of everything I pass – the jagged tree stump hunched to my left, the nettle patch to my right – like a list of directions, afraid on some level that I'm about to get lost. Then again, wasn't that the point of coming here?

Being in the woods brings with it an almost immediate sense of physical calm, the same safety I felt nestled between the impossibly tall buildings in Manhattan. Maybe all I need to be mentally stable is to live in a place where I'm always dwarfed by my surroundings. Last night's dream lingers. I still feel half-asleep, and if I stopped to listen I think I'd hear my mum's voice in the rustle of wind through branches.

As it turns out, there's a clear path to the lake cut directly through the woods, and even I can't get lost. Before long I can make out a clearing in the trees ahead of me, and blue rippling through the gaps, and I'm finally at the lake. There's a small cabin tucked into the lakeside, jutting out into the water beside a pier where boats are moored, but I see no signs of activity. If I were really bold, I'd go and knock on the door, maybe even try the handle, but this can wait.

Back in the woods, I stop dead in my tracks without immediately knowing why. Seeing a person here seems impossible; a shard of ice at the centre of a bonfire, and yet. She's pale, her hair long and dark and lank, dressed in a slightly dusty white dress with wide shoulders and a high collar, its shape reminiscent of a medical gown.

'Hi,' I manage, eventually.

She looks through me, eyes wide and slightly glazed. And before I can say anything else she has turned, moving smoothly but swiftly away through the undergrowth.

'Caitlin!'

I snap around just in time to see Jake running towards me, jaw set.

'What are you doing out here?'

He looks shaken, and when I turn back the girl has vanished.

'Having a walk. Didn't you see my note?'

He shakes his head, a hand on the small of my back, and I let him guide me back towards the house.

'I was worried. Come on.'

'Sorry – I did leave a note. With a smiley face and every-thing. With fresh coffee!'

My playfulness isn't returned. He's rigid beside me, and I can't bring myself to speak again. Back in the kitchen, I sit silently at the table as he pours us two mugs of coffee from the pot, now barely lukewarm.

The counter is dotted with ingredients – bacon, carton of eggs, a tall tin of extra virgin olive oil.

'Were you making breakfast?'

'I was going to.' Every word clipped.

'We still can,' I try, my words an anxious staccato beat. I should go over to him, touch him, say what I can't with words.

'Sorry,' I say instead, quietly. 'I really didn't think you'd mind.'

'It's fine,' Jake says, after a long beat that says it isn't.

We drink in silence. The breakfast ingredients stare me down, accusatory, and I can't believe I've ruined this.

'Who was that girl?'

'Who?'

'The girl, in the woods. She was right in front of me, she'd just run off when you called me. You must have seen her.'

He shakes his head, shrugs with his mouth and shoulders at once.

'You didn't?'

'I only saw you.'

'That's weird,' I say, ignoring the flip of my stomach at the way he says these words. 'Does anyone else live around here?'

'Sure, there's a couple of other houses. Not that close, maybe a mile or so away. She could have been from across the lake.'

That cabin I saw, incongruously manmade amidst the wilderness.

'I saw... I guess it was a house. A cabin. It didn't look occupied, down by the lake. Maybe she lives there?'

Abruptly, he seizes my hands and pulls me to my feet so hard I topple against him.

'Let's make breakfast,' he murmurs, our foreheads pressed together, our eyes perfectly aligned.

'You've cheered up.'

He kisses me, and I stop asking questions.

But as I'm whisking eggs, Jake's hands light on either side of my waist, I can sense he's somewhere else.

'So, what time are your parents getting here?'

'Soon. They're driving up right now.'

'What did you say they do?'

'My dad's a high school history teacher. My mom temps a lot, secretary stuff mostly. She was a stay-at-home mom for years.'

He takes the whisk from me, pours the eggs into the now-sizzling oil.

'You know, though, let's not talk about them too much while they're not here. I don't want to psych you out.'

I stand awkwardly as he serves out eggs and bacon that I suddenly can't imagine eating, take a seat across from him and try to smile. Jake's posture is determinedly casual, almost studied, one ankle resting on the opposite knee in a perfect relaxed L, as he cuts and spears forkfuls with one hand, but that stiffness is back. I can see the tension in his muscles. His foot spasms with every few bites, and my appetite withers further.

'Are you okay?' I ask finally, because I can't stand it any longer. Then I hear it. The door swinging open, and Jake springs to his feet like he's been electrocuted, a look I've never seen in his eyes.

'Stay here,' he barks, and jogs into the hall.

Outside I hear hushed, urgent voices, and inch around the corner trying to stay out of sight. Jake is gesticulating wildly at a woman whose face I can't see. His mum, surely. But nothing about this feels right.

The front door is open behind her, and outside there are more voices. Not whispering, and not just two or three. It sounds like a crowd of tourists has somehow stumbled upon this place, this perfectly isolated place.

'Jake.'

Dreamlike, I don't even realize I'm walking until I'm beside him, and the woman is looking intently at me. She's tall, regal, silvery hair swept over one shoulder, and though she must be in her fifties there is something indefinably quick about her, like she could spring into action in a heartbeat.

'Jake, what's going on? Is this your mum?'

I look hopefully at her as she smiles, and have to catch myself from staggering backwards. Her eyes look black to me and there's terror in my spine, sudden and fierce.

'Caitlin, just go back into the kitchen for a second, okay?'

'No.'

'Will you just—'

The woman moves past me, gesturing over her head as she does, and a procession follows her. None of them look at me.

They are young, twenty-somethings and less, most with a subtly unkempt look about them like they've been sleeping outside. Several have dirt on their faces and clothes, and every second person carries a tent.

'Take your gear out back,' a strong female voice calls from the rear of the line.

I watch them, dumbly, dazed. There are five in total, all of them young, followed by another fifty-something woman with short bowl-cut hair.

'What the hell is this?' I ask, my voice deadly quiet. Then louder, when Jake stays silent, 'What?'

Nausea is churning even before he replies. I know what this is, and I don't know what this is.

'It's my family.'

'What?'

I stare at him.

'This is... This is a family. It's where I've been living for the last two years. Since I left home, after I came back from Afghanistan. Kris kind of introduced me to this place, and it changed my life, and I wanted you to experience it.'

'You lied to me?'

I'm reminded of the first school dance I ever attended, when I was eleven. My all-girls' school had organized an evening of carefully supervised mixing with the associated all-boys' school, as if a single night would make up for spending your formative years segregated from people of the opposite sex. I stood there all night with my two best friends Felicity and Amy. Felicity was willowy and delicate, even then, and she was asked to dance swiftly and often by the few boys who dared to make the voyage across the empty dance floor. Amy and I were left to stand awkwardly near the drinks table, pretending not to mind.

Finally, a boy asked me to dance. I don't even remember if he was good-looking or not – all I remember is the thrill of being asked. Being seen dancing with him.

The next day at school, Heather Bowman sidled up to

me, took me by the arm and told me, gently and with eyes like venom, that the boy had only danced with me for a joke. His friend had done the same to Amy.

'I just thought you should know,' she said with paper sympathy, her perfect cascade of blonde hair swaying gently in the afternoon breeze.

I remember two things about this. One is how fervently I laughed it off, told her that I didn't care either way, but that I worried for Amy because she could be so sensitive. The other is how stupid I felt. Because of course the boy had not really wanted to dance with me. I had frizzy hair and braces and thirty extra pounds of not-just-puppy-fat back then. Of course.

That same feeling sears through me now, hot and prickly. Of course.

As I push past the crowd of strangers I can feel their eyes on me, looking now, and I don't meet their collective gaze.

'Caitlin, wait—' I hear Jake say behind me. I push forward and focus on the sunlight, feel his hand on my wrist.

'Don't touch me.'

It feels good, snatching my hand back, like striking him in reverse.

'I can explain. This wasn't meant to happen like this, they weren't meant to be back until later—'

'Who is "they"? Who are these people?'

But no, I'm giving him the power back, even by asking and waiting for a response.

'Actually, I don't care. I just wish I'd known before I let you bring me out into the middle of fucking nowhere.'

'Don't swear, please. It's not... it's not good here.'

'It's not… Are you serious?'

All those jokes about horror movies, and I don't see myself as much of a final girl. More like the first girl, the sacrificial lamb who gets reeled in by the first boy who gives her a second glance, and can't even drive herself to safety.

'Are your parents here?'

'No.'

At last. Honesty.

'Were your parents ever going to be here?'

He closes his eyes, wincing.

'No,' I answer for him, in a winded whisper.

'I haven't seen my parents in a very long time.'

'Is your dad really a teacher? Do they really live upstate? Is anything you've told me true?'

'Yes. Everything I've told you is true, I haven't lied to you.'

'Oh, wow. Okay.'

All I want is to go back in time by half an hour, back to when he enclosed me and I let him, because he felt like the first sure thing I'd had in years.

He has never looked more appealing, his morning hair still dishevelled, one lock flopping over his forehead like some kind of aftershave commercial. His T-shirt rumpled by sleep. My tears dried into the fabric.

'Okay,' I murmur to myself and not to him. 'Okay.'

I turn around and begin walking away, back towards the woods, because this is all that makes sense. I have no phone, no computer, no way of communicating, no way of looking up train times or maps or walking directions. The sun is already beating down hard even now, at mid-morning, and if I can get to the shade I'll be able to think straight.

'Caitlin, come on. Where are you going?'

'I'm going to the woods.'

He follows me, and doesn't talk, and the silence and shade of the trees doesn't make any of this easier. I feel light-headed, my body tingling with something like electricity. My legs feel hollow.

'What is this place?'

'It's hard to explain.'

'Try.'

'It's just that... I think anything I say is only going to make you more mad, and it's not really my job to explain this part—'

'It's not your job? What are you, a Mormon? Or, I don't know, a Scientologist? Is this a church?'

I'm casting around wildly in my head for the names of more creepy religious organizations, already trying to fit this experience into a box that will make sense as an anecdote back home. The time Scientology tried to recruit me.

'Hell no, it's not a church. It's more like a... a healing group.'

'A healing group.'

I bite back a hysterical giggle.

'So, what made you pick on me? I looked like I needed healing?'

'It wasn't like that.'

His denials are getting more and more half-hearted, and I feel myself growing angrier as he grows quieter, trying to fill the void left by his ebbing energy.

'Were you in New York specifically looking for someone like me? Someone easily led, foreign, alone, clearly a bit broken?'

'You're not broken—'

'I'm getting out of here.'

'Okay, look, if that's really what you want nobody's going to stop you.'

'Great, so show me where the bus station is.'

'You need to talk to Don, he can get you a ride to the terminal. That cabin that you saw by the lake, that's his office, but I don't think he's there right now—'

'So find him. I'll wait for him there.'

I turn and start walking, and it's almost a relief when I don't feel Jake's presence at my side. Almost.

I don't look back, breaking into a jog as the glinting water appears in the distance. I try to focus only on that, and not the memory of Jake's arms around my waist, the solidity of his gaze on mine and how urgently I wanted to believe in him. Done. Done. Done.

CHAPTER SEVEN

The first thing I notice is the lake.

The cabin is almost on the water, and from the doorway it looks afloat. A swathe of silver-blue, laid out so unmoving it could be ice, like it wouldn't give under your weight. Beyond is the forest, and from the line of dark trees behind the lake there's no way of knowing how far back it goes. For miles, I imagine.

I was surprised to find the door unlocked, my knocks going unanswered, and though decorum tells me I should wait outside there is something irresistible to me about this space, beckoning me in. Everything inside the office is dark wood and silver, a natural extension from the outside landscape. Before the panoramic windows is a neat mahogany desk, a stack of manila folders on one corner. A spherical paperweight, a leather place mat, a row of three pens. A chunky black laptop that might have been new in the late nineties. Bookshelves line the walls, the left mostly filled with large hardback volumes, the right a mixture of paperbacks and what look like leaflets.

I pull out one leather-bound book, looking for distraction more than anything. *The Interpretation of Dreams* by Sigmund Freud, an old well-worn edition with '$9' hand-written on the inside of its cover.

The idea of decoding dreams has never held much weight for me. My mum went through a phase, during one of her more lucid periods on an antipsychotic that worked, where it obsessed her. She had an encyclopaedia of dream interpretation – less weighty than the Freud, more pictures – which she kept on hand at all times.

'Did you have any dreams you remember last night?' she'd ask, eyes wide and hopeful, and I'd rack my brain and play for time and usually make something up. Having her back was still so novel then, having her able to construct a sentence without losing her train of thought halfway through, or cutting herself off to snap at a voice only she could hear.

One of the dreams I improvised wildly on the spot involved being late for a significant interview and finding myself trapped in our house with a river suddenly running through the living room. The river was wide, wider in fact than the room had been, but I knew that it could be crossed because we had done it before, and this river had always been a part of our lives. But in my anxiety I'd forgotten how to cross, and forgotten too where the phone was to call for help.

As dreams go, it seemed inconsequential, but it kept Mum happily occupied for a morning as she pored over the different elements – lateness anxiety, locked doors, river – and I listened, happily, to her making sense of something.

A door shuts quietly to my right and I jump.

'Hey there. Sorry to keep you waiting. I'm Don.'

He crosses to me and shakes my hand in two smooth, confident motions. He's in his fifties, probably: tall, lean-faced, soft around the middle, crumpled shirt tucked into dark trousers. He looks like someone's teacher.

'Hi. Caitlin,' I get out, sounding more sullen than I intend.

'And you are from... London?'

'Did Jake tell you that?'

'Educated guess.'

He gestures towards two leather sofas placed opposite each other, and we sit.

'So. Caitlin. What brings you here?'

'Well, Jake brought me here. Against my will,' I snap, hoping to galvanize myself.

'Against your will?' The skin between his eyebrows creases.

'Well, I mean... He told me that his family lived here. We just had this whole thing in Manhattan, and he told me that he wanted to bring me here to meet his family. But that clearly wasn't true.'

'Well, that depends on your definition of family. For Jake, that's the role we've filled.'

I think of Jake's stories. His parents taking him to the city in summer, his father showing him how to make a table out of driftwood.

'I'm pretty sure that's not what he meant. This whole thing was just a ploy, so he could try and recruit me for... whatever this is.'

'I promise, no one is trying to recruit you. Lord knows we're a long way from being that organized.'

I look down at my hands, a knitted bundle in my lap.

'I'd really just like to go.'

'That's fine, Caitlin. I just want you to understand why you're leaving before you do.'

There's something in this that makes me feel chastised, despite how clearly I'm in the right.

'Because I've been lied to and led on and humiliated for a week, and I would like it to be over.'

'You feel betrayed by Jake.'

'Yes.'

'Is that all?'

'Sorry?'

He grimaces apologetically, hands raised as he seems to ponder his phrasing.

'What I'm asking is, are you feeling anything else besides betrayal? Anything that was going on before you two met?'

His eyes are boring into mine, and on a petulant impulse I refuse to look away.

'Why would I talk to you about my feelings?'

'I apologize. I know I must seem odd to you. I help people to talk about what they're feeling, look at it, make sense of it. Sometimes I can help to change the way a person thinks, to make their patterns less destructive, or less depressed, or less self-defeating. Other times I can't. But that's what this place is.'

'What, like… therapy camp? That's what you're running?'

'Call it what you like. I still haven't found a name for it. All I know is that there's something about getting out of the city. Sometimes that's magic in itself. It can transform a person, especially New York people. The city can really get into your bones if you let it.'

He's retrieved two bottles of water from a pack beside his desk, and hands me one.

I think about staying here. And about going back to Manhattan, assuming I can even find somebody to drive me away. Both options seem impossible, and I'm suddenly so tired that I let my head fall and press the heels of my hands against my eyelids, glow-worms dancing in the dark.

'I'm sorry,' Don says, his voice sounding far away. 'I know this is a lot to take in. I don't know why Jake lied to you.'

I stay silent.

'Why don't you stay for tonight? You're not going to make the bus back from Monticello now anyway, and if you don't mind me being honest, you seem shattered. Like you could use a decent night's sleep.'

The dreams of my mother and the events of this morning feel seamless to me, one long aching jumble of loss. The only thing I want is to stay here, in this cool dark office with water and books.

'Okay. That would be good,' I manage, not trusting myself to look up at him.

'All right. Why don't you stay here for now, get yourself hydrated, feel free to read a little more of that Freud. We'll get you a room.'

I feel the air shift as he passes me, and focus on the sound of branches rustling outside.

Once the door shuts behind him, I turn to the book in my lap. After flipping pages for a while, I finally settle on a chapter entitled 'The Wolf Man'. This rings a bell, and I suspect maybe it came up during my psychology studies at school, where I consistently went beyond the required reading out of sheer curiosity. I spent hours under the fluorescent lighting of Highgate Library, reading about delusions and hallucinations and the prodromal phase of schizophrenia, scaring myself with accounts of descent into madness.

Pankejeff went to Freud with 'nervous problems' that made him feel there was a veil cutting him off from the world, a feeling I now understand. He resisted psychoanalysis, until he didn't any more. And then comes Pankejeff's own description of the dream that would make him infamous: a dream in which he was terrified by the sight of white wolves crouched in the tree outside his window, their ears pricked, ready to pounce. 'I had had such a clear and lifelike picture of the window opening and the wolves sitting on the tree,' he writes, and this particular line feels directed squarely at me; the uncanny feeling when a dream has so closely replicated your physical surroundings that solid things no longer seem solid. Freud's conclusion, upon hearing Pankejeff's story, was that the dream somehow represented a traumatic experience where he had witnessed his parents having sex. This is a logical leap I can't follow, no matter how many times I re-read the passage.

The small print and rapid thought processes of the book have made me drowsy, and I rest my head against the soft leather of Don's sofa. Behind my eyelids, white wolves gather against a backdrop of pale, slender trees, their outlines bright worms against the black. They seem familiar, gentle, like a sentinel standing guard, and it strikes me that Pankejeff must have been disturbed to see these creatures as anything but a comfort.

A hand on my shoulder wakes me what feels like only a moment later.

'Hey.'

I jolt upright, disoriented, my contact lenses dried uncomfortably in my eyes. Through a cloudy film I see Don, and someone else behind him.

'God, sorry, I just closed my eyes for a second—'

'Not a problem,' says Don with a smile. 'Looks like you needed the rest. I've only been gone about a half hour.'

The girl behind him steps forward as I stand, holding out a hand and beaming. She's maybe my age or even younger, honey-blonde hair cropped just a bit too short to suit her cherubic face, tanned and tall in denim shorts and a white tank top.

'Hey there. I'm Tyra.'

'Hi,' I smile back.

'I'm gonna show you to your room. You're gonna be bunking with me for right now.'

'Tyra will take care of you. But I'll see you again later on,' Don says, clapping a hand briefly on my shoulder as we leave.

Outside, the now-midday sun is merciless as we cross into the woods, heading back towards the house.

'So, you want a tour?'

'Um—' I'm conscious of my belongings still sitting in the room I'd shared with Jake. 'I should probably go and get my stuff first, move it to the new room?'

'That's all taken care of. You just had the one suitcase and your purse, right?'

'Um, yeah. They were in the bedroom.'

'We've switched it all over for ya, but you can take a quick look in a sec and make sure we didn't leave anything behind.'

'Then, yeah, a tour would be great.'

'So we just came from Don's place, which is that room down by the lake. There's not much else on that side of the forest, he likes his space, and that's where he holds sessions.'

'His sessions? Like therapy?'

'Whatever you wanna call it. I like to call 'em my check-ins.'

'What are those like?'

We're walking slowly back through the woods, close to where I saw the strange, ghost-like girl in white this morning. Tyra pulls her lips into a hard line.

'There's not really much in the way of rules here, but one of the big ones is that you can't talk about your sessions with anyone else. Not to be a spoilsport. Don just thinks it's not real helpful to invite feedback from other people when you're in the middle of the process. But you'll find all this out for yourself, anyways.'

'I don't think so.' Off her quizzical look, I carry on. 'I mean, I just don't think I'm really cut out for one-on-one therapy. I'm not going to be here for very long.'

She gives me an odd look, friendly but bemused, and doesn't answer.

'So, how long have you been here?'

'Two years – little bit over.'

'Oh, wow.' I want to ask what brought her here. She can't

be older than me, which means she came when she was just a teenager. Has she even finished school? 'So do you leave sometimes, to see family, or…?'

'I don't have any family. So this right here is the way to the carriage house.'

She says these two things with equal weight and sentiment, and leads me away from the main track, down a path that doesn't look like one until you're walking along it.

'A lot of people sleep up there in the big house where you were, but personally I prefer rooming in the carriage house, the rooms are a little bigger and it's a little separate. You get more space, and also more *space*, you know?'

It's still not clear to me exactly what we're walking towards. There looks to be nothing up ahead but more trees, growing denser and denser.

'This is actually the shortcut,' Tyra says, as if sensing my confusion. 'The main route from the carriage house up to the big house is way clearer, I'll take you up that way in a sec. But this is handy if you're coming from the lake – just don't take it when it's dark, you'll never find your way.'

'I can believe that.'

'So, you're from London?'

Her accent sounds vaguely Southern to me, but I'm not sure if the daisy dukes she's wearing are warping my impression of her.

'Don't think we've got anybody else from overseas here. There's Sean, he's from Toronto – you'll probably meet him tonight.'

'How about you? Where are you from?'

'I'm from Celina, Texas. Little town just about an hour

outside of Dallas. I thought I was a long way from home, but nothing compared to you.'

'I'm going back soon.'

We've finally reached the carriage house, and I'm grateful for the distraction from my knotting thoughts. I'm going back soon. I am not going back soon. Both equally true, and equally impossible.

'Come on in,' Tyra smiles, holding the wood-beamed door open for me. Inside is a narrow entryway, opening out into a kitchenette on the left side with an old-fashioned stovetop kettle and microwave. Tyra leads me down the corridor into the first of three bedrooms, where my suitcase and satchel are laid out neatly atop a bare mattress.

Beside them is a pile of bedding: pillows, sheets, a scratchy-looking blanket. Another mattress, fully made with rumpled sheets, lies against the opposite wall, and a bedside table bears what I assume are Tyra's few belongings: glasses case, toothbrush and paste, hairbrush, a slim paperback with yellowing pages.

'Bathroom's right across the hall, and there's another way down at the end. That's your bed right there – I promise, these mattresses are super comfy – and you can put your stuff in that little cabinet. There's a drawer too for, like, your personal stuff. So does this look like everything, or do you wanna check back in on your old room?'

'Oh no, this looks great,' I say immediately, before even looking properly. 'Let's carry on with the tour.'

'So, two of these rooms are empty right now,' she says, pushing doors gently ajar as we move further down the hall. 'That one used to be Kris's, and this last one here is Dale and

Sean's. They're out on a run right now, but you should meet them later. We do a lot of workouts here, it's a big part of the program. Running, swimming, bodyweight stuff, lots of circuit work. *Mens sana in corpore sano.*'

It's so incongruous, Tyra quoting Latin at me, and it's clear that she's parroting the phrase from elsewhere. Or am I just being a terrible snob, assuming the small-town Texas girl doesn't know Latin?

'Do you like to run?'

We're back outside now, exiting through the back door, which Tyra locks behind her.

'In theory. I like the idea of it, but I've never really... I'm not much of an athlete.'

'Well, you look pretty fit, I'm sure you'll be totally fine.'

It's pathetic how much this pleases me. I am aware I've been eating less food, and less frequently, since coming to New York, without the three-meals-a-day structure imposed upon me and the new concern of money.

Money. I haven't even considered this. I have no idea how many dollars I have left, and I doubt anywhere within several miles is going to take my Barclays debit card.

'How does it work here with payment?'

'Payment?'

'Yeah, like – if I'm staying tonight, and having dinner and everything, how much is that going to cost? I may not have that much cash on me, I need to check when we get back to the room.'

She looks at me in total confusion.

'You don't have to pay for anything. There's no charges here, it's not like that.'

'It's not... Wow. Okay, thanks.'

'Don't thank me,' she shrugs, still looking vaguely thrown. 'I mean, it's... It's been so long since I even thought about money.'

'But how does that work? How does the organization run itself, how does Don keep it going, his therapy and everything, if nobody's paying?'

'You'll have to ask him, I guess. So, this is the way you'd normally take if you're going up to the main house, which is where we have group and awareness training. In summer we usually have our meals out there on the front lawn – there's a big grill out there and campfires and stuff. It's awesome. Thursday is steak night.'

We're taking a wide, grassy slope up to the main house, the carriage house already hidden by foliage behind us. I'm conscious of the sun beating down on my lunar-pale skin, burning already, probably. If I scraped my nails down one arm now, the skin beneath would whiten into tracks.

Tyra has probably never worn sunblock in her life. She looks like she applies baby oil to sunbathe and comes away bronze all over, the kind of golden glow I never see back home. We look like members of two entirely different species: her long-limbed and effortlessly cool in shorts, me pale and puffy in black jeans that only magnify the heat, encasing my lower body like tin foil around an oven-roasted joint.

I want to ask her about family. Tyra does not look like a girl with no family, and yet probably neither do I.

'So, I guess y'all already got round a lot of the big house last night, right?'

'Yeah, I mean – we got here pretty late, so we mostly just stuck to the kitchen and then that bedroom. A lot of the others were locked.'

'Yeah, we always lock 'em when we're gone. Most of us were out on a vision quest last night, that's why the place was so empty.'

'A vision quest?'

'Yeah – that's just my name for it. Kind of silly, I'm not sure where I even came up with it. It's like a camping trip. You'll find out.'

She keeps saying things along these lines, and it seems pointless to say yet again that I'm not staying long. She must think I've actually signed up for this.

'Well, this is the porch here, and we eat out on the lawn usually, where those tables are. We grow a lot of our own fruits and vegetables, but I think Barb's doing a grocery run today.'

'Where do you go to get groceries?'

'Monticello, I guess.'

She doesn't sound sure, nor particularly concerned, just as she hadn't seemed interested in money. Having known Tyra for fifteen minutes, the defining personality trait I'm picking up is contentment, and a lack of curiosity. Which, thinking about it, might be the same thing.

'So this right here's the kitchen, which you know,' and as we pass through I try not to look at the table where I'd sat this morning, the countertop which is now clear, the breakfast ingredients long gone.

'Dinner's the only meal we all eat together, so you're kind of free to graze throughout the day. Ruth and Barb go out for groceries once a week – they'll pretty much get everything you need, but if there's anything specific you want just ask.'

She shows me around the rest of the ground floor, its dark wood and patterned wallpaper and faded furniture. There's a living room with an open fire and armchairs arranged in clusters, their haphazard placement somehow strange alongside the elegant sash windows and polished wood floor. There is no sign at all that anyone lives here. It feels like an impression of a family home put together by someone who has never set foot in one, designed to look normal rather than to feel it.

'What's through there?' I gesture towards a pair of glass-panelled doors on the room's inner wall, through which I can see the kind of dimmed sunlight that suggests a conservatory or greenhouse.

'That's the mind room. That one's a little hard to explain – you should find out tomorrow, actually, so hold your horses for now.'

The living room leads into a much smaller dining room, a large oak table taking up most of the space with mismatched chairs arranged around its rim.

'We haven't really eaten in here much lately, the weather's been so great we've been outside since March. But when it gets cold we'll be back in here for dinners.'

She offers to show me upstairs, but from last night I know the basic layout – six bedrooms or more, a bathroom at either end of the corridor – and there is nothing I want less right now than to catch even a glimpse of the room where Jake held me last night. That bedroom is a black hole in my memory, a non-event, negative space.

I make my excuses to Tyra, who looks slightly disappointed to be cut off mid-tour, and run back down the slope to the carriage house. The sun has passed behind cloud, and without the blazing sunlight the corridor looks dark, our room cold and foreboding.

I sit on the mattress, my limbs too heavy to even contemplate unfolding sheets and stuffing pillow into pillowcase, and listen to the sound of my own breathing. This, at least, is constant. This I can trust.

CHAPTER EIGHT

By the evening, I'm feeling almost human again. I take a long shower with the water turned almost hot enough to scald, and the sting wrenches feeling back into my numb skin until the memory of that pale, silent girl in the woods has almost faded like a dream.

It will be fine. I will be fine. Already I'm beginning to absorb this as a temporary moment of madness that I'll look back on as an adventure. I'll stay here just for tonight, make polite conversation with Tyra and whoever else, eat some steak in the evening sunshine. And tomorrow morning, I will get on a bus and then I'll be back in Manhattan. Alone. Without a next step. I'll check back into my spartan hotel room with its rattling air conditioner and its view of the brick wall across the street, and its absolute lack of anything to distract me from the fact that I have no plan. And probably, by now, no money.

'Focus on the next moment,' is one of the only helpful

things the university counsellor said to me. 'Think about what you're going to do in the next day, and if that's too much then the next hour, and even the next ten minutes.'

My next step is making my bed. The one after that is putting makeup on, and this is like a tiny adrenalin shot because my eyes look brighter, my skin more dewy, my cheekbones more defined than I remember them. It feels like days since I've looked properly at my own face. Country air must agree with me, or maybe the emotional stress does.

I wish I'd thought to bring jewellery with me. Maybe my dad will already have packed up my belongings, stored them up in our attic behind the boxes of Christmas ornaments. He'll be glad for the extra space, and probably for the chance to make extra money from a lodger, though I pity whatever unsuspecting student ends up renting my room.

Forget that house. Forget it.

'Hey!'

Tyra bounds in flushed with sweat-slicked hair in a high ponytail, wearing Lycra shorts and a long camisole.

'God, my glutes are killing me,' she moans, stripping off in two fluid motions.

'Good workout?'

I'm busying myself with putting each item of makeup very slowly back into its bag, carefully averting my eyes.

'It was all right, but the heat just kills me. Whatcha been doing all afternoon?'

Fortunately she doesn't really seem interested in the answer.

After she's showered and dressed in another pair of denim cutoffs, we walk over to the front lawn, which has transformed into a hub of activity. The silver-haired woman from earlier husks corn cobs alongside two young men, her neck-to-ankle dress incongruous next to their loose-hanging tank tops.

Further down at the base of the slope, another older woman and a dark-haired girl stand over a steel grill which looks close to industrial-sized, big enough to cook ten steaks at once. There's a low stone set into the lawn like a circular wall, and as we get closer I realize it's a fire pit, a few blankets scattered at its edges.

'Let's introduce you to some folks,' Tyra says, leading me in a half-jog over to the corn table.

'Dale, Sean, this is Caitlin.'

The shorter of the two looks up and beams at me, holding out a bronzed hand.

'I'm Dale. Good to meet you.'

Sean is taller, paler, his hair strawberry-blond and his shoulders freckled in the sun. He nods at me, polite but not warm, and says, 'So you're the new recruit.'

'Oh, well, no—' I start, but Tyra's gently angling me towards the woman.

'Ruth. Did you meet Caitlin?'

'Too briefly,' she smiles, and I think back to this morning, her black eyes and how I literally recoiled. In the peachy evening light she is serene, benign, her eyes a dewy grey.

'Hi. Sorry about earlier.'

'There's a lot to take in,' she says with a faint smile, and takes my hand in her cool chalky palm.

'Hope you like corn,' Tyra chirps.

'I do like corn,' I smile at her, politely releasing myself from Ruth's grasp.

'We make it good – garlic oil and red chilli peppers,' Dale says eagerly, and I feel my face aching with the effort of smiling back.

Tyra beckons me onwards, swatting absently at a fly that's buzzing around my hairline.

'You got any bug spray on? They'll bite you half to death out here once the sun sets.'

'Damn, no, I forgot to bring any.'

'There'll be some in the big house, I'll go get it later.'

'Thanks.'

'Ruth's been here longer than anyone, you know,' she says with something like reverence, descending the slope in a lolloping trot.

'How long?'

'Gosh, I don't even know. A long time. She knew Don before any of us.'

'How about Dale and Sean?'

'Umm... Dale's been here a long time too. Sean got here around when I did, I think.'

Barb, a short and round-faced woman with her hair cut in a pudding-bowl bob, shakes my hand with such gusto I fear for my connective tissue.

'Good to meet you, hun,' she smiles, and I hold onto her hand just slightly longer than I need to. The woman behind her regards me silently, dark hair framing her pale face like half-drawn curtains, and I recognize her from the forest this morning with a strange jolt. It is unmistakably the same person, but up close her face is nothing like I remember it. From a distance in the woods she appeared childlike, but visible fine lines around her eyes and on her forehead mark her out as unmistakably a woman, probably in her thirties.

'Oh, I think we—' I start, but she has already turned away and is walking steadily back towards the house, arms and shoulders rigid as though held down.

'Don't mind her,' Barb murmurs. 'She doesn't mean any harm, Mary, she's just a little skittish around new people.'

'I can relate.'

'Nah, I've known you two minutes and I can already tell you're good with people. Got a way about you. A sweetness.'

'Oh. Thanks.'

'So, have you met everyone yet?'

'We're getting there,' Tyra cuts in, nibbling on a sugar snap pea from one of the multiple bowls nearby. 'There's Kris, but...'

As she trails off, Barb looks suddenly stricken, as though some invisible line has been crossed.

'I um... I think I met Kris,' I say eventually, trying to break the silence. 'In Manhattan, he lent Jake his car to drive up here.'

'That's not his car,' Barb says sharply. 'It's ours. Kris just borrowed it.'

'If you wanna call it that,' Tyra mutters darkly.

There are steaks now, vast slabs of red brought over by Sean on two piled plates, and as he fires up the grill I stick close to Barb, helping her to finish off husking twenty or so cobs of corn. I want to ask more about Kris, why the mere mention of his name seems treacherous, but now does not feel like the time.

'So, how many of you are there in total here?'

'Right now there's ten of us,' says Barb. 'Abby should be out in a bit, she's still dolling herself up after that circuit training, or whatever the heck it was you all did this afternoon.'

'Do not remind me,' Tyra groans. 'Pretty sure I'm not going to be walking much tomorrow. It was like Hell Week all over again.'

'You need to take it easy,' Barb tells her gently.

'Don't you worry, I'm gonna eat it all back tonight. I'll be fine to get out there again tomorrow.'

'Tomorrow's the mind for you,' Barb replies.

I'm still trying to unravel this weird sentence when I see him. Jake is here, and of course he had to wear the sky-blue shirt, the one he wore on the ferry when he asked me to come here, the one that offsets his eyes so perfectly a lump forms in my throat to look at him.

'Let's eat!' Barb cries out, gesturing to the nearby picnic tables. I've been starving for hours, thinking of steak, and now my stomach is a knot.

'Where's Don?' I ask as we sit, desperate for anything to distract me.

'He doesn't always eat with us – depends on his schedule. He'll be out later to lead circle, though.'

I decide against asking what the circle is. Just get through this evening. Think of the bus.

The steak is so unimaginably good I don't have to try hard to enjoy it. There's an odd lack of any carbohydrates on offer – along with the corn on the cob there are grilled peppers, sugar snap peas and green beans, which taste nothing like the over-boiled monstrosities I remember from school dinners. I can't help thinking a baked potato would really tie this meal together, not that I'm about to suggest it.

Barb also offers me a kind of alcohol – 'Home-brewed!' – which I decline. The last thing I need is to be less in control of myself right now, though Barb's friendly, solid presence makes me feel so safe I almost relent. The smell of the drink – rich and dense, like mead – makes me think of home again, the pub east of Hampstead Heath on a steep down-ward slope of Highgate Road, its sign advertising 'ALE. CIDER. MEAT.'

Our table is filled out by Tyra, Dale and Sean, and I'm grateful not to have to contribute much to the conversation, nor to be anywhere near Jake who's taken a seat at the other table. In no time it's dusk, the sun finally vanishing behind the line of darkening trees on the horizon, and I think soon I can excuse myself, slope off to bed and be done with the whole thing.

'Time for circle,' someone murmurs, and the table empties in an instant, everyone moving en masse towards the fire pit where flames are now flickering.

'You know, I think I might just get an early night,' I whisper desperately to Barb. 'I'm going to get the bus back to Manhattan tomorrow morning, so—'

But she's already guiding me gently over towards the fire pit, whispering 'Trust me,' and I do.

Everyone is cross-legged on the ground like school-children awaiting assembly, and when Don arrives everyone sits up a little straighter, as he settles into the only chair and looks around.

'Thank you all for being here. None of what we do would

be possible without you. We are here for each other, and we are nothing without each other.'

I do an inward double take as everyone around me repeats this final sentence in unison: 'We are here for each other, and we are nothing without each other.'

'And we have a newcomer.'

Oh, God.

'Everyone, I assume you've already met Caitlin.'

And everyone turns to look at me with the same welcoming smile, some more sincere than others. Even Mary, whose face I didn't imagine was capable of such an expression.

'Caitlin, thank you for joining us.'

'Thanks for having me.'

'Has anybody explained to you yet how circle works?'

'No.'

'It's self-explanatory, if you're familiar with support groups. Every other evening, we gather around the fire pit here and talk things through. One person will share – it might be their story, how they came to be here, or thoughts they've been having. Anything they feel they need to get off their chest. Once the share is done, everyone is encouraged to offer feedback. Often the share will wind up leading us into a broader discussion, but we try to keep the focus on the sharer for at least a half hour or so. Does that all make sense?'

I nod. If he asks me to share, I'm making a run for the trees.

'Was there anything that anyone wanted to raise from last night, before Barb gets started?' He looks expectantly around the group. 'Ruth said it was a fairly mellow one.'

A few murmurs of agreement at this. I hear a mumbled 'spectacular' from Sean, while Dale shakes his head in silent awe, eyes closed as though the sheer memory of last night is too much to handle.

'So nothing to discuss from last night?'

'I think not,' Ruth says softly, after a moment of silence. 'Nothing appropriate for circle.'

'Well, all right then,' Don says. 'Barb, all yours.'

'Thanks, Don.' Barb leans forward, rubbing her hands nervously once or twice down her thighs. 'Boy, you know, you tell a story this often, you'd think it ought to get easier to start.'

Beside her, Ruth reaches out a supportive arm and strokes her shoulder, a circular motion that looks almost ritualistic.

'You know how they say about some people that they got married too young?' she starts. 'Well, I was the opposite of that. I got married too old. Too old, because once you're in your forties and single your whole view changes. Your wits get dull, your choices get narrow, and you stop thinking there's an abundance because there just isn't any more.'

'You're speaking in second-person truisms,' Don says sharply. 'It's a defence mechanism, and you know better.'

I feel stung on Barb's behalf, but she seems unfazed.

'I do. Don't know why I'm finding this so tough today. I was forty-four when I met my husband, and I'd wanted to get married ever since I can remember. I knew which friends I was gonna have as my bridesmaids in middle school, I knew where I was gonna have it, what my first dance was gonna be. I had it all figured out, except for the man part. That whole thing just never really clicked for me.

'I kept myself busy in my twenties and thirties – I became a nurse, got my diploma, worked a lot of double shifts. Told myself I was saving up to have a family, without figuring the other stuff you have to do to get there. My mom was real sick too, so I didn't have a lot of time to do personal ads or go to parties or get set up on dates. Fast forward to forty-four, I'd pretty much given up.

'And that's when I met Arthur. And he swept me off my feet. Flowers, weekend vacations in Montauk, the whole kit and caboodle. I met him online, and you know, this was in 2004, so I was pretty sceptical about the whole thing. Signed up mostly to keep my sister quiet. But Arthur came along, and he made it real tough to have a lot of misgivings. He was perfect. Handsome – kind of a silver fox, even then – smart, good job, wanted kids, even though I knew I was pushing it biological clock-wise. He proposed after four months, and I didn't hesitate.'

Watching her, so steadfast, I'm sure I have to be wrong about where this story is going. She talks about the wedding – modest, city hall, not exactly her dream but good enough – and how she ignored the warning signs for too long.

'Arthur was always finnicky about things, and he'd turn nasty if something wasn't done right. On our second date, he gave our waiter a dressing down because my appetizer took a few minutes longer to arrive than his did. There were lots of things like that. And somehow it just never occurred to me that he'd ever turn on me.

'I spent a lot of my time apologizing. I'd quit my job by then, so I spent most of my days just trying to figure him out, trying to please him, planning how to make him happy.

And every time I managed it, every time we had a nice evening with no fighting, it was the best feeling in the world. It was like I'd won. But I was winning less and less often, and still I kept playing. Had to keep believing I'd get that lucky hand again one day.'

'How long did this go on for, Barb?' Don asks.

'Six years,' she replies, after a painful pause. 'Christmas 2010, when he landed me in the ER with twelve stitches, that's when I finally got out. He'd never hit me before, if you can believe that. Wish he had, because then you can look at yourself in the mirror and see the proof. My bruises were all in my head, in my soul, and that makes them easy to ignore.'

'It allows for ambiguity,' Don supplies. 'For interpretation.'

'Exactly. So it took me that long. Six years. But I didn't really get free of him until I came here.'

'Let's hear that part of the story, now.'

Don's eyes flick briefly to me, and I realize that this is for my benefit. Barb describes how her husband tracked her down, begged her to take her back, and though she was lonely and scared and almost penniless without him she said no.

'My sister found a support group nearby for women who... you know. And that's where I met Ruth. And the rest is history.'

Ruth now has both her hands wrapped around Barb's, their fingers interlocked like a lattice basket.

'She befriended me. Made the world seem a little less dark. She was a nurse too, so I guess the nurturing came natural to her. And I guess she saw something in me – the same thing we all saw in each other, that need.'

'The need to connect,' Ruth nods.

'And to escape,' Barb adds.

'And to detoxify,' Don says, and the three words sound suddenly like a mantra. Connect. Escape. Detoxify. 'That's why we're all here.'

I know I'm staring but I just can't stop. Sean is now delivering a monologue about the absence of connection in our modern world, and I tune in and out, his voice more lulling than engaging. Every now and then my ears prick up in fear when it sounds like I may be singled out for attention, but I think I'm over-estimating my importance as the newcomer.

A nudge at my elbow finally stirs me. Tyra smiles encouragingly, and I scramble to my feet along with the others, legs tingling painfully with pins and needles.

'We are here for each other, and we are nothing without each other,' everyone repeats once more, and I mouth along numbly.

'Thank you all,' Don says with a quick flick of his palm, and everyone scatters, like an invisible drawstring around the group has been loosened.

I feel woozy and disoriented, phantom flames still dancing before my eyes so that the darkness is confusing. I want to say something to Barb, something supportive, but everything I can think of seems like the wrong thing. Instead I close my eyes for a few moments, trying to find equilibrium.

'Caitlin.'

He's standing beside the now-abandoned fire, looking deep into it.

'Come here a moment,' Don says, not turning around, and I do. 'What did you make of all that?'

'It was great, it was really interesting.'

'You don't have to be nice,' he says quietly, not unkindly. 'I think you've spent a lot of your life being nice at your own expense.'

'I'm not sure what I think. All the caring and sharing isn't really me.'

'I wonder why that is.'

He sounds like he really does wonder.

'But Barb's story was amazing.'

'Yes, she's quite a spirit. You should talk to her more on your own time, she's very open. A lot more comfortable one-on-one.'

'That makes two of us.'

'We try to do a mix of group and individual therapy here. I think the group dynamic is important when it comes to shaking off some of the more damaging aspects of American society. We're such a culture of rugged individualists – any hint of community, of concern for your fellow man, and you're a socialist.'

'I was worried you were going to pick on me,' I admit. 'Ask me to share or something.'

'I wouldn't put you on the spot like that on your first night. I would like to hear your story, though.'

'There's not much to tell.'

'I doubt that.'

I look away from him, back into the flames, which seem less intense in comparison to Don's gaze. He doesn't seem like a man whose interest is easily earned.

'Is it just you that does one-on-one therapy?'

'Yes, Ruth and Barb sometimes lead circle, but only I

conduct individual therapy. Anything else would be wildly irresponsible – they're not certified. I used to be a psycho-therapist.'

'Really?'

'Had my own practice on the Upper East Side, I was there for a little over a decade. Great years, many of them. But it's a strange profession, because you get into it imagining that you're going to help people. What you come to realize – too late, in my case – is that the system isn't designed to help people. It's actually rigged against you, if that's your goal. It's not that I didn't do good work in that time, or that I didn't have patients who meant the world to me. But I realized I could do more good striking out on my own.'

'And that's why you founded this place?'

'Founded sounds so structured. I came out here six years ago just to clear my own head. But Ruth and a few others, they'd been patients of mine for years, and they followed me out here to continue sessions, even though I'd officially stopped practising. It evolved from there. There's never been a plan, which is why we don't have a name, or a website, or anything of the sort. Sean's been badgering me about that lately, saying we need a web presence.'

I laugh out loud at his bemused pronunciation of this phrase.

'I hope you'll stay a while.'

'I... I don't think I can. I should really go back tomorrow.'

'What do you need to get back to?'

My rapidly dwindling bank balance. My lack of any connections in Manhattan at all. The reality that I will have to go home. The latter is still unthinkable, and I force myself not to contemplate it for too long. I have to go home. I will never go home.

'Nothing,' I answer. 'But I came here under false pretences, and I just don't feel comfortable staying.'

'Do you feel comfortable right now, with me?'

'Yes.'

'And are you curious at all about what we do here? How we help people to detoxify emotionally, to connect?'

'Yes.'

'Then you should stay. Even just for a few days. Look, it's an open-door policy, easy come, easy go. There's a bus back to Manhattan every day from Monticello. But I'd like to hear your story, if you'll let me. I'd like you to feel safe. I get the sense that you haven't in a while.'

I look harder into the fire, my eyes stinging, and say yes.

CHAPTER NINE

All I remember from the next morning is pain.

Tyra wakes me up at dawn, pale light barely lapping the edges of half-drawn shutters, and my eyes are dry and scratchy as she beams down at me.

'It's time for your induction!'

'What?'

'Your induction. It's just a fancy term for showing you the ropes. Strength training, core work, HIIT intervals, that kind of stuff.'

She could quite literally be speaking a foreign language.

'Fridays are always morning workouts. But don't worry, I'm feeling pretty beat up myself after yesterday, so I'll go easy on you.'

'Um.' I struggle for words, overcome by the horror of this moment. My bed – the same hard mattress that had seemed so uninviting yesterday – now feels like the most welcoming cocoon in the world. 'Is it light yet?'

'It will be soon,' Tyra grins. 'If we get out there in ten we can see the sunrise.'

And we do, and even as I'm still struggling to make sense of the world through my sleep-sticky eyes and the overwhelming sense of doom that has become part of my morning routine, there is no denying the beauty of this dawn. The sun mounts slowly in threads of red and gold, the air sweeter than I'd noticed yesterday, foreign after so long in the smoggy city.

Induction, as it turns out, is just Tyra talk-yelling me through a seemingly endless sequence of weight-bearing exercises. They remind me dimly of the 1980s-era fitness video I used to watch my mum do growing up, in which a perma-grinning blonde in a leotard walked you through exercises like 'Wash the windows!' and 'Go skiing!', as though assigning meaning to these repetitive motions would make them feel less absurd.

This is resistance training, Tyra says, aimed at building muscle and improving my body composition. My body could not possibly feel less composed as I struggle to hold myself in a high plank for the allotted thirty seconds.

'Girls don't have a lot of upper body strength naturally. We're kind of imbalanced that way, so it's real important for us to build it up.'

I grunt in response, focusing on keeping my weight spread evenly over my arms and legs, hands beneath my shoulders, spine flat and not arched.

'You ever heard the expression "Pain is weakness leaving the body"?'

'No, but it sounds like a lie.'

'It's true! I think so, at any rate. A lot of the time when

your body tells you you can't do something, it's really just an invitation to push yourself through the burn.'

It's a strange thing, listening to Tyra speak. On the one hand, I know that nothing can possibly be as easy as her maxims make it sound, and on the other hand they seem impeccably logical. Like this network of straightforward wisdom has always existed, if I'd just been open to it. And maybe life really can be this simple.

After what feels like several hours of high planks, low planks, side planks, push-ups, mountain climbers and more, my muscles are quivering involuntarily and sweat is pouring into my eyes.

'All right, that should do it,' Tyra says, giving me momentary hope. 'Let's move on to cardio. You always wanna do your strength work before cardio, because that way your body's gonna have to start burning fat for fuel during your cardio. Plus your form will probably suck if you do strength after cardio, because your muscles are already fatigued.'

Cardio consists of 'sprint drills' – running as fast as possible between two points and bending to touch each one as you reach it, which sounds easier than it turns out to be – along with jumping jacks, some basic kickboxing moves and a short run down to the lake that would have been longer had my pride not finally given way to exhaustion. The stitch in my side and the mounting stiffness in my neck and shoulders force me, finally, to admit I'm done.

'That's okay,' Tyra says encouragingly, as I press a fist into my side to try to dispel the stitch. 'I was expecting you to clock out way before now. You did real well for your first time, I'm impressed.'

And I can only assume it's the endorphin rush, but when I emerge later freshly showered and join Tyra at a picnic table, I feel invincible. I wish Jake would appear like he did last night, because I now feel I could stand the sight of him, could even smile breezily at him and say 'Morning!'

He's nowhere to be seen, but Dale does join us for breakfast, carrying a plate piled high with what turn out to be banana-nut pancakes. I'm not sure if they're the best thing I've ever eaten or if ravenous hunger is warping my tastebuds, but either way only propriety keeps me from inhaling my entire plateful at once.

'You know what's amazing about these pancakes?' Dale asks, passing me a jar of runny honey to pour over my own.

'Everything?'

He laughs.

'They're totally wheat-free. And dairy-free. They only have four ingredients – banana, eggs, almond butter and cashew butter. The cashew butter is what gives them that kind of cookie dough taste.'

'Wow. I didn't even know you could make pancakes without flour.'

'I know, right? Most people don't. Have you heard of paleo?'

I shake my head, mouth too full to respond.

'It's the paleolithic diet – basically caveman food. It's how we eat here.'

'Oh boy, here comes the hard sell. Get comfy,' Tyra groans, headbutting his bicep in mock-despair.

'No more pancakes for you, bitch,' Dale answers mildly. 'Okay. So the Stone Age began with the invention of stone tools, and it lasted up until the beginning of the agricultural revolution, about ten thousand years ago. And back then, we were hunter-gatherers, right? So everything we ate, we either hunted, foraged or fished. There were no grains, there was no dairy because we had no domesticated cattle, so what we ate was meat, fish, fruits, nuts and seeds. What the paleo diet does is mimic that.'

'Basically, you can't eat carbs,' Tyra interjects.

'Not true, and you know it. These pancakes we're eating right now are packed with carbs – fruit has a ton of carbs, and so do veggies. The four main food groups you need to avoid are grains, dairy products, vegetable oils and refined sugar. Which are the four major ingredients in most junk food, which the American diet is saturated with. And that's why our children are obese, our hormones are all out of whack and we're dying faster than ever from heart disease and diabetes.'

'Okay, I only have one question about this. Can you eat chocolate?' I ask.

'Dark chocolate, sure. So long as it doesn't have milk solids and as little sugar as possible, you're good.'

'Okay, I'm in.'

'Honestly, it took me a couple of months to adjust, and I wanted to kill him for that entire time,' Tyra says. 'But much as I miss biscuits and gravy – and my God, I do – I've gotta admit that I've never, ever felt better in my life than on this diet. My skin cleared up like magic, and I'd always had real bad skin.'

'Me too,' I admit, suddenly self-conscious. In my post-exercise elation, I hadn't even thought of putting on makeup.

'Few weeks on paleo, that'll clear right up. And you'll probably find you have more energy, you sleep better, you're more alert—'

'You get way less bloated,' Tyra interrupts. 'I don't know how Aunt Flo treats you when she comes to town, but she was always pretty rough on me, and I swear after I switched to paleo that all pretty much disappeared.'

Dale makes a protesting sound in the back of his throat, mid-sip of coffee.

'Girl, really? Can you not?'

'Hush your mouth, Dale. Caitlin and I are having a woman-to-woman moment here, and let me tell you, this is a serious issue for us. This is dealbreaker stuff, right here, this could turn her onto paleo forever.'

'She's already on board! Easiest convert ever!'

'Well, you know, I say that now,' I laugh, 'but I can already imagine I might regret it next time I get a cheese craving.'

'Ugh, don't talk to me about cheese,' Tyra moans. 'I just have to pretend like it doesn't exist. Which thankfully is pretty easy 'cause Barb and Ruth do all the grocery shopping, not that we buy a whole lot from the store.'

'Yeah, we're mostly self-sustaining. All this land you see around here is part of the estate, Don owns it, and we grow pretty much all our own fruits and vegetables here. There's black walnut trees out back – wish we could grow more nuts but the winters up here are too cold for it, so we buy organic almonds and cashews, make our own nut butters. There's a farm a few miles north of here where we get all our meat and honey, and we fish for trout and bass in Catskill Creek.'

'And Dale makes pancakes, among other things.'

'Among a lot of other things. I'm cooking up some sweet potato brownies for later – seriously, don't knock 'em till you've tried 'em.'

I'm already starting to feel better about my decision to stay for a few days – this place is essentially free bootcamp, and I've always wondered what it would be like to be truly lean, in the best shape of my life. Why not here? These people seemed impossibly strange to me yesterday, but looking at Dale and Tyra now I have no idea why.

After breakfast, we go for a gentle hike around a short looping trail that runs parallel to the lake. Dale asks me a lot of questions about where I'm from, and is almost alarmingly impressed when I tell him I was at Oxford.

'You may be the smartest person I've ever met. Just, like, by default,' he tells me solemnly.

'Well, you should meet some of the people I went to university with. They're not all geniuses, by any stretch.'

'I wouldn't know. I'm still not over getting rejected from Syracuse. I swear if I'd gotten in there instead of fucking Schenectady Community College, I wouldn't have dropped out. I'd have been, like, at least seventy per cent less likely to drop out.'

'You keep telling yourself that, darlin',' Tyra says, earning a playful dig in the ribs from Dale.

'So, are you worried that the mind part isn't going to work on her?' Dale asks, looking meaningfully at me.

'No, why?'

'She might be too smart. Like, I'm not even kidding, I think she has to be the smartest person who's ever come through here.'

'She is pretty smart.'

This has gone from charming to uncomfortable, their flattery concealing what feels like passive-aggression. Am I acting like I think I'm too good for them? Maybe what I think is playful has come off as condescending. Then again, maybe I'm overthinking all of this.

I smile in what I hope is a humble, curious way, but they're not actually looking at me.

'I feel like if you're too smart, like if you're really in your own head to begin with, then maybe thought-stopping isn't going to work.'

'No, that's the whole point of it, like Don always says. It's people who think too hard that need it the most. God knows I do.'

'Need what?' I finally interject.

'So most days are divided up into two segments, morning and afternoon. And for each of those segments you'll do one of four things: body work, mind work, yard work or soul work.'

'So, body work is what I did this morning?'

'You got it. Yard work is just what it sounds like: gardening, weeding, planting things, cooking, cleaning, whatever needs doing around the place. Soul work is your sessions with Don – has he mentioned those?'

I nod. I wish now that I'd asked Don exactly when I'd be able to have my first one-on-one with him.

'And then there's mind work. Which is kind of hard to explain, and I know I'm going to mess it up if I try. Tyra?'

'Gosh, it is tough to explain. We should probably leave it to Ruth.'

'Come on, give me a clue. Something. You said "thought-stopping" – is that just what it sounds like?'

'Yeah,' Dale says reluctantly, even though he brought the subject up in the first place. 'Thought-stopping is basically making a choice not to have a certain thought. It can be a certain kind of thought, or a specific one – like, let's say you worry obsessively about germs, right? Like an obsessive compulsive thing. And it's getting so bad that it's a distraction from your everyday life, all you can think about is germs and all the places they might be. So with thought-stopping, you learn to recognize those thoughts as they come to you, and just say "stop". Don't acknowledge them, don't entertain them, you literally block them out of your mind.'

'You have to see your thoughts as separate from you,' Tyra chips in. 'You're not controlled by your thoughts, you control them. You can turn them on and off.'

'I mean... does that really work? Doesn't thinking about stopping the thoughts just make you have them even more?'

'It's just a different mindset,' Dale says, nodding sympathetically. 'There's some literature that you can read on it, but I feel like you really just need to speak to Ruth.'

Back at the big house for the afternoon, my introductory mind session with Ruth goes about as well as I expect. Like hypnosis, I suspect that her particular brand of 'thought-stopping' only works if you already believe that it will, which to my mind makes it more or less useless. But something about Ruth, her serene, impervious gaze, makes it impossible to say no.

So I sit with her in the window seat of the sun-dappled

front room, toying with the tassels on a faded cushion as she talks, and try to look as though I am eager to learn.

She begins by walking me through the very same breathing technique Jake taught me, on the bench in Washington Square Park, and the association is far from relaxing. She notices I'm on edge, and tells me that thoughts are tangible things, separate from ourselves, and that we have both the right and the responsibility to take control over our thoughts.

She gives me five symbols on a sheet of paper – a house, a tree, a mountain, a pond and the sun – and asks me to draw a picture using them.

'Draw whatever comes to you first, wherever you think these five things should go in relation to each other. Just go with your instincts.'

I grit my teeth and draw the picture, feeling ridiculous with every turn of the pencil because, honestly, how many different ways are there to position the sun in relation to a house? I wonder what conclusions she would draw about me if I drew the sun beneath the house like it was buried in the earth, or put the pond on top of the mountain.

She tells me more about awareness, and how thoughts are weapons that can work either for you or against you. She says that she has had her own problematic thoughts, persistent and nagging self-doubt that left her incapacitated in life for years, until she finally learned to simply not accept the thoughts any longer. It's a good story, but the way she says it makes me sure that it's somebody else's. This woman has never lacked confidence in her life, this much I'm sure of.

'What's a vision quest?' I ask, interrupting her just to see what will happen.

'I'm sorry?'

'Tyra mentioned it last night. I've been wondering.'

'A vision quest?' She looks momentarily puzzled. 'I suppose that must be Tyra and her way with words. She means the overnight trips we embark upon from time to time. Out in the woods.'

'You were coming back from one, yesterday morning. Right?'

She nods.

'So, it's a camping trip. Isn't it? Why did Tyra call it a vision quest?'

'You would have to ask her. Certainly, there is a spiritual element to what occurs out in the wilderness. My priority is always to get people back in touch with themselves, and being returned to nature allows for that reawakening process to begin. There are a lot of toxins in the world outside, things that will get into your bloodstream if you let them, and I'm speaking of more than just physical toxins. That's why the mind work is such an important complement to the body work we do here.'

After another monologue about the importance of stopping your thoughts before they stop you, Ruth offers me tea, which I accept largely out of desperation for something else to focus on. The tea is too sweet, with a heavy, bitter aftertaste – I can tell the bag has been left to steep for too long – but nevertheless the warmth of it gives me patience for the next task Ruth assigns me, which would otherwise have been the final straw. Leading me into the greenhouse-like space that Tyra had called 'the mind room' yesterday, she positions me gently against one wall, instructs me to close my eyes and focus on being in the moment.

'When you're ready,' she says, her voice growing quieter as she moves away from me, 'start walking, as slowly as you possibly can. Focus on each individual step, think about the entire movement of your foot from the minute it leaves the ground, and take as long as you physically can over it. And focus.'

I wonder if this is some kind of coordination test, like the police asking you to walk in a straight line. In any case, the tea has calmed me, and I manage to walk in slow motion for what feels like at least ten minutes before boredom wins out.

Ruth tells me this is good for a first timer, and that the goal of this task is to achieve something like meditation by focusing on bodily motion. All it has done is make me sleepy. This morning's exercise and this afternoon's mental acrobatics have combined to leave me weak-limbed, and when I finally escape back to the carriage house I flop straight onto my mattress and doze, listening to the rustle of branches and the distant, persistent cry of an agitated bird.

Dinner is a more languid, less structured affair than last night, though possibly it only seems that way because I'm so tired. Barb has made chilli, which we eat with some strange-tasting rice that turns out to be made from cauliflower, and Dale offers me some of the alcohol that I turned down last night. I didn't even think I liked home-brews, but suddenly the mere thought is enough to make me salivate, and I don't think it's as much about the smell or the taste as the possibility of belonging.

I meet Otis and Abby, the only two people to whom I wasn't introduced last night, a stocky black guy and equally chunky red-haired girl both in their late teens. They are friendly and smiling and ask me about my day, and don't seem to mind when I have very little to say besides good, it was good, it was so good.

There is no circle, and no sign of Don, which I'm told is usual for Friday nights. Friday night is party night, is a phrase that sticks in my mind from nowhere, and plays on a slow, dizzy loop. Is it a song lyric? It sounds like it should be.

Jake is at the next table, eating in what looks like semi-silence with Sean and Ruth and Mary, a stark contrast to our increasingly boisterous group. He meets my eye at one point, and I smile at him before I can catch myself, then look quickly away and back at Dale, and ask him just how exactly this beverage we're all drinking fits into the paleo lifestyle.

He tells me that it's Apfelwein, a cider made from apples and corn sugar and therefore totally within paleo boundaries, and I find the word 'Apfelwein' suddenly hilarious and repeat it again and again until Tyra starts to imitate me, and Dale looks at us both like we're lunatics and I lean against Tyra's bronzed shoulder and giggle helplessly, feeling loose-limbed and blissful.

Back in our room, I'm too full of chilli and cider and Dale's promised sweet potato brownies to sleep immediately. I lie in a daze and look up at the ceiling's latticework of slim wooden planks, and drift into a dream where I am watching the bus back to Manhattan depart from Monticello station, which my brain has painted as a single wooden signpost in the middle of a desert. The bus looks dusty and has blacked-out glass like a limousine, its back windows gaping like eyes as it drives away.

Half-asleep, my last thought is strangely clear: It won't come back for me.

CHAPTER TEN

By the following evening, I am ready to kill someone for a pitcher of Apfelwein. After waking up with razors in my throat and a headache throbbing upwards from the back of my skull, I'm launched straight into another full morning of strength training by Tyra.

'Just high on life, is what I am,' she says, when I ask what she's on and if I can have some of it. 'And you will be too, after this session!'

I don't realize until we're outside and sweating underneath the midday sun just how late we slept. In contrast to yesterday's crack-of-dawn wakeup call, today I haven't even seen the morning.

'Good to know you guys have a healthy appreciation for Saturday lie-ins,' I comment, mid-lunge. I'm pleased to discover that I seem to have more strength in my lower body than my arms and shoulders, which are still screaming from yesterday. My efforts this morning don't feel as pathetic.

'Oh,' Tyra laughs. 'Yeah, that's true – everybody needs their beauty sleep before Saturday night.'

'Why, what's Saturday night?'

'Boy, I forgot, I guess nobody told you this yet. Saturdays we have all-night circle. We start a little later than usual, maybe like nine, and we'll go through till the sun comes up.'

'And then... do you sleep in the day tomorrow?'

'Nope, we go straight into the day as normal. You sleep real well when it comes to Sunday night, which is what's great – you'll get a solid twelve or thirteen hours tomorrow night, really sets you up for the week.'

This sounds more or less like torture to me. In the summer I turned seventeen, I got into the habit of staying up until four or five in the morning, writing short stories and watching films and reading blog posts online, all to avoid really thinking about what was happening in the house. My internal clock lost its rhythm, and when the school term began again I would lie awake for hours, anxiety knotting in my chest as the minutes on my digital clock passed and passed, sure that I would never sleep again.

I had to take pills, in the end, the one and only time I ever have. Since then, I've been deadly afraid of lying in for too long, or staying awake too late, or doing anything that will take me mentally outside the lines. So much for that. If this is the hidden cost to free bootcamp, I'm not sure it's worth it.

'Don't worry,' Tyra hastens to add, seeing my discomfort. 'You don't have to do it if you don't want to. I almost didn't do it my first week, because Lord knows I need my sleep. But it's actually good for your body to have a sleepless night once in a while, like how letting a battery run all the way down makes it charge for longer. Long as you make up for it the next night, it's a good thing.'

'Do you do this every week?'

'Pretty much every Saturday night, yeah, unless there's a vision quest instead. We don't stay up all night on those, it'd be tough to hike all those miles back home on no sleep. Somebody does always stay up to keep guard while we're out camping, though, because of the bears.'

'There are bears here?'

'Just black bears,' Tyra says, as if this is supposed to soothe me. 'They're not like grizzlies, they don't really attack unless you give them a reason to.'

After the endorphin rush wears off, my headache actually gets worse and worse as the afternoon wears on. Just as I think I can't possibly feel any more strange, I walk into the kitchen to find Jake gutting a fish that is twice the size of his arm.

'Um. Hi.'

'Hey!' He lets the knife clatter to the counter, the fish sliced half-open and glistening.

'Don't let me interrupt.'

There are four more fish of the same size lined up on the table behind him, their mouths hanging open in anticipation.

'You're not. Just prepping some trout.'

'Did you catch it?'

'No, but it is fresh caught. I'm just filleting and skinning it ready to grill later.'

'I guess that's something your dad taught you, like when he showed you how to make furniture out of driftwood.

One of those summers that you spent with him at this house, which has been in your family for generations.'

I really had every intention of keeping this civil.

With a weary grimace, Jake picks up the knife again and slices the trout's head off in one smooth motion, then slides the blade into its backbone. It's obscene that he can look this appealing up to his elbows in fish guts. Maybe I'll write a poem about this, or a country song: 'He Gutted That Fish Like He Gutted My Heart'. The lyrics write themselves, if only I could play the guitar.

'Don't you want a real knife?'

He's using his Swiss Army knife, the one that turned out to be engraved with his initials. I'd kept making fun of him for that back in the city, until the night we walked across the Brooklyn Bridge and bought cheap wine in the Clark Street subway station, and drank it on the waterfront looking across at the impossible Manhattan skyline. His pocket corkscrew saved the day when we realized it wasn't a screw-top.

'This one works. Three-inch blade's plenty.'

'So, talk me through it.'

He blinks at me.

'You want me to talk you through the fish-filleting process?'

'Yes. Yes, I do.'

'I'm butterflying it now, so both the fish and the knife have to be upside down, like this.' He flips the fish on its back, holds it aloft and turns the knife so its blade is facing upwards, and slowly slides the fish down onto it. 'You want to slice open from the ribcage, and then you're going to turn the knife over like this and cut along the backbone.

And you repeat that on the other side of the fish, so you end up with this.'

The fish is now laid open in two shining pink folds, a thick ridge of grey bone set along its centre.

'Let me try.'

I hold out my hand, and after a second of hesitation he hands me the knife.

'Okay, so next you need to take out the bone structure here, so you want to slip your knife right underneath this grey part, and make sure not to cut the skin—'

He takes gentle hold of my arm, guiding me towards the right spot, and after a second I turn to glare at him.

'No, this is not like you're Patrick Swayze showing me how to make pottery, okay? Don't try to turn this into a sexy reconciliation moment.'

'I wasn't... What?'

'Never mind,' I snap, wishing I hadn't weakened my argument with the obligatory film reference. I slice the bones out with more gusto than the poor trout probably deserves. 'Just tell me what to cut into next.'

He shows me how to feel out the small remaining bones with my fingers, and I cut them out carefully with the very tip of the blade before handing the knife back to Jake. I draw the line at cutting off heads.

'Sorry I lied to you,' he says, so quiet I almost don't hear him.

'So am I.' And then, putting something together in my head, I ask, 'That apartment. The one you said your uncle owned...'

'It's Don's,' he nods. 'I really thought I was helping. Bringing you here.'

'So why not just be honest? Why was the whole story with the family necessary?'

'I was being honest. This is my family.'

'Don't play semantics, you know that's not what you told me.'

'Would you have come? If I'd told you the truth?'

His shoulder brushes mine, and I leave before I lose the will to do it.

Dinner is later than usual, the entire day shifted forward in anticipation of the extended night. By the time we sit down to grilled trout, yams and baked spinach it's already dark, the sound of crickets encircling the house in soothing waves.

I've somehow ended up on the opposite table to yesterday, and so spend most of dinner avoiding Jake's gaze. He's looking at me, I know, and it must be clear to everyone else too.

'The fish is good,' I say, bullishly breaking the silence, determined to show him I'm fine. 'Tastes so fresh.' But inside all I'm wondering is how much do they know? They must know Jake brought me here. But do they know how we met, and how he persuaded me to come with him? The heady seduction in Manhattan, the family homestead upstate, this could all be a practised routine, and I'm just the latest in a long line of wide-eyed, besotted girls he's recruited.

I look over at Tyra and Abby, giggling over what looks like a small insect that's crawling across their table, and wonder if he brought them here too. I find it hard to imagine Mary has ever not been here. Something about Mary grates on me, though she has done nothing, nor said anything, to earn my ire. That first strange morning in the woods aside

I have never seen her alone; she's always close to Ruth or Barb or both, clinging to them like a limpet, and she strikes me as too old to have so little independence. Over-indulged.

Jake frowns in confusion as I glare at him, and I promise myself that I will ask Tyra how she came here when I next get the chance. I pour out a half-mug of cider and drink it down in four gulps, relishing the burn in my chest and the sting on my tongue. I'm going to need this.

The arrival of Don, who emerges slowly from the trees that wrap around the house on one side, is everyone's cue to begin circle. And for once I'm eager. I reach the fire pit at a jog and spring onto the ground next to Tyra and Dale, who grin warmly at me, Dale handing over a full mug.

'All right, thank you all for being here,' Don begins. 'I hope you're all feeling well rested. Just a couple of ground-rules reminders before we get started. First off, this is an all-night circle, so we go right through from now until sunrise. Anyone who does not want to take part, you're welcome to leave now, but please make that decision now and not later.'

He pauses for a long beat, looking down at the ground as if in deference to those who choose to leave, but nobody moves.

'All right,' he continues with a decisive clap. 'We have a newcomer in our midst, so let's do a quick refresher here. First off, as ever, we are here for each other and we are nothing without each other.'

Everyone repeats this in unison once again and I join in, sensing rather than seeing Don's eyes on me.

'All-night circle works just like regular circle, except that everybody gets a turn. As always, you don't necessarily have to speak about your own past – you can speak more generally about things that might be troubling you, or thoughts that you've been having. Remember that you will get out of circle what you put into it, and that it's worth pushing out of your comfort zone sometimes. If you're too comfortable, you're not growing, and if you're not growing you're stagnating.'

On his left Ruth nods, solemnly and repeatedly, and I hear Tyra murmur, 'So true.'

'I think one of the most important lessons we learn in life is that real family is hard to come by,' Don continues. 'The family you're born with are not necessarily the family you need, or the family you'll keep, and that's a lesson the world will teach you sooner or later. I think a lot of us here can speak to that. Would anyone like to begin on that subject?'

'I guess that's my cue,' comes Dale's voice. He shifts on the ground, rearranging his limbs one atop the other until he looks half-folded up. 'Well. My story. Turns out that all that "It gets better" shit doesn't really apply in every situation. Sure, it gets better if your only problem is being the one gay kid in a super-Republican town, and getting picked on by the other kids at school or whatever. That stuff actually does get better, because you get to go home at the end of the day, and you get to know you're graduating and going to college, and only sociopaths actually believe that high school is the best days of your life, right?'

A few supportive laughs from the circle at this.

'But just to be clear, it does not get better,' Dale continues. 'When your actual family tells you that your existence is a sin against Jesus, and your dad cries on your birthday because he's so torn up that he spawned a sodomite, and your mom makes up an older college girlfriend named Melissa because it's easier to do that than tell the neighbours the truth… It turns out none of that gets better after high school. It actually gets worse.'

He's crumbling a sweet potato brownie between his fingers, throwing the balled-up pieces into the fire pit like the flames are tiny hungry birds.

'My high school graduation was in the summer of '09. And my parents attended, because you gotta keep up appearances, but they didn't say a word to me on the ride home. I'd read all of the stuff online, you know, the how-to guides on coming out. I read a very informative article online which listed, like, twenty-four awesome viral ways that people had come out to their parents, and I kind of started thinking that maybe it would be okay, you know? We live in enlightened times, I wasn't giving my folks enough credit.

'I knew better, but still there was this part of me that thought they wouldn't turn their backs on me. They're my family, they love me no matter what, home is the place where when you go there, they have to take you in. That is fucking bullshit.'

His voice falters on the last syllable. Beside him, Tyra is openly crying, gripping his free hand fiercely with both of her own.

'Tyra, is there anything you'd like to contribute?' Don asks gently.

'No,' she says in a tremulous half-whisper, 'not right now. I'm just… The hardest thing I've ever had to learn is that family doesn't mean what you think it means. All you want is for them to love you no matter what, and it's not gonna happen.'

'True family is hard to come by,' Don says. 'I think most

of us here have come to know that, one way or another. There is not enough real love in the world, and that's a hard lesson to learn, just as you say, Tyra.'

Dale continues his share, moving on to the story of how he left home, after a fight with his father that makes me physically wince as he describes it, though the violence is all verbal. How does anybody turn on their child like this, so deliberately and savagely? My parents never rejected me, and if anything I rejected them, because whose choice was it to leave my dad alone that night with no note and no goodbye? There are people here who would kill to have a home to go back to.

The notion of sharing fills me with even greater dread than before, because now I feel fraudulent on top of nervous. And I know that if we move clockwise, it will be my turn after Dale.

'So that's when I met Kris,' Dale's saying now, 'in my first week of college in Schenectady. Couple of weeks later, I guess, he invited me up here for a little retreat, just to clear my head, but at that point I'd already decided to drop out. And... yeah. I found what I needed here.'

Everyone is invited to share their thoughts on Dale's story, and I stay silent as Barb and Abby express sympathy he must have heard before, telling him how sweet and good and deserving of better he is, and Don mentions again the importance of finding real family.

'You know, they say you can't choose your family, but I don't believe that to be true,' he concludes. 'I see evidence to the contrary every day, among you all. Caitlin, what do you think?'

I'm not prepared for this, and blink dumbly across the flames at him.

'About family?'

He doesn't reply, just looks steadily at me, and he knows I'm stalling.

'I haven't really ever experienced chosen family. I've been too busy with my real one.'

'And what do you think makes family "real"?'

'Real, as in blood relatives. Shared genetics. I'm an only child, so I'm really just talking about my parents.'

'Your parents have kept you busy?'

I'm absolutely not up for this conversation, which already feels like it's turning into an interrogation.

'Yeah, both my parents are… complicated people. But I have to say, listening to Dale's story, I don't feel like I have the right to complain about them now. That's so awful.' I look to Dale apologetically, feeling somehow intrusive, and he quirks up the edge of his mouth warmly.

'There are no comparisons here,' Ruth says, speaking for the first time this evening. 'Don't put your pain down beside another's and allow their shadow to make it small. Your pain matters.'

'It just feels wrong, complaining about them.'

Because my mum is dead and my dad is maybe worried about me or maybe too drunk to know I'm gone, and either way the mere thought of them is making me sick with guilt. Soon enough he'll be dead too, which will at least make things easier to categorize.

There's a silence that seems to last forever, during which I struggle for composure.

'I get what Caitlin's saying,' comes Jake's voice. 'My folks were great too, couldn't really have asked for much more. But sometimes the best things in your life are the things you want to escape.'

'That's how you found it after Afghanistan, isn't it?'

'Yes, sir.'

I want him to go on, but instead he talks about the town where he grew up, and much of what he says are things I've heard before. On our second night together we sat on a bench by the Hudson River and he told me about Hamilton, New York, a small town recently voted one of America's friendliest, and how he hadn't figured out his family was poor until middle school.

There are so many things I'd wanted to ask him since that night, about the army especially, about the dreams he had and the one morning I woke up to find him staring into the air with corpse-blank eyes. I'd been assuming I'd have all the time in the world to ask him these things. Now I can't ask him, and I can barely admit to myself that I care, because girls with self-respect do not ache for men who never really wanted them.

'Haven't you all heard most of this before?' I ask Tyra quietly. 'I mean, if this all-night thing happens every week then haven't you all heard each other's stories?'

'Yeah, but it's never really the same story. It's different every time. And we don't always tell them in a straight line.'

As the night wears on time begins to lose its shape, and I lean against Tyra and listen to Otis explain how he'd dropped out of high school after sustaining a knee injury that forced him to stop playing football, crushing his dreams of a college scholarship and sending him into a depression so deep he considered suicide.

'If you hadn't brought me here, I would've been done,' he says,

Five years, he's been here at the house. The thought is so inconceivable that it only exists in my mind for a moment, and I can't keep a handle on it before it fades into the warm blur that has consumed the rest of my thoughts.

When the very first streaks of dawn light begin to seep over the horizon, Don stands.

'All right, everyone. This has been exceptional, tonight, you're all such examples to me, and I trust you to sustain the energy level through to sunrise.'

There's a general murmur of agreement, and Ruth shoots Don a glance I can't read.

'Caitlin, I'll see you in the morning.'

I turn, startled, but he's already moving rapidly into the woods, his retreating shadow blending seamlessly into those of the trees until he's just one elongated shape among hundreds.

'You're up,' Barb says, giving me an encouraging smile as I turn back towards the fire. 'You know where to go, right, you've been to his cabin?'

'Yeah. Yeah, I have.'

'You just make sure you take a brisk little walk right before-hand, shake yourself out after tonight. You want to be awake and alert for this. Nobody ever forgets their first session.'

CHAPTER ELEVEN

There is too much light.

The sun seems to rise all at once in a hideous burst, bleaching everything sickly beige, and though it isn't hot yet my mouth is dry.

As everyone rises unsteadily to their feet, Dale and Sean extinguishing the fire's final embers, I creep away to a corner behind the carriage house and watch a shadow gradually recede into sunlight. My head is pounding, jagged jolts pulsing along the back of my skull and neck, muscles I didn't know I had screeching every time I move. All I can imagine doing is crawling into bed.

'You'll be sore for a while, real sore,' Tyra said yesterday as we finished our last circuit, when I was too dizzy and exhilarated to believe her. Now even walking gingerly into the house feels like a triumph.

Inside the house I lean against the door, listening to the heavy thunk-thunk-thunk of the pendulum clock, trying to fight back a clammy wave of nausea. It seems to take forever for that next hour to pass, as I drink as much water as I can stomach and try unsuccessfully to doze at the table, the clock's metallic rhythm following me into half-dreams.

Trying to move my head as little as possible, I make the walk over to Don's cabin still feeling dimly sick. The trees seem too large and dark around me like a cartoon forest, and I can't understand how I ever found them soothing.

It's only when Don answers the door, looking crisp and serious, that it occurs to me I should have changed my clothes.

'Morning, Caitlin.'

I had washed my face to get the smoke and sweat off, but my jeans are grass-stained and I feel filthy. Pulling my cardigan tighter around me, I try to smile.

'Come on in,' Don says, gesturing towards the sofa.

Lying on the coffee table is *The Interpretation of Dreams*, more or less exactly where I left it a few days ago.

'In case you wanted to pick up where you left off,' Don says, taking a seat.

'Sorry about that. Just taking your book off the shelf, that was rude.'

'That's what they're there for – goodness knows I wish more young people took an interest in reading. Are you keen on dream interpretation?'

'Not really. My mum was, so I picked up a bit from her.'

'It's useful in a lot of ways, but it can be a distraction in others. Was your mother a very analytical person?'

I huff out a laugh.

'Really?'

'What's that?'

'You're really going to start by asking about my mother? With a book by Freud sitting on the table? My irony meter may break.'

'Point taken,' Don says with a smile. 'Not much gets past you, does it?'

I say nothing, looking around his office. It looks different from how I remember it – lighter, less grand, and there's a musty, woodsy smell like mothballs.

'So, Caitlin. What would you like to talk about?'

'No idea. I'm not sure why I'm here.'

'Why are you here?'

'I just said, I'm not sure.'

'I mean here, in general. It was my understanding that you planned on leaving the day after you arrived.'

'I do. I'm leaving tomorrow, probably.'

He looks at me steadily, hands knitted into a contemplative sphere.

'Here's why I don't believe that: you don't strike me as a person who's easily led. If you'd wanted to leave, you would have. And if you didn't want to come here this morning, to my office, you wouldn't have.'

'I'm English, I was just being polite.'

'I think you do want to be here. For now, anyway. So what do you say we drop all the "one foot out the door" business? We both know better.'

I'm too blindsided by this to reply for a moment.

'Okay.'

'Good. So, what would you like to talk about?'

'How do you usually start?'

'I know this isn't going to seem very helpful, but there truly is no usual. Everyone approaches therapy differently, every person is different, every session is different.'

I should have predicted he would say this.

'But I can tell you'd be more comfortable within a framework. So, if you like, I can start by asking you some questions about yourself.'

'Do I have to answer them?'

'Not if you're uncomfortable. But I would ask that you keep an open mind, and you try to make yourself as vulnerable to the process as you can.'

I'm looking hard at a particularly dark knot of wood on his coffee table, its edges exploding into the grain like fireworks.

'And selfishly, I admit I'm curious. I feel I only know a very little bit about you, and you're a subject of some fascination here. We don't get a lot of exotic foreigners passing through.'

'I'm hardly exotic.'

'Have you noticed that you tend to dismiss a compliment the moment you get it? That's not uncommon. For someone with low self-esteem, accepting a compliment can be very frightening because it threatens their reality.'

'I don't have low self-esteem.'

'No?' He scans me with his eyes. 'Maybe not. But you are running away from something.'

The woodwork looks like a galaxy to me, gentle loops and dark curlicues spreading outwards from deep-brown planet shapes, disappearing into the paler wood.

'You could say that.'

'You ran all the way across an ocean, but you're still not safe.'

A chill goes through me, sudden and sharp, and when I ask 'What does that mean?' my voice sounds strange.

'Do you feel safe?'

'No.'

'When was the last time you felt safe?'

I don't know how to answer this. There must have been a time, back before I understood what schizophrenia meant. Maybe pockets of time after that, even, when my mum told me something comforting that I actually believed, or the internet's phrasing of a prognosis flooded me momentarily with relief.

'At home,' I say at last. 'A while ago.'

'Where is home?'

'London. Highgate. But I was away at university in Oxford for the last three years.'

'I used to have a colleague who got his doctorate at Oxford. Very smart man. Some days, when he seemed blue and I'd ask him why, he'd say he was missing the spires.'

'Dreaming spires, yeah. It's an easy place to miss.'

'Did you enjoy university?'

'Mostly. My first term was hard, just because I felt like a fraud for being there at all, like I'd managed to fool them. Then I grew into it and realized basically everyone feels that way at Oxbridge.'

'And you say you felt safe at home. Yet you left.'

'No, I said that the last time I felt safe was at home. That's not the same thing.'

He waits, expectantly. I've often wished I were better at leaving silences unfilled.

'My mum... this is sort of a long story.'

'We've got time. As much as you want.'

'She always had some problems, when I was growing up. There would be periods she was just gone for a few days at a time, or in bed every afternoon when I got home from school. But she was still a good mum, you know, very loving, sewed name-tags into my school clothes, talked to me about things. When I was about ten, she changed. She taped cardboard onto the windows of our house and made a den up in the attic, because she thought the government was tracking her brain waves and white blood cell count. She thought she was infected with a disease and they would come to quarantine her – or sometimes she thought they were listening in on our conversations. I sort of thought it was a game.'

I had spent a full day and night in the attic with her, tucked up in a coverless duvet that gave us little static shocks every time we moved, and in the dim warmth all I had felt was loved.

'They won't find us here, sweetie,' she'd whispered, her breath tickly-warm against my ear, and I'd laughed and cuddled into her saying no, never, never never never.

In the morning, my dad lifted me into the cold air and carried me downstairs, ignoring my screams of protest. Later that day my mum was gone, and I didn't see her again for a month, and when I did it was in a room with grey walls and narrow windows, and she was glassy-eyed and cold and her hands kept shaking.

'Go on,' Don prompts me.

'So, yeah. This went on for years before she was hospitalized and they diagnosed her with schizophrenia. She went on medicine, and when she came back she was...'

I choke on the word 'better'.

'A zombie?'

'That's not what I was going to say.' But it's not wrong, either.

'I don't mean to put words in your mouth. I've just seen an awful lot of patients get diagnosed and immediately medicated so far up to their eyeballs that they never really get treated. They're docile, their symptoms are masked, but they're not really being helped. It's one of the many failures of our healthcare system.'

'Yeah. Well, she was different. Slept a lot. Moved slowly, talked slowly, never really got excited or upset about anything.'

We'd been living with a ghost for years before she died, is how my dad put it in one of his rare reflective moments.

'Where was your father in all this?'

'He was there, around. I guess you could call it supportive, in a passive way. He wasn't affectionate, but he put up with it all. Just drank.'

'And your mother is dead.'

'Yes.' It doesn't strike me as odd that he knows this. 'Lung cancer. She had emphysema before then, for years, but she never stopped smoking. I think for all the different drugs they tried her on over the years, the only thing that ever really calmed her down when she was psychotic were cigarettes. I knew she was going to die if she didn't stop smoking, but I also knew she would never stop smoking, not even for a day. She tried for a morning, once.'

I'm aware that I'm talking very fast, and also that I have never said these particular things out loud.

'So the lung cancer didn't even feel like a surprise. It was like "well, of course", what did I think was going to happen? And what did she think was going to happen? You don't keep smoking with emphysema unless you've got a death wish.'

That's what someone on an internet forum had written, and it had stuck with me, echoing horribly in my brain as my mum's cough worsened, as her inhalers stopped making any difference, as she lost the ability to walk up even one flight of stairs. Towards the end her lips took on a near-constant blue tinge, and when she was asleep she looked dead already.

'What are you thinking?' Don asks me, quietly. I've been silent for a while, afraid to start motor-mouthing again.

'I'm starving. Sorry, that's literally the first thought that came into my head.'

He chuckles, standing.

'Let me guess – the paleolithic regime is taking some adjusting?'

'I was really on board at first, and now all I can think about is carbs. Baked ones, specifically.'

'All right, you're going to have to promise me that this stays between us. Ruth would stage a coup if she knew I had these.'

He retrieves from his desk a bright blue package, and as it comes into focus my mouth fills with saliva.

'Oh my God, you have Oreos.'

We eat in silence, and I'm too absorbed in the taste to consider until much later how awkward this moment could have been.

'So, you're not entirely on board with the paleo plan?' I ask him.

'Oh, I let Ruth and Barb call the shots there,' Don answers with a wry smile. 'The house is their domain. Ruth is all about eliminating physical toxins, living as naturally as possible. I'm a little more focused on emotional toxins. But they're two sides of the same coin.'

'I changed my mind,' I say next.

'What's that?'

'I changed my mind. Before, I said the last time I felt safe was at home, but that's not right. I felt safe on the plane, coming here.'

'The plane. Tell me why.'

'I didn't want the flight to end. Being suspended in the air like that, you're just… You're so hermetically sealed off in this little world, where people bring you stuff on trays and nobody in your life can reach you, and there's that humming of the plane's engines to help you sleep.' I pause, biting the top layer off another Oreo. 'I know that probably makes me sound insane.'

'It doesn't. You express yourself very well.'

'Yeah, but articulate people can still be nuts.'

'You are quite extraordinary.'

He says it so offhandedly that I'm not sure I heard him right.

'Never doubt that,' he says, off my look of surprise. 'I knew it within a few minutes of meeting you. And what you say about the plane only makes me more certain that you need to be here.'

'Why?'

'Because this is the closest you're going to get to being that sealed off without leaving the ground. If you do choose to stay here, you're agreeing to be cut off from the outside world. No contact with family or friends, no leaving the grounds, no phone or internet access, no news. It's all part of the detoxification process.'

'Does everybody here live like that? Some people have been here for years, haven't they?'

'Not everybody lives that way all the time. People come and go as they like, once they've found their place within the group, but the initial period is quite sacred. That period of total detoxification from the world is what gives you back your power, power you can draw on throughout the rest of your life. Wherever that may be.'

'So people come here and then leave, go back to their lives?'

'Nine times out of ten, that's what happens. The folks you've met here, they've all chosen to come back for their own reasons. Most people come, they stay for a few months, get straightened out, then they leave. Go back to their lives, as you say. But for that initial period, their lives must cease to exist.'

I'm more than halfway there. My phone is drowned, no one knows where I am, and there's nothing about this final step that feels wrong. And Don's presence encloses me as I nod.

'Want to take a break?' he asks me after a while.

'No, I'm okay. I think the sugar's kicking in.'

'I always meant to ask you, why did you pick out that Freud book in particular?'

'I don't remember. Everything was sort of a blur that morning.'

'Do you remember which part you were reading?'

'Yeah, it was the story about the Wolf Man. It kind of annoyed me, actually.'

'Why?'

'It just seemed so arbitrary. This guy had a dream about seeing wolves outside his bedroom, and Freud decided that this represented his parents having sex and basically bullied him into agreeing.'

'Maybe that's the analyst's job – to offer the patient an interpretation of their life.'

'But there's interpretation and then there's just making stuff up. People aren't stories you can just rewrite.'

'So you think Freud overstepped the line?'

'Yeah, it seemed like he messed him up even more by telling him this story about himself. I hope that's not what you're about to do here.'

Don chuckles warmly. 'I doubt I could rewrite you even if I wanted to.'

I wish you would, is what I almost say.

'I'm keen that I leave this first session with a fully rounded sketch of your circumstances. So. What happened to make you leave London?'

'My mum dying wasn't enough?'

'You said that was a year ago. What changed, a month ago?'

I close my eyes and think of that glass, sticking out behind the side table. If I hadn't seen it, if I'd entered the room a few seconds later, maybe I'd still be in Highgate living in wilful denial.

'My dad started drinking again. And he lied about it, again. He's been a drinker for years, but I barely noticed for a long time. He never exactly got drunk, because he's a big guy, high tolerance, very functional. But he was working less and less, missing deadlines, pissing off his editors. He was a freelance journalist, a really good one – long-form profiles, some criticism. He won awards, back in the nineties.'

'You felt he was wasting his talent.'

'Oh yeah. And he'd started getting these symptoms, which he never hid very well – swollen ankles and feet, that was the big one.'

I had Googled, of course, and what I'd found had terrified me. I had printed out the NHS website's list of symptoms and left it on his desk, hoping he would understand without my needing to say the words. We had never had that kind of relationship.

'The doctor told him that he had to stop drinking, that his liver was damaged but if he stopped now, it wouldn't get any worse. He promised he would. He promised a lot, and he went back on promises a lot. And that night, I got home and he had been drinking, and I just couldn't. It felt insane.'

'What felt insane?'

'That I was going to have to watch him die too.'

I've stood up because I can't stand sitting down any more, and the words hanging in the air are too much.

'So that's why I left,' I say to disperse them, then walk a few paces around the sofa, unsteady on my feet.

'You seem agitated.'

'I'm fine.'

'Tell me exactly what's going through your head.'

'I'm worried that I haven't said a lot of this very well, and that we don't have enough time for me to tell you everything properly. I'll forget what I have and haven't told you in between sessions, you'll forget things because I talk too fast, I'll forget important details because I assume you know them, and you won't understand me because of that. I've never tried to make this make sense to someone else before.'

'Take a deep breath.'

I obey.

CHAPTER TWELVE

One afternoon a strange thing happens, though it seems less strange to me every time I look back on it. As I'm walking through the woods from Don's cabin I freeze, a flash of red through the branches stops me mid-pace, the colour alien. It's a car. As I inch closer for a better view I see Ruth striding forth and a man emerging from the driver's seat, greying hair, beer belly, thoroughly benign-looking.

Instead of emerging, I linger behind a tree feeling suddenly exposed, straining to hear their conversation. The lawn is deserted but for Ruth and the stranger, and I have no desire to be a part of this.

'… got myself turned around somewhere near Hurleyville,' the man is saying, holding up his cellphone like a gesture of surrender. 'Ran out of battery on this thing. You happen to have a phone I could use, just to call my wife? She's a worrier.'

'I can't help you,' Ruth says calmly. 'I'm sorry.'

The man looks nonplussed. His reply is too quiet for me to hear, but it looks urgent, worried, right hand hooked awkwardly into his belt loop as he gestures with the other.

'You need to leave now,' Ruth says, still calm but much louder, no room for argument. She watches him, arms folded over her torso, unblinking, until finally he backs away. His brakes screech as he reverses hard out of the driveway, leaving tyre tracks deep enough for me to see from this distance. I wait until Ruth has retreated inside the kitchen to risk cutting through to the carriage house, and spend the rest of the evening trying not to think about the lost man and his dead cellphone and his anxious wife. A worrier, he'd said, which is a phrase my teachers used to use about me. I hope he found help.

The next morning, as I'm setting out for a run with Tyra, the tyre tracks are gone.

Gardening has never been my thing, and after a week of near-relentless yard work I'm more convinced than ever that I have a black thumb. Sweat and soil and some kind of indefinable grit stinging my eyes, I'm on my hands and knees packing soil around my seventeenth chard hole. Barb had made this look effortless when she demonstrated it, but now the ground is barely yielding, each miniature burial taking what feels like an hour.

'You signed on for this,' I had muttered to myself on my first day of chard duty, and I did. I volunteered for extra yard work in order to avoid more mind work, that interminable walking from one side of the 'mind room' to the other, all with Ruth hovering silently at my elbow like a wraith. There is nothing here I hate more – it's horribly tedious and leaves me feeling drained and slow – and after three sessions I no longer feel guilty about stating my preference.

So yard work it is. And though it may never come naturally to me, there is something soothing in the repetitive loop of sowing seed clusters into little holes.

What I much prefer, but have only so far been allowed to do once, is cooking. Barb and Dale take charge of this on a rota, cooking food in giant batches that require a second person to assist with chopping and measuring. I'd spent a blissful day helping Dale to make a week's worth of food: sweet potato brownies, paleo granola and butternut squash stew, marinated chicken breasts, poached salmon, black bean chilli.

I'd seen the process behind the mysterious cauliflower rice that remains a staple food at dinner: steam several heads of cauliflower, then chop them finely in a tiny but powerful processor to get the grain-like final product. Unconvinced by the faintly bitter taste, I'd persuaded Dale to let me add salt and olive oil and mash the results together to make something that more closely resembled mashed potato than rice, and was all the better for it.

The only constant here is activity. Morning and afternoon segments, every hour accounted for, reminding me of school timetables and their soothing lines. There is never an idle moment, barely time to draw breath, and each night I go to bed exhausted and sleep deeply.

The sensation of being truly physically spent at the end of every day is novel and delicious, and lying awake steeped in anxious looping thoughts feels like a distant memory, like something that happened to a different person. Things here feel solid, constant.

'Hey.'

I squint upwards into the sun, wiping sweat from my eyes as Sean's face comes into focus. He hasn't spoken a word to me since our first meeting, much less sought me out.

'Hi!'

'Did I startle you?'

He doesn't sound apologetic, but I shake my head anyway.

'Do you have a second?'

'Absolutely.'

I stand up cautiously, bending at the waist to stretch out my scrunched up vertebrae.

Sean leads me up a gradually widening path onto a main road, which I had no idea was so close. I can't remember hearing anything that sounds like traffic noise.

'Are we safe to be walking along here?' I ask, as we follow the road's undulation round a sharp corner that could only be a blind turn for any oncoming car.

'Oh yeah, there's barely any traffic. I've seen maybe four cars drive along here in my entire time.'

'This whole place is still a mystery to me, I have no idea where anything is in relation to anything else. I suppose I'll work it out eventually.'

'Probably not,' Sean says evenly.

Just when the silence is growing so unbearable that I'm considering saying something about the weather, he says: 'So, are you ready for a challenge?'

'Er, what kind?'

'I'm guessing you've heard about Hell Week by now?'

'I haven't. Not a fan, based on the name.'

'It's a marine term, part of SEAL training. It's basically trial by fire, five days of pushing your body to its absolute limits – minimal sleep, minimal food, continuous physical activity.'

'Were you in the SEALs?'

'Yeah. Can't you tell?' he says, sarcasm thinly spread. 'No, we do a modified version. Ours is more like bootcamp, but it's still five days, still not much sleep or food, still pushing yourself as far as you can go.'

'Do you do this often?'

'No, you can't do it often. A few times a year, but we're doing it now. Starting the day after tomorrow.'

'Who's we?'

'Me, Dale, Otis, Tyra, probably Jake. Everyone who's anyone.'

I'm just going with the assumption that everything Sean says is sardonic, because it's impossible to tell from his monotone.

'You're asking if I want to join you?'

'It's kind of a rite of passage.'

'Baptism of fire. I'll think about it.'

I don't have to think about it for long. There was a time, not very long ago at all, when a physical trial by fire would have sounded like my very worst nightmare. But I'm now several workouts into Tyra's regime, and I've noticed the difference in my performance with thrilling rapidity. After years of feeling flabby and stagnant, regardless of whether I looked that way to the outside world, it's a rush to feel physically capable.

And I want more. Even from a salesman as bad as Sean.

'Hey you!'

Tyra's at my arm before I'm even fully inside the carriage house, beaming, eager as a puppy, and I'm so relieved to see her.

'So Sean found you?'

'Yeah,' and I pause, glancing over my shoulder to make sure he's out of earshot. 'He was the last person I expected to be hearing about intense exercise from.'

'Why d'you say that?'

'He's just kind of... indoors-y looking.' Pale. Quiet. Lacking in muscle tone. I could be describing myself, and we both know it.

'You should have seen him when he got here. But he's super committed, after Dale converted him it was like—' Tyra snaps her fingers. 'So, you're in?'

I tell her yes, and she tells me more about Hell Week, which is really just Hell Five Days ('but believe you me, it'll feel a whole lot longer than a week!'). We'll begin each day at six, with a light warmup jog of two or three miles, after which we'll eat a small breakfast.

'Here's the catch, though: that's our only meal for the day.'

'No food at all for the next twenty-four hours?' I'm not even trying to keep the fear out of my voice. She has already described what the rest of the day will entail: heavy weight training, boxing, more running, swimming across the lake, then a ten-mile hike back to the house.

'No, that's the whole thing. Your body reacts totally differently if you're exercising in a fasted state – you start burning through your stored sugar, which is exactly what we want.

Kris always said that if you want to really get to the root of yourself, when you're trying to be mindful, it's best to do it on an empty stomach.'

'But is that healthy, fasting for a day at a time and exercising that hard?'

'Heck yes, it's healthy. You just gotta be sure and drink a lot of water. And on that fifth evening, boy, we're gonna feast it up. I can't tell you how much better food tastes after Hell Week, you just gotta experience it for yourself.'

I must still be looking sceptical, because she sighs.

'Look, if you don't want to do it you definitely don't have to. It's your call.'

But the next morning I'm lacing up my trainers as the birds have just barely begun to sing outside, trying to think of anything but the word 'hell'.

My stomach is growling already. I should have eaten more at dinner last night – the untouched chilli and cauliflower left on my plate haunts me now – but I wasn't hungry and now it's going to be five full days until I get to eat properly.

'Gooooood morning!' Dale chirps, holding out his hands to simultaneously high five Tyra and me. Sean is solemn beside him, grey hoodie pulled up over his head.

'Is Jake coming?'

'No, he's sitting this one out.'

Thank God.

Dale takes us through some dynamic warmup moves, practically pulsating with unspent energy next to me.

'Sean, you got our route mapped out right?'

'We're just doing the first mile of the lakeside loop, there and back,' Sean nods.

'Somebody hasn't been to bed yet,' Dale mutters, his gaze fixed back at the house. I turn to see Mary, pale and still as ever, watching us from an upstairs window.

And something savage goes through me, because I am part of something and she is not. I've been the pale bystander before and now I'm in colour, alive, blood pumping. I belong.

'All right, let's race it on the first mile. You ready?'

'Hell yes.'

I run the mile faster than Tyra and Sean, landing light on the balls of my feet as Tyra instructed me. This technique never made sense before but now it feels effortless, as natural as breathing, and I could run forever. Dale and I are neck and neck for a while, and though he pulls ahead his eyes are wide and impressed when I reach our makeshift finish line.

'Don't peak too soon – we've got a whole day of this ahead.'

'I could do this forever.'

I'm barely hungry when the time comes to eat breakfast, forcing down the nut-based paleo oatmeal and half banana because all I want is to get back out there. My head is spinning from the reality of being athletic, being able to feel my heart and lungs and muscles working this hard and this effectively.

This high sustains me through the weight training, which is a level up from anything I've done with Tyra before. Dale's chirpy promise to 'start out light' turns out to mean lifting a ten-pound barbell over my head, and I barely make it through three reps before giving up.

'Keep your back straight, don't dip it,' Tyra instructs me as we switch back to bodyweight training, my wrists and shoulders burning as I hold myself up in a plank and alternate pulling my legs into my chest. My muscle strength has not improved as rapidly as my running, but I grit my way through the entire set and resist the urge to collapse.

'Okay, we're gonna take this next run at a real easy pace,' Tyra says, after we've taken a break to hydrate and stretch. 'And I mean easy, we're just trying to loosen up after all that resistance, we don't need to be breaking any records here.'

It's a lot easier resisting the urge to sprint now that my leg muscles feel like a truck has run over them, but still I'm careful to keep pace with the others, because I will not fall behind.

At a clearing in the trees we pause for more water, then split into girl-girl boy-boy and box, Tyra talking me through basic jabs and punches.

'So, you've started your sessions with Don?' Tyra asks later, as we sit waiting for the sun to dry our sweat.

'Yeah, I have. I've only had two so far.'

'Pretty amazing, right?'

'I thought we weren't meant to talk about our sessions.'

Tyra told me this herself, I remember now.

'We're not,' Sean chips in, 'but good luck trying to stop Tyra talking about anything.'

'I know, I know, I did say that, but man, I remember my first sessions... I just felt like I was walking on air. I'm jealous of you, getting to have your first sessions—'

'You don't have to tell us anything,' Dale interrupts. 'I can tell from the look on your face how you're feeling about it. It's hard to put into words what he does.'

I nod, because this is as good an excuse as any, and he's not wrong. I have no desire to try to put what happens in Don's office into words for anyone else to interpret.

I do want to ask about the ribbons, though. A few days ago as I wove my way slowly back through the forest from Don's, half-lost, I noticed for the first time a flash of orange, standing out like a lightning bolt. I still don't understand how I could have missed it before. A bright, tangerine ribbon, and as I drew closer to it I saw another in the near distance, and they guided me back to the path towards the carriage house. A trail of bright breadcrumbs.

I can't see any ribbons now, and I decide not to mention them. By the time we've hiked the ten miles around the lake the sun is close to setting, and I feel a chill descending despite the warm air.

'I'm going to run the last part of this. We're nearly back, right?'

'You are on,' Dale whoops, and when I outrun him by several seconds he wheels around to gape at me, his eyes and mouth wide open in exaggerated shock.

'Girl, what the hell has gotten into you? You're a machine!'

And I am.

By the fifth day, everything hurts and yet nothing does. I'm dizzy and dazed but laser-focused, my entire body light, my hunger pains long gone. We have slept very little – five hours a night, and much of that patchy and shallow – and right now I can't imagine what appeal sleep ever held.

Our final run is seven miles, slow and steady, and though

my hips and knees ache with every step the movement itself is effortless. Hell doesn't seem even close to the right word to describe what this week has been, though there have been moments when I felt I might be dying.

'And we! Are! Done!' Dale screams out as we pass through the final row of trees and emerge onto the front lawn, Sean collapsing dramatically onto his side in the foetal position. 'That was Hell Week, boys and girls.'

'Do we get a prize?' I gasp out, accepting a bottle of water from Barb as she emerges from the house, beaming.

'Way to go, hun,' she murmurs to me. 'That's one hell of a thing you did. Everybody thinks they're capable of so much less than they are. That's the first thing you learn, being here.'

It's true. I dreamed last night of my PE teacher, and of the Year Seven netball lessons that I dreaded like an execution, but in the dream I was playing Goal Attack and I never hesitated for a second. I can feel my personal history being rewritten, in my own mind if nowhere else.

'Wait till you see what's been cooking for you all,' Ruth says to the four of us.

'Oh my God, I am gonna murder that meat,' Dale moans. 'That meat isn't gonna know what hit it.'

The evening's meal doesn't disappoint, and when it comes down to it neither does my appetite. There's a vast salad of beetroot, avocado and mixed seeds with chicken, another of kale, chard and asparagus with pine nuts, slabs of steak served with sweet potato mash and baked mushrooms, spicy chicken wings with guacamole, and I suspect it would all taste just as good even if I weren't ravenous. The cider goes to my head far more quickly than usual, despite how much I'm eating, and when I sway Ruth appears out of nowhere to steady me.

'Do you feel stronger?' she asks, hand lingering light on my elbow.

'I feel like I'm about to pass out.'

'But inside. Do you feel as though you're better prepared, now, for what's to come?'

I have no idea how to answer her question, so I laugh a little, and sidle away towards the fire pit where circle is about to begin.

Jake and Don arrive together, coming from the direction of Don's cabin, and I'm not prepared for how strange it feels to see them side by side.

'Evening, everyone,' Don calls out jovially, taking up his usual seat by the fire pit as everyone scrambles to join him with their blankets and mugs of cider.

'So, I understand a few of you are coming off a Hell Week. Let's have a quick show of hands.'

The four of us wave, and everyone else applauds.

'Well, I just think that's great,' Don continues. 'It's one of the few things from my SEAL days that I wanted to bring with me back into the world. The thing they don't tell you about Hell Week is that it's not really about the physical – it's about mental discipline.'

Of course Don was in the SEALs. Sean's oddly specific knowledge of their training rituals now makes sense. After the usual introductory chorus – 'We are here for each other, and we are nothing without each other' – Tyra pipes up.

'I know it's been a while since I shared this with y'all,

and I guess I've got some new perspective on things recently. On what brought me here.'

She shifts on her blanket, tucking her long legs up underneath her and knotting her fingers together, then re-knotting them as though getting a stronger grip on herself.

'I loved growing up in Celina. I had pretty much the high school dream – I was a cheerleader, fell in love with the quarterback, he gave me a promise ring at our junior prom. And I gave him a lot more than that. I gave him everything.

'I was always real good, went to church every Sunday with my folks, knew in my bones that sex before marriage was a sin. But with Nate, none of that mattered, because I knew I was gonna marry him. It just felt right, I knew it was right.'

I know where this is going, because clichés are clichés for a reason.

'I tried to deny it to myself at first. I was late, never had been before, but I was stressed with the SATs and that had to be why. I got sick in the mornings, but it was probably something I ate. Almost left it too late for anything to be done.'

She grimaces, rubbing her arms as if trying to get rid of a chill, and Ruth reaches out to touch her hair briefly.

'My daddy knows practically everyone in town, so I was too scared to go buy a test in case somebody told him. Had to drive two towns over before I found the nerve. And then I had to buy two more tests, 'cause I wouldn't believe the first one. Prayed so hard it was wrong.

'Telling my parents was the worst thing I've ever had to do. They wanted me to have it, and I knew I couldn't. I mean, just physically, the idea of...' She shudders. 'Being ripped open like that, camel through the eye of a needle, I just… there was no way. And I told them, it's my right. I get to choose. They did not agree.

'Nate's parents had money, so he paid for me to get it done. We'd always talked about going to New York, so we flew all the way there, had some stupid idea we'd turn it into a romantic vacation, like I wasn't going to be curled up having the worst cramps. Like we weren't ending a life. And I knew I couldn't go back home after that.'

'Why?'

She looks at me in surprise.

'I mean, your parents… They wouldn't have taken you back?'

'Never, after that. My mom would never speak up against him, not ever, and he was real clear. You get that procedure, you're no child of mine. He'd always been hard like that.'

I've never seen Tyra this steely, and suddenly everything I've experienced of her – the bubbly, boundless energy, the simple-minded satisfaction with things as they are, feels admirable.

'That's all, I guess. Except… Well, it's like Kris used to say, about family. I know this now, beyond anything, there is no family except the one you choose for yourself. Blood means nothing when it comes down to it. It's the people who choose to give a crap about you that you have to hold onto.'

'Amen,' Dale says quietly, pulling Tyra into his side with one arm and toasting with his mug in the other.

'Thank you, Tyra,' Ruth says. 'I think that's a sentiment we can all appreciate here.'

After circle wraps up for the night, I force my aching

muscles into motion and sidle over to Tyra and Dale, feeling closer to both of them than ever before. Tyra's eyes are a little red, but she's giggling and looks like something has been lifted from her.

'I always thought he might be kinda sweet on you,' she's saying to Dale, throwing an arm around me as I ease myself down beside her.

'Kris? Girl, how many times do I have to say it? I don't think Kris was ever sweet on anybody. He's an ace if I ever saw one.'

'What's an ace?' I ask.

'Asexual. Swings no ways.' Dale looks across at me with a pointedly raised eyebrow. 'How about you?'

'Me?' I swallow. 'I'm... I like men.'

'Yeah you do,' he grins, raising his mug to me. 'Good for you, girl. Jake's hot.'

'Dale!' Tyra says, slapping him lightly on the arm. 'You'll have to excuse him, he never did learn to mind his own beeswax.'

'It's fine,' I say, and to my surprise it really is. I'm laughing. Jake *is* hot, and of course it's no secret to anyone how I came to be here. Why should it be?

Time becomes shapeless as the night draws on, but it feels like long after midnight when I return from the house to find Jake helping himself to a refill from the barrel of freshly brewed cider, his skin flushed from the fire.

'I have a question for you, soldier,' I say, feeling newly bold. The nickname slips out like it's habit, though I don't think I've called him that since our first night together at the diner, when he'd still seemed like I dreamed him.

'Shoot.'

'Why don't you ever talk about the war? At circle, or just ever. It's a huge part of your life, and I just realized... you don't talk about it.'

'Wow. All right, you went there.'

'I'm not asking for gory details. It's just... curious to me, because everyone's all about sharing their life stories, their traumas. A big part of yours hasn't come up.'

'I talk about that stuff with Don, sometimes,' Jake says, after a long pause. 'But I've put a lot of energy into not thinking about it. Not letting those thoughts happen.'

'Thought-stopping,' I murmur.

'Yeah. It's what made me function again. There's nowhere else to put that stuff. Normal people think they want to hear it, but they don't. Trust me.'

'Can I ask you something else?'

He puts a hand to his chin, pretending to ponder.

'I mean, I feel like I'm at a disadvantage because we don't have the ketchup bottle of truth any more. We should be alternating questions.'

'While we're on that subject, I don't think cheeseburgers and malt shakes were exactly on the paleo plan.'

'I won't tell if you won't.'

'I won't. If you answer my second question.'

His hand brushes mine as he refills my mug, and I want to kiss him so urgently I can barely breathe.

'Go on,' he prompts.

'What did you think was going to happen? When you brought me here, what did you think was going to happen with us?'

'What do you mean?'

'I mean, did you think we were going to be together? Here?'
He looks away, suddenly awkward.

'Well, yeah. That was... I mean, I hoped. I hoped you'd
just kind of slot right in, and we could stay the way we were.
Maybe it was dumb.'

It was, but I can't bring myself to tell him so.

'Everyone!'

Don's voice cuts so sharply through the night that I jump,
his tone unusually stiff.

'We have a surprise visitor! Well, I say visitor, but everyone
here knows he's a lot more than that.'

I squint through the darkness at the rangy figure beside
Don. It's Kris, bags in hand, his elongated shadow spider-like
against the flames.

'Sorry to arrive outside of visiting hours,' he says abruptly,
and though both he and Don are smiling there's a chill in the
air that has nothing to do with the night.

'That Manhattan traffic, it'll get you every time,' Don
says cheerfully. 'Let's get you a drink, son.'

Jake has moved forward to grab Kris's bags, greeting him
with a hug that looks uneasy even from where I'm standing.
Ruth is frozen in place, Barb at her shoulder.

'What is he doing here?' I hear a voice say behind me.
It's Abby, stopped in mid-motion with soapy plate in hand.
'He can't just...'

'The rules don't apply to him,' Otis replies.

I open my mouth, but can't find the words to insert myself
into this conversation, and I'm weirdly drawn towards Kris.
He's listening intently to Jake's low, urgent words, head

bobbing intermittently in what should be a nod, but looks closer to a spasm.

'Hey, Kris.'

He looks straight through me. And just like that, circle is over for the night.

CHAPTER THIRTEEN

I arrive too early for my next session with Don, and immediately regret it. I should have paused after knocking, should have stopped as soon as I heard something amiss, because the sounds from the other side of the door don't sound human. High-pitched wails, like something wild being split in half, and as I push the door open I see they're coming from Kris. He's folded in on himself, clinging to Don, his face twisted, and I can't tell whether Don is hugging or restraining him.

I flee before Don has time to turn around, but of course he will know it was me that intruded, and this disturbs me as much as the thing itself. I don't want him to see me as a person who bulldozes, oblivious, into other people's pain. Why didn't I wait?

Running back through the woods I almost trip over Tyra, who's planting bulbs in a soil bed near the edge of the woods.

'Sorry,' I manage, winded for reasons that have nothing

to do with the run. I don't get breathless from light exertion any more.

'Whoa there! Weren't you going to Don's this morning?'

'Um… I was meant to.' I falter. 'But Kris is in there, and he…'

Tyra rolls her eyes.

'Yeah, don't hold your breath for your session. Kris was always waltzing into Don's place unannounced, taking up more than his share of time, even before.'

'Before he left.'

'Right. He's always been kind of like Don's little pet, you know? But it's different now. It should be different now, anyway.'

'You don't like him much, do you?'

She frowns, looking down at her hands in the dirt.

'He used to be the best one of us,' she says carefully. 'The very best one. That's what's scary about it.'

I leave her to her task, sensing that to ask any more would be pushing it right now. When I get back to Don's and muster up the courage to knock, he opens the door with an apologetic smile, and there is no sign of Kris.

'Can I ask you about what just happened?' I say, before we've sat down.

'What would you like to ask me?'

'Nothing particular, I suppose. I just… didn't mean to intrude.'

'You weren't. I'm sorry that you had to see that. Our session had run over, but Kris was in no state to leave.'

'Is he okay?'

'I'm not sure I could describe him that way.'

'Am I not meant to ask you about other patients?'

'Well, traditional rules would say that I can't tell you about anyone else,' Don replies. 'But here our approach is a little more focused on communication, and on sharing our burdens between the group.'

'Do you talk to anyone else about me?'

'No. Never. Not you.'

'Why not?'

'Because you're special.'

'I bet you say that to everyone.'

'Look, I don't think I've made any secret of the fact that I feel a connection with you, beyond what's normal. We're on the same wavelength. Would you agree?'

I smile.

'We are.'

'I have always – fantasized is a strong word, but I have always wondered about the possibility of having a patient who is my intellectual equal. Somebody curious, somebody academic, somebody imaginative. I had more or less given up on ever finding them.'

'Nobody else here matches up?'

'I love each and every one of the people here. Every time a person makes that choice, to reach out, to detoxify, to accept help rather than let the world poison them – that's a beautiful thing. But I simply haven't ever met anyone like you before in all my years of practice. You are unusually engaging.'

'Thank you.'

'I've been meaning to apologize to you. After every session, I feel almost guilty because I feel my responses aren't as fast off the mark as they should be. I'm not used to having to keep up with my patients.'

'You're keeping up fine.'

'You look like you want to ask me something else,' he prompts.

'Yeah. So... Kris went away, right? He left for a while, and people didn't seem happy that he left.'

Don hisses a breath through his teeth.

'It's complicated. People are free to come and go as they please here, as I said before. But Kris, I confess, I didn't see coming. Nobody did. I'm not even sure that he did. He got it into his head suddenly that he needed to go back to the city, and he left in... difficult circumstances. I'll just say that.'

'How do Kris and Jake know each other?'

'I believe they connected at a veterans' support group, a short time after Jake returned home. He was having some difficulty readjusting to the world, some PTSD, though he'd never want me to use that term. And as you say, Kris brought him here. Kris was one of the very first people to join us here, in fact.'

'How long ago?'

'Oh, years. It can be hard, coming out of the military, for anyone not from that background to understand you. I held pro bono group therapy sessions for veterans, back in the city, and Kris came along one day, sat scrunched up into himself, didn't say a word for the entire time. He never came back, but he took my card. And two years later, I got a call from him. Like fate. That's really all I can tell you.'

'Okay. Well, there was something else I wanted to talk about today.'

'Please.'

'Something weird happened to me in New York,' I begin, testing the waters, watching him for any flicker of recognition. Have I told this story before? Trying to distinguish one session from another in my memory has become impossible, their edges slippery with déjà vu, and I'm never certain whether I'm repeating myself.

'Would you like to talk about it?'

'I think I should. It was before I met Jake, a week after I arrived.'

'You were alone for that period?'

'Except for small talk with cashiers, yeah. I've always been good on my own, but a week was a lot even for me. And I'd started feeling odd. Sort of detached from my body – I'd wake up in the morning with my heart just pounding, so hard I could feel it in my ears, and I felt this surge of adrenalin, or energy, or something in my muscles, but I couldn't move.'

'This happened to you every morning?'

'Most mornings. When I woke up and realized – God, I'm actually in New York, I've actually done this thing. I've run away. And before I could distract myself with activities there'd be this feeling of doom, like something awful was about to happen, and I didn't know what or how.'

'Have you felt anything like this before?'

'Never that intensely. But the really weird thing happened on the first night I actually felt lonely. I wanted to be out with people, which is strange because I usually hate being out in a group. But it felt like I was in this big city full of people and possibilities, and I was just watching it all go by like a ghost.'

'The city can be a very lonely place,' Don nods.

'So I ended up in a bar. I don't really know what I was thinking, I had some fantasy that I'd end up making friends, or at least having a conversation. And people did talk to me there. But I couldn't talk back, in the end. Something came over me, like a fog, or like I was looking into a funhouse mirror. Nothing around me felt real. I thought there was dry ice or something in the bar because it looked like there was actual fog, like I couldn't see shapes properly, and everything was too loud.'

'Did you have the feeling of watching yourself from above?'

'Yeah, actually. And the room was sort of looming around me, it was awful. It felt like I was in there forever, hours and hours, and finally I just ran out.'

'How much time had actually passed?'

'Barely half an hour. It was like I'd been in a wormhole. And I just...'

'Are you all right?'

'I just feel a bit dizzy. Remembering that.'

'Your body remembers it in ways your mind doesn't. Muscle memory. Drink this.'

I accept the steaming tea he pours out from a blue pot, sipping it slowly.

'Thanks.'

'Was that the end of it?'

'Yeah. I went to sleep eventually and the next morning I felt mostly back to normal, ish. So long as I didn't think too much about it.'

'Have you experienced anything similar since?'

'No, not really. Should I be worried?'

'Why do you ask that, Caitlin?'

I'm on my feet now, walking slowly back and forth to get blood flow back to my head.

'I mean, does this sound like something? Something diagnosable?'

'You're worried that what you experienced may have been the onset of a mental illness. You've always worried about this.'

'Given my family history, it seems like a concern. I don't know, this definitely felt like... something.' I pause, looking carefully at him, watching for any signs that he is secretly worried for me.

'What I'll say is that it does sound dissociative in nature, but I'm not sure it's anything you need to be concerned about.'

'Dissociative, like multiple personalities?'

'No, no, entirely different thing. I'm talking about a dissociative state, not dissociative identity disorder.'

'I was in a dissociative state?'

'Possibly. Probably, based on what you've described. You may have been in and out of it for a lot of that first week or so, without realizing. Being alone in the city can do funny things to a person.'

I stay silent, processing this.

'What's the earliest age you can remember being afraid of mental illness?' he asks.

'God, I don't know – probably as soon as my mum was diagnosed, around twelve or thirteen. I got obsessed with reading about schizophrenia and psychosis, while she was away in hospital. I was trying to prepare. I went to the library and read every single book I could find, took notes and everything, and once I'd exhausted those I started looking for the early signs.'

'In yourself?'

'Not at first – I just wanted to know what the warning signs might hypothetically be, before the actual symptoms. There's this period where you can supposedly spot warning signs of a psychotic break before it happens. Have you heard of that?'

'I have. The prodromal phase,' he nods.

'But such subtle things that you could basically read it into any normal person's behaviour – mild depression, anxiety, insomnia, fatigue. All of which I had, by the way.'

'What were the more specific signs?'

'There was one that always stuck in my mind. It was a bit like a Rorschach blot, only with words. The person was asked to name the similarities between an apple and a banana. A healthy person would say they were both fruit, but in people prone to psychosis, they wouldn't say the obvious. They'd say something like "They both have skin".'

'And what would you have said?'

'I have no idea. That's what made me so anxious. I think I probably would have said the fruit thing, but once I'd read it the skin answer seemed perfectly reasonable too, and how could I be sure I wouldn't have said that?'

'There is nothing more dangerous than self-diagnosis.'

'But this is how I drove myself nuts – metaphorically – for years, just lying in wait for my symptoms to start, obsessing over every sleepless night or movement in the corner of my eye. So what does a dissociative state mean, if that's what I had?'

'Quite possibly nothing. You were in a stressful situation, you'd been alone for a week, away from home and amidst all these hostile forces. Since we're on the subject of studies, here's one – psychosis is far more common in urban environments than rural ones.'

'So city life can drive you mad?' I mean this half as a joke.

'I think it can exacerbate a problem. That's why I knew, when I struck out on my own, that I had to set up shop way out here. The countryside can't save you, but you've got a better shot at getting your head straight.'

'I do feel more stable here. The structure, the activity, but then I worry I'm just distracting myself from whatever's going on in my head. Maybe I'm just a time bomb.'

'You still think you're in your prodromal phase.'

'What do you think?'

'I think you should take a deep breath, and give yourself a break, and keep coming back here so that we can dig into this more. I'm not worried about you.'

'Okay.' I try to believe him. I have to believe him.

'May I ask you a favour?' he asks, after a long silence.

'Okay.'

'You agreed very swiftly.'

'Well, you're giving me free room and board, food, therapy… It's the least I can do.'

'You need to get out of the transactional mindset. But since it serves my purpose, I'll forgive it for now.'

'So what's the favour?'

'May I call you Kate?'

'Why?'

'I keep stumbling over Caitlin. Not that it's a difficult

name to say, but you just don't seem like a Caitlin to me. Maybe it's because I'm seeing you become a different person. It's what tends to happen to people here.'

'Yeah. I am, I think.'

'I keep wanting to call you Kate. And sometimes, I think it's best not to fight an instinct like that.'

No one has ever shortened my name. I learned from an early age how to say 'Caitlin with a C and two Is', and now I'm struggling to recall why it mattered.

'Kate is fine,' I say eventually.

'Thank you, Kate. Can I share something with you?'

'Sure.'

'It's a story from my past – the long distant past, now. Back when I had just started practising in Manhattan, and I still believed I could save people.'

'You don't believe that now?'

'I believe that people can choose to save themselves, but that they usually don't. The people who come here, they're the ones who've made the choice to reach out a hand instead of drowning.

'You asked me a few sessions ago what had made me stop practising. I'd like to tell you this story first, if I might – I think it'll help to illustrate where I'm coming from.'

I nod, and he continues.

'My second ever patient was a young girl called Robin, around your age. Very bright, very astute, and very attuned to her own mind. So much so that it was difficult for us to make much progress at first, because she was so defensive.'

'Why did she come to see you?'

'She had been cutting herself, and pulling out her hair.

Otherwise she seemed well adjusted, she was doing well at NYU, she had been a high-achieving student through high school, very responsible. Her biggest concern was that her family never find out that she was coming to see me.'

'I can understand that.'

'Of course you can. You remind me somewhat of her. Not her self-destruction, but her resilience, and her stubborn self-reliance. I've never met anyone more disbelieving of other people's ability to help them. She had always been the stabilizing force in her family, for her younger siblings in particular – her parents' marriage had been very dysfunctional. We were making progress, significant progress, when she abruptly left me a voicemail saying that she wanted to stop therapy. That it was doing her more harm than good. That's… more or less the worst case scenario, for a therapist.'

'For a patient to leave?'

'For a patient to leave without the proper exit steps. It can be extraordinarily damaging – therapy is about opening somebody up, making them vulnerable in ways that they weren't before. It has to be done responsibly, and stopping without notice is like walking out of the operating theatre before the surgeon's had a chance to sew you back up. I was frantic. But there's nothing you can do, in that situation, she was over eighteen and I couldn't reasonably say she was a danger to herself or anyone else.'

'Did you see her again?'

'That was the part of the story I was going to leave out.' Don looks on edge now, uncharacteristically so.

'Why?'

'Because I don't want to frighten you, Kate.'

'What do you mean?'

'Almost exactly seven months after she left me, a colleague at Creedmoor contacted me. That's a psychiatric hospital in Queens – Robin had been found wandering on the train tracks, in what appeared to be a catatonic state. She didn't respond to treatment, which isn't unusual with catatonic schizophrenia – they had administered Thorazine, I believe, which had actually worsened her symptoms.'

'Do you know what happened to her?'

'I visited her once, but she didn't seem aware that I was in the room. Which was to be expected. The last I heard, they were going to try ECT.'

'Like in *One Flew Over the Cuckoo's Nest*?'

'The treatment has advanced a little since then.'

'Do you know what happened to her?'

'I don't. I cut myself off from it, asked my colleague not to tell me any more unless there was good news. I had seen enough to suspect that hers wasn't going to be a happy ending.'

'Do you think you could have helped her? If she hadn't stopped coming to you, would she have been okay?'

'Look, I'm not omnipotent. And it would be irresponsible for me to make guesses about what could have happened. But I do think that seven months where she was untreated – that was like a gap under the door, if you will. Just wide enough for a draught to creep in, and the illness to take hold.'

'So therapy is like draught-proofing.'

'Consistent therapy can be. It doesn't mean the wind

outside goes away, but it's got more layers of insulation to get through.'

'That's comforting.'

'Are you and Jake still involved?' he asks me later, the question I've been dreading for weeks.

'Do I have to answer that?'

'You don't have to answer anything. But bear in mind that secrets don't tend to stay that way for very long around here.'

'No, we're not involved. I'm not really sure what we are.'

'The first time we met, you seemed so angry at him that I didn't think the two of you would ever reconcile.'

'We haven't. But I don't hate him like I should either.'

'Why should you?'

'I mean, he lied to me, he led me on, he let me think that he was interested in me all just to bring me here.'

'But was bringing you here such a bad thing?' Don asks.

'No, not in the end. But I still don't agree with his methods. Does he do that a lot?'

'Bring people here? Not at all. It's not something that we set out to do, necessarily, but when someone leaves to go back out in the world, sometimes they'll come across a person they think would fit in. From what Jake has told me – which isn't much, by the way – that's what he saw in you. And he wasn't wrong, was he?'

'Kris brought Jake here, the first time. And they seem kind of...'

'Kind of what?'

'I don't know. Tense. I never know exactly what to think when they're together. And what exactly does it mean, to be a person who would fit in here?'

'I suppose it's a desire to be understood. In your case, Jake saw someone who deserved better than the hand she'd been dealt. Someone who deserved to be taken care of for a change, rather than always having to be the strong one.'

'I've never felt strong. Not once. Not until I came here.'

'Why did you run so far?'

'I don't remember the moment of deciding, but I just had to get out of the house, and somehow the next step became getting out of the country.'

'This wasn't the first time you'd had this confrontation with your father.'

'No. He'd promised to quit drinking and then backslid so many times before, to the point where I'd stopped really giving it any weight when he said it. I'm not sure why it hit me so hard that night.'

'Maybe that was the moment you realized that you could do better. That you could find a better place for yourself, where you wouldn't have to always be on your guard against being let down. That's a powerful moment.'

'I still am on my guard, though. I haven't ever really trusted anyone not to flake out on me. And that's okay – people are just fragile.'

'Not all people. There are people who will anchor you, if you let them.'

'Like you?'

'Do I seem fragile to you?'

'No. You seem solid, like steel. I feel dizzy.'

'You're sleep-deprived. How did it go, last night?'

'It was amazing. We were up so high, we were climbing for hours before we stopped to set up camp. Tyra swears she saw a bear, but the others didn't believe her. Is it true that there aren't grizzly bears here?'

'No, just black bears, which are pretty docile unless you get between them and their cubs. Problem is, you won't always know when that's the case.'

'That's less comforting than what Dale said.'

'Safety in numbers, Kate. I'd never want you going out there alone.'

'I can guarantee you I will not be doing that.'

'You look exhausted.'

'What time is it?'

'It's a little after one. Look, this isn't usually how it works, but would you like to take a nap here?'

'Yes. Please.'

'Keep this between us. You're really meant to stay awake straight through after these outings, you know, but I think you could use some rest. Are you comfortable on the couch?'

'Very. But I don't want to cause any trouble with the others.'

'You'll be safe here. Nobody can see you. Just close your eyes, you're all right. You're fine.'

You're fine.

CHAPTER FOURTEEN

The ribbons have moved.

It takes me a few circular attempts at finding my way back to the house before I settle on this explanation. I'd set out from Don's cabin after our latest session, afloat on the hazy calm that always follows me out, but already I can't remember exactly where I came from, and the ribbons are not guiding me the way they usually do. Following them has become subconscious, a reflex, but reflex only works if your environment is predictable.

I retrace my footsteps and stand still in front of the last ribbons I saw, as though looking at it long enough will reveal my path. There is no next ribbon to be seen, and they have never led me to this point before. Nothing around me is familiar.

Find the lake. The advice comes to me fully formed, as though the words have been spoken to me before, though I can't remember when or why. If I find the lake, I can reverse-engineer my steps back to the house. I hope.

Despite how lost I am, I don't feel afraid – the forest is safe again and has felt so for some time now, associated in my mind only with trips to and from Don's. It's not until I finally glimpse shimmering water through the leaves that my heart starts pounding, though I don't understand why until I emerge into a clearing. Kris is by the water, his back to me. I walk backwards, determined to make a clean escape, and though a twig snaps under my foot I'm sure I've got away with it.

'Don't leave on my account,' he says loudly, and I freeze.

'Hi! Sorry, I was just – I'm lost.'

I edge out into the open, let the sun shine on my face. Kris is hunched down by the water like he's ready to jump in, but he's fully clothed and doesn't seem like the type for spontaneous feats of athleticism. He's different from the man I met in New York, though I can't put my finger on how. He's as restless and spindly as ever but smaller, as though something has been drained from him.

'I've been meaning to ask, what were you doing in the city?' I ask, trying for friendly. 'When you brought us the car, it seemed like you lived in Manhattan. Were you working there, or…?'

Nothing in his stance indicates he's heard me. I suppose he has good reason to be angry with me now, at least.

'I'm sorry about the other day. At Don's – I shouldn't have just come in like that. I didn't mean to intrude.'

Looking at him now, it's hard to believe those terrible wails could ever have emerged from him. He's perfectly still and silent, his face placid when I finally move close enough to see it.

'Don't you have somewhere to be?' I ask, sounding peevish. It seems incongruous for anyone to be this still here. There is always purpose, always activity, always something scheduled. Kris does not fit.

'Probably. I've lost track of the schedule. You'll have to fill me in.'

'Well, I'm weeding this afternoon, helping Barb, and then an evening hike with Tyra and Abby.' Today is a fasting day, and our hike is in lieu of an evening meal, designed to distract us from hunger. 'I think Jake and some of the others are going to get wood this afternoon,' I offer. 'For the fire. You should go with them.'

'I'll pass.'

I want desperately to ask what's going on with him and Jake, why they always sit on different tables at dinner and don't seem to speak at all any more.

'You should lead circle sometime,' I tell him. 'You're too drawn into yourself. The whole point of being here is to share.'

'Everybody here knows my story.'

'I don't.'

He doesn't respond to this either, and I finally give up and turn back, my bearings returning. When I've almost reached the trees Kris says my name, and I start at the sound.

'Caitlin.'

'Yes?'

'He'll get tired of you too, in the end. It's what he does.'

I keep walking. It's only much later in the day that I realize I'm not sure which of them he means.

★

I meet Tyra and Abby on the edge of the forest at sunset, the warm light bringing out the honey-and-roses shades of their hair. I'm light-headed from hunger, but my legs feel strong and my lungs open as we begin our walk. There's a kind of freedom in the discovery that I can, in fact, go a day or more without food. I used to be a slave to my own hunger, irrationally terrified of going too long without a snack, rushing to tend to my blood sugar the moment I felt a twinge in my stomach. This feels better, cleaner. My head as uncluttered as my gut.

We're setting out on a ten-mile loop around the forest perimeter, skirting the lake at its north and southernmost edges, and already the air is tangibly cooling. The summer is over, I suppose.

We walk in silence, Tyra looking as close to solemn as I've ever seen her, and I wish Dale were here with his Tigger-ish energy.

'How did you come here?' I blurt out, not sure which of them I'm asking. Apparently my weird interlude with Kris has reignited my desire for answers from everyone.

'Otis,' Abby answers straight away. 'We were in the same church, back in Rochester, and he just approached me one day with this pitch. I thought he was gonna ask me out on a date.'

She sounds rueful.

'I know the feeling,' I murmur.

'But instead he invited me here. And I haven't wanted to leave since.'

'How long?'

'I guess it'd be a couple of years? I'm not sure.'

Something about this seems odd, but I'm more interested to hear Tyra's answer. It's her story that has been bugging me, ever since hearing her tell it at circle, and I've tried in vain to fill in the gaps for myself. I turn expectantly to her.

'Kind of similar for me,' she says, eyes on the ground. 'Except it was Ruth who came up to me – actually outside the clinic in New York. I guess I was looking lost.'

'What did she say to you?'

'She said, "You look like you need someone to take care of you." I had Nate with me at the time, but even so it hit home. I took her number, and gave her a call after he bailed. It was like she knew.'

I wouldn't be entirely shocked to discover that Ruth has some kind of extrasensory powers. I see her sometimes in the woods, walking with Barb or with Mary, and have to firmly remind myself that there is no way she can hear my thoughts when I look at her.

'Your boyfriend left you? After all that?'

She nods, smiling tightly.

'Left a real nice note. Saying he knew I'd be better off without him, that he knew I couldn't go back to Texas but he had to. He was going to college there, couldn't throw all that away.'

'What a dick,' I say.

Abby laughs, but it takes Tyra a few seconds to join in.

Five miles in, we stop for a water break and flop down on the forest floor, leaves and tiny insects rustling calmly beneath us.

'You know Mary hasn't been seen in days?'

This is a characteristically dramatic statement from Abby,

who I'm gradually coming to know as an engaging but unreliable storyteller.

'I saw her at the window yesterday,' Tyra shrugs.

'Yeah, but like, she hasn't been out. She hasn't come to meals, hasn't been at circle—'

'Like we'd even notice the difference.'

'What's going on with her?' I ask. 'Can she not speak?'

'I'm not sure there's a word to describe what the heck she is,' Tyra says, mouth skewed in concentration as she reties her shoelace.

'How long has she been here?'

'Longer than any of us, that's for sure. I used to figure she was a ghost who kind of came with the place,' Abby replies. 'But then the way I heard it, she followed Don out here from Manhattan.'

'We shouldn't be talking about this,' Tyra cuts in, looking uncharacteristically stern all of a sudden. 'Abby, come on.'

Abby nods, her eyes going dull, and I almost yell in protest.

'Wait, how did she know Don before?'

'Enough,' Tyra says.

'Speaking of Don,' Abby says, turning to me with renewed focus. 'How are your sessions going?'

I bite my tongue deliberately, the sharp rush of pain clarifying my thoughts as I choose my next words.

'They're amazing. I wish I had more than two a week. I wish I'd known someone like him at home.'

'There is nobody else like Don,' Abby replies. 'He's one of a kind. It's a rare privilege, to meet a man like that and have him give you his time so freely, like he gives it to all of us.'

'What do you like the most about him?' asks Tyra, her

voice now dreamlike and playful, like a child playing I Spy. My head is spinning, and I let the dizziness take me, closing my eyes and listening hard to Abby's reply.

'God, that's so hard. I think… I like how he pays so much attention to everything I say. I know he's really listening. He quotes things back at me I barely remember saying myself.'

'Caitlin?'

The spinning slows, gradually.

'He's not fragile. I know I can tell him things, and he can handle them, he can take them on, they won't break him. He makes me feel held.'

'I wish so much he was my dad,' Tyra says, out of the blue. And I reach out and find her hand amidst the earth and twigs.

Fasting days do not exclude cider. We're allowed to drink it, and tea, in unlimited quantities, which makes more sense the less I think about it. The hunger makes me a cheap date, and it helps that I turn up to circle already feeling half-drunk.

'Is this normal?' I'd asked Tyra in our last mile of walking, my head feeling almost detached from my body. 'I feel like… I feel incredible. Like I'm thinking clearly for the first time in my life.'

At the time I knew the words sounded dramatic, but looking back on what I said now it doesn't feel wrong. Nothing feels wrong.

Dale pours me a second mug of tangy-bitter apple, and with every sip I feel my body growing looser and my soul growing stronger. And when Ruth slips over to me as if from nowhere, her bony hand barely brushing my shoulder, I feel nothing but warmth for her.

'We've been talking,' she murmurs, 'and we think it's time. I think it's time. Don thinks it's time. Don't you think it's time?'

And I do, yes. I do.

I float rather than walk across to the fire, my feet moving so swiftly they're a blur beneath me.

Everyone is already gathered there, cross-legged on the ground, their faces lovingly upturned in the moonlight. It takes an effort for me to look away from Jake, the angles of his face making my chest constrict slightly, but he's not looking anywhere near me.

'We are here for each other, and we are nothing without each other,' goes the singsong, and I join in more fervently than ever because never have these words made so much sense to me.

Tyra and Barb are on either side of me, their smiles encircling me, and I am ready. It is time.

'Everyone, this is a very special occasion,' Don begins, shooting a brief warm glance in my direction. 'I'm sure you'll all agree that a person never forgets their first share.'

A general hum of agreement at this.

'And hearing somebody else's first share is no less significant. It's a privilege. It is the foundation of everything that we do here. And tonight, we have a first share.'

Everyone looks to me again, their eyes gentle.

'Most of us – I can venture to say all of us – haven't known Kate for very long,' Don continues. 'But I think I speak for more than just myself when I say that getting to know her has been a pleasure. She's quite an extraordinary young woman, and I think we can all learn a lot from her story. Katy – whenever you're ready.'

I blink hard past the stinging in my eyes, my cheeks aching. And I speak to him, not to the group.

'I just have to start by saying, Jake… Thanks for bringing me here.'

I look over to him but his eyes are fixed on the middle distance now.

'I didn't understand before,' I press on. 'It took me a while, but you were right. I do belong here, and I never would have worked that out on my own. I'm not sure how you knew, so long before I did, what I needed.'

He looks briefly in my direction, gives me the ghost of a smile, and I move on. I tell my story. My voice doesn't shake despite the eyes on me, as I talk about the night I left London. I wonder if my dad has gone to the police, despite my note, reported me as missing. I suppose they could trace my passport to New York, but they will never find me here.

In a few months' time, maybe a year, he will give up on me. He will move on, and be creatively inspired by the pain of my disappearance, assuming he's sober enough to feel it. He will, perhaps, write a heartfelt first-person essay about it for the *Guardian Weekend* magazine, 'A Father's Agony', and even the most embittered commenters online won't be able to come up with much to criticize about its nuanced turns of phrase, its restrained portrait of unspeakable pain. He'll probably get a memoir out of it.

I go back further in time, tell the circle about my mum's diagnosis, her paranoia and the delusions I helped to foster.

I tell them almost all of it, but hold back a few key details, because there are things I want only Don to know.

There is something inherently cathartic about storytelling beside an open fire, I think, because when I finish I feel impossibly relaxed. I lean against Barb, who squeezes me and whispers, 'I'm proud of you, honey,' and listen to everyone say sweet things.

But I'm also only half-focused on the group now, because Jake and Kris are speaking quietly to each other, heads bowed and tense.

'None of us ever really know our families—' Otis is saying, but he freezes in mid-sentence as Don holds up a hand.

'Jake, Kris. What's going on?'

'Do you have something you'd like to share with the class?' Tyra blurts out in a high giggle, jarring the silence.

Jake opens his mouth as if to apologize, but Kris jumps in first.

'I'm sorry to interrupt, sir. But I'm just wondering if it isn't time for Jake to share his origin story. His real one, not whatever *Ordinary People* bullshit he's been spouting this year.'

'I don't like your tone, Kris,' Barb says sharply.

'I don't like liars, Barb. Not here. And it seems to me there's a few people here who don't know the real Jake. Funny enough, it was Caitlin talking about her crazy mother that made me think of it.'

Heat rises in my stomach, but before I can even begin to formulate a response Jake is on his feet, dragging Kris up with him like a bag of bones. 'Hey, no disrespect,' Kris says to me pleasantly, shaking out of Jake's grip. 'After hearing your story, I finally get why Jake's got such a hard-on for you.'

Then he's folded over double from Jake's sucker punch, Don yelling something incoherent as Dale and Sean dash to pull them apart.

'Katy, you want to hear this, right? The real story behind your beau, the reason I got him here in the first place?'

I stare back at him, and at Jake who seems equally speechless.

'He had an episode,' Kris hisses, struggling out of Dale's grasp. 'Poor little toy soldier, broken apart like shrapnel and never put back together right. You can only play the well-adjusted boy next door for so long, no matter how many times you tell that story—'

'Enough.'

It takes me a moment to identify the voice that says this. It sounds nothing like Ruth at all, reedy and hollow and almost possessed, and her stare is enough to finally silence Kris. Jake is gone then, a blur of blue fabric vanishing into the trees.

Don makes a single, sharp beckoning gesture, and Kris follows him without a word towards the cabin, one hand pressed to his chin where Jake punched him. Their retreating forms leave behind bewildered silence.

'Kate, honey—'

Barb reaches out an arm to me and I try to smile, but find myself turning instead, and walking, and then running. The fire isn't warm enough any more, and all I want is his skin on mine. No more walking away.

In the forest I feel blind and yet certain, following what

I somehow know to be his path. He's close, and before long I see his back, the angles of his shoulder blades through his shirt as he stands still and breathes into his hands.

Catching up, I grab his arm and twist him to me, his bicep tense under my palm.

'Hey—'

His gaze is fixed, and there's too much I want to say and too much that I don't.

At long last he speaks, low and soft.

'Thought you'd never look at me that way again.'

'Jake,' I breathe, and his hands are in my hair as he pushes me back against tree bark, his mouth hard on mine, the forest folding itself heavy around us.

CHAPTER FIFTEEN

When Jake tells me the real story, under sun-dappled trees just after dawn, it comes as a surprise. I haven't had time to over-analyse, to turn what Kris said over and over in my mind, because for once my mind has been perfectly still.

We'd danced around the forest floor in slow motion, the intermittent hooting of an owl our only music, and I'd kissed him until I could hardly breathe and almost torn at his shirt, so desperate to get to his skin. I've thought often about what this moment would be and have never imagined it this effortless, like falling, my body in surrender. Through the night, as we slept, I kept glimpsing things out of the corner of my eye, darting shapes that whispered, but I pressed my face hard against Jake's neck, and in the morning they were gone.

'He wasn't lying,' is what Jake says, his words humming against my cheek. My dress is still on, his shirt spread over me like an extra blanket.

'Hmm?'

'Kris. He wasn't lying.'

I prop myself up cautiously on my elbow. My body doesn't feel changed, as I'd imagined it would when I finally had sex, but my head is spinning and I lean back against him, trying to focus my eyes on a fixed point.

'You tell your own story enough times at circle and even you start to get sick of it. You want to rewrite it, edit out some stuff.'

'Like what?'

'I wasn't right, after I got home. I wasn't right, I wasn't safe. My shoulder hurt all the time, and I figured my head would get clearer once I came off the pain meds, but everything just got fuzzier. My family didn't seem real, some of the time, like they weren't really there, or I wasn't really there. There was a period where I really thought I was dreaming, and I kept expecting to wake up in my bunk.'

'Dissociative?' I have learned this, of course, the correct terminology.

'That's what the shrink called it,' he says, looking at me with mild surprise. 'My mom made me go, but I never went back after that first time. This guy had no idea, he hadn't been in combat, he wasn't ex-military, he'd just read all these words in a book and there he was trying to tell me how to "reintegrate into society". But there was this support group, and that was the compromise I found to keep my mom happy.'

'And that's where you met Kris?'

'Yep. Just another veteran, I thought. I guess he saw me looking doubtful and so he latched onto me, told me about this place. He called it "a refuge", but I wasn't ready yet. I thought I was dealing with things at home. I was handling the dreams okay, not having too many of them during the day.'

'You had nightmares during the day?'

'Flashbacks, maybe. It's like a daydream, only I'm not aware of anything around me, impossible to wake up. It's like a wall got broken down in my head. Things that should be separate started bleeding into each other.'

I think about how wretched his sleep looked that one night I awoke, how much like drowning it seemed, and push myself back against him, my head nuzzled under his chin.

'I thought it was under control. But then I woke up with, uh—' I feel his Adam's apple bob against my scalp. 'I woke up on the ground, and my head was killing me, and my dad was there, standing over me, still. And my sister was crying, holding her throat, we were in her bedroom. I'd dragged her up out of bed and tried to strangle her.'

A kind of low hum goes through me, almost a shiver, but I'm too tightly pressed against Jake to feel much.

'And I had no memory of it. I couldn't even tell her why, if it was a nightmare, if I'd thought she was an intruder, I'd mistaken her for the enemy. I kept thinking the whole thing would be easier if I could explain it, but there was nothing. My head was like a shell, just sand and echoes inside.'

I'm running my hand absently up and down his chest, a motion designed to soothe myself as much as him.

'And that's when I left. I had Kris's number, so that was it. We went to the city first, he wore me down a little, and then I met Don. And the rest is history.'

'Wow.'

'This is your opportunity to run for the hills, by the way. I wouldn't blame you.'

'I'm not running anywhere, soldier.'

But there's more. The thing I really want to ask is on the tip of my tongue, has been there all night and maybe longer, ever since I first saw how Kris looked at Jake the afternoon we left Manhattan, like something he'd lost.

We lie still and silent, the story settling quietly into the dirt. I know logically I should be afraid of him now, looking back on all those nights I spent in bed with him, the night I just spent alone with him in the woods. But I still feel safe, like a warm fog has fallen over me and him and everything here, and nothing sharp or anxious can pierce it.

Even the headache building upwards from my neck feels more like a dull tickle than real pain, and Jake massages the base of my skull gently when I mention it, my forehead pressing into the dirt as his sinewy fingers knead out the tension.

'What time is it?' I mumble at last, my words muffled.

'Who knows?' The subtext of his reply is closer to 'Who cares?', and with his hands still working over my scalp it's hard to summon up much of a response.

'Why me?'

'Huh?'

'Why did you choose me? At Jennifer's party, when you came over. What did you see in me?'

His hands gradually still against my neck.

'You looked lost. Pretty and lost.'

'Pretty lost. I was. Were you at that party looking to recruit someone?'

'It's complicated. We don't call it that. Maybe Kris would call it that.'

'He recruited you?'

'It didn't feel like that.'

'It never does, I imagine.'

He's silent for a long time, then drops a kiss onto my forehead and tugs me to my feet.

'Let's stay gone.'

'We've already been gone all night.'

I pull him, half playfully and half not, back towards the house. It seems deserted when we get back, the fire pit cold, the lawn empty and quiet. I have no handle on days any more, but I think I am due at Don's this morning, and Jake leaves to take a shower before I can ask him if he remembers the schedule for today.

The face of the pendulum clock has a crack in it, a jagged scar that distorts the numbers into garbled segments. Looking at it I can't see any point of impact, no sign that it's been hit – only the crack, almost like it occurred naturally. No matter how long I look at the shattered face, its numbers don't make sense to me – the small hand and big hand don't align with anything I can read. But the sun has risen, and that's good enough.

When I reach the kitchen, it's as though a valve has been opened and all my energy drained, and I feel ragged and floppy as I sit at the kitchen table, resting my head in unsteady hands. There's whispering behind me, so, good, some of the others must be awake. I'll wait for them to emerge, and maybe they will make breakfast and the rushing in my ears will stop.

'Morning, sunshine.'

I turn to find Barb behind me with a tightness in her face.

'Hi! Sorry we disappeared last night. We were—'

'None of my business, Kate,' she cuts me off. 'But you both ought to get yourselves changed and ready to go.'

'Go where?'

'Don't you remember? Today's an outing. We're all hiking up into the mountains, camping overnight, getting in touch with the silence. Well, gosh, I guess this'll be your first time.'

'A vision quest? I think... I'm meant to have a session with Don this morning.'

'You'll see him when you get back.'

And the finality of this forces me into submission.

While Barb packs supplies into a large canvas bag, I go back to the carriage house to shower and change, my appetite gone. We'll be away all night, and the weather is turning cold, so I pull on two extra layers on top of my vest and jeans. Tyra's bed is still made, cold to the touch.

'Bring a bathing suit,' Abby yells as she passes in the corridor.

'Wait, what?'

She's already gone, so I choose to ignore her. I have never been much of a swimmer.

It's already early afternoon by the time everyone has assembled on the veranda, and Tyra finally emerges from the house with a sheepish grin.

'What happened to you?'

'I had a little too much of that apple goodness last night,' she giggles, clutching conspiratorially at my arm. 'Thank the Lord, Don let me sleep on the couch in his cabin.'

I pull my arm out of her grip, unsettled by the weight of what she's just said.

My stomach has been rumbling for so long that the sensation has now become routine, and when Barb presses a banana into my hand it takes me a moment to register what it is.

'You're gonna need your strength,' she explains. 'We'll be ascending about one-and-a-half thousand feet all told, and not eating dinner till we set up camp. You look about ready to keel over.'

The veranda is getting full now, Dale waving his finger in the air in a counting motion, but I can see at a glance who is missing.

'No Jake, no Kris.'

'There's a shocker,' someone mutters to my left.

'Jake will be here,' I say without really knowing why. He was so reluctant to return to the house earlier, but I still find it hard to imagine he'd abandon me in this. Not after last night. I still can't shake the feeling that Don will be expecting me, but no, none of this can be happening without his say-so. If I am going on a vision quest this morning, it can only be because he wants me to.

'All right, we'll give them five more minutes,' Dale sighs.

Five more minutes pass in near silence. I keep my eyes trained to the ground, conscious of the glares being directed my way. Growing angrier at Jake with every second.

'Let's go,' I burst out at last. 'Let's just go, you're right.'

Barb leads the way with Otis at her side, setting off into the forest as the sun grows brighter and more bleach-like, an autumn chill in the air.

Tyra, Abby, Dale and Sean move together in a knot, talking quietly with their heads bowed, and I wish I hadn't pulled away from her so hard. Now I'm on the outskirts. Mary brings up the rear with Ruth, looking as close to normal as I've ever seen her in jeans and trainers, but still as though a heavy breeze could knock her down.

It's a relief not to have to talk, I realize after several minutes of rhythmic footsteps. One foot in front of the other, the slope beneath my feet steadily sharpening, this is like meditation. Jake's absence becoming less punishing with every one-two, one-two, one-two. I listen hard to the air in front of me, trying to pick up any hint of what Tyra is murmuring. Trying not to think of her in Don's cabin.

Later, we rest beside a roaring waterfall, jagged rocks framing its descent. And as though working from a cue sheet I have not been given, the others begin to strip off their clothes. Only Ruth remains still, settling herself quietly on the ground beside our abandoned backpacks and tents, fully covered as always.

'It's that time again,' Dale says with mock-excitement that might not be mock. 'You ready?'

'Me?'

Abby was not joking. Everybody looks purpose-built for this, even Barb in her stretchy one-piece, and they're looking expectantly at me. So to hell with it.

I take off my hoodie and long-sleeved tee and camisole, pull off my jeans, almost like I'm watching somebody else perform this strange striptease. There was a time when undressing in front of anyone was unthinkable. But my body feels harder and smaller than it ever has, and standing before them all in my underwear is close to exhilarating. Easy-going girl. Swims-in-her-underwear girl.

But even that girl falters when she sees the drop.

'Last in, first out, Kate,' says Sean sharply, eyes fixed on me.

'You're seriously... you want me to jump?'

'It's a tradition. Rite of passage, if you will.'

'I can't. That's insane, look at those rocks.'

'It's fine, seriously, nobody ever hits the rocks. It's not how the angle of descent works.'

I look around, searching for support.

'I know you can do it,' Don says, though he isn't here.

And I gather the adrenalin tight into my chest and leap, legs tucked, bones braced to be shattered. My landing feels like flight.

Later, everything is fuzzy at the edges, and my stomach is hurting from laughter that I can feel more than hear, tearing through me in hysterical jerks. We have set up camp for the night in a clearing ringed by trees, their tangled branches stretched overhead like a thatched roof. There is food and a new brewed drink that tastes different from the cider, richer and more like wine.

'Why is Ruth always so covered up?' I ask Dale, feeling reckless enough not to care whether she's in earshot. She isn't, I don't think, because he shows no reluctance in answering.

'She hates the sun. Thinks it's corrosive.'

'Like, she burns easily?'

He shrugs.

'I guess.'

The evening had begun with structure, each one of us going round in turn and naming what we had left behind, the thing we had escaped in the outside world by coming here. Dale said judgement. Barb said fear. I fretted all throughout about what to say, but when it came to my turn I said 'Decay' before I'd had time to consciously form the word.

Decay.

'What's a black bear really gonna do, anyways?' Sean is asking loudly, and this strikes me as an excellent question, but I can't find the right words to tell him so. He and Dale are building a fire, I think, but they're too fuzzy and I'm too drowsy to really know.

'Sorry Jake was a no-show,' Abby says somewhere to my left, and I laugh because it doesn't matter, I understand, he had his reasons and when I get back tomorrow I will tell him.

'Everything just makes sense here,' I hear, and it takes me a second to realize that I've said it. Then I repeat it, again and again, and the words don't lose their meaning as I lie back and listen to the rustling of leaves at my ears, imagining the hundreds of insects crawling beneath me in the dirt.

I'm so serenely numb that it takes a moment for me to process what the sudden pressure is. A hand, cool and rough and very small, has slipped into mine, and I turn to see Mary kneeling beside me with an urgent expression I have never seen her wear before. The others are far away, and I realize I must have been asleep.

'Hey—'

But she shushes me, and this makes sense because even to my own ears my voice sounds harsh, like I'm disturbing something. She pulls me gently behind her, leading me away from the path and through the narrow gaps between trees, down and down for so long that I start to realize I will never find my way back.

When I look back on this moment I will remember the shapes of branches and little else.

The shape that matters, I don't see until I am almost directly beneath it, and even when I do it makes no sense to me. An elongated silhouette half-obscured by branches, my first thought is that it's a series of birds' nests strung together like a vertical daisy chain, but this of course is madness.

The shape of it is clear. The lolling head and broken neck, the spindly limbs swaying just so in the breeze. Kris has never looked so serene.

CHAPTER SIXTEEN

Dead bodies do not look alike.

This should be obvious. They look no more or less alike than living bodies, and yet I'm disappointed by how unprepared I was.

Kris has been dead for hours, his lips blue, his skin chilly as I grasp his wrist. And everything moves very fast after this.

I must be making noise, enough to be heard back at camp, because they come. Dale first, running, then Sean and Otis a short way behind him. The air fills with shouts and I shrink back against a tree, feeling myself become smaller and smaller against it.

Dale and Sean cut him down, lay him out on the forest floor like timber.

Someone is crying, wailing like wind against a sheer wall, but it's not me. I'm frozen, limbs locked, mind empty. Until someone lays a hand on my shoulder and I jolt like I've been shocked. The fog is back. The fog is good, and needs to stay in place, and would everyone just be quiet. Please.

And after a while, nobody tries to touch me any more, and the fog settles around me. I am invisible, or close enough, as we gather together and begin to make our way back onto the forest path. Tyra and Abby are huddled together as one, letting out hushed sounds of horror as they pass me without a second glance.

Dale and Sean linger several paces behind us in their awkward burdened shuffle, the painful bundle of blankets held aloft between them, and this becomes like a game for me and I suspect for us all. Don't look back. Don't look.

My dad tried to stop me from seeing my mum's body – in a rare moment of sensitivity – on that sweltering summer's day in the hospital basement. We had sat on chairs that seemed unforgiving by design, my overheated skin sticking to the plastic in the shorts I shouldn't have worn. I've never looked good in shorts, had chosen that day of all days to try to convince myself otherwise.

Stay here, he had said, but when it came to it he didn't move. The nurse waited expectantly, his smile a study in sympathetic caution, as my dad sat motionless with his eyes fixed on the opposite wall.

'I'll do it,' I'd said, and followed his white-coated back into a narrow, shallow room whose walls I will never forget.

In my half-blind state I have lost track of Mary, and I don't see her again until dawn, when our numb trek back downhill to the house finally concludes and I see her, watching like always, from the veranda.

I barely take note, though. There's only one person I need

to find, now that the fog has lifted with the first rays of morning sun.

My back hurts and finally I realize how hard I have been shaking, hard enough to judder bones out of joint, practically. Someone has put a blanket over my shoulders.

'Where's Jake?' I ask, my voice too quiet to be heard. I ask again and still nobody hears me, so at last I give up and veer off towards the house alone, cold morning air brushing my shoulders as the blanket drops to the ground.

I find him in the bedroom that was ours for a night, heavy-limbed at the edge of the bed. He looks held together by a thread, eyes two red-rimmed bruises as he looks up at me. I climb onto his lap and hold on tight, arms wound around his neck, trying to press myself into him.

'You're freezing,' he whispers against my shoulder, his voice cracking as I kiss his hair. And I'll never understand him and Kris, but I know how much there was between them.

'I'm so sorry.'

He holds onto me hard enough to bruise, and it strikes me that I've never felt someone else's tears on my skin before.

The next evening, I help Abby and Otis lay siege to the weeds covering the front lawn. The house has become a blinding flurry of activity today, more propulsive and intense than the usual routine, and without its coherence. There's no rhyme or order to what anyone is doing, no timetable for the day, no clearly defined divisions into mind, body, soul and yard work. It's well into the evening and no preparations have been made for dinner.

The weeds need to go, and this feels as important as anything I've ever done in my life.

'Been mowing it too low,' Otis had muttered as he handed me a sharp spade. 'Weakens the grass, lets light get at the soil so little critters like this can grow. We gotta start cutting this at three inches, maybe even higher.'

We're weeding by hand, yanking whole plants out by the root and digging around in the vacant space to make sure no root pieces remain behind. Root means rot. Pull all the sprouts to starve and kill the weed. For deep-rooted dandelions, I use the sharp spade to push hard into the soil, angling its tip towards the plant's centre and pry it upwards into my hand.

Soothing. The pattern of it. When weed and roots are all out, I smooth the soil, smother in some compost, and patch over the area with lawn seed. Good as new, and maybe they'll bury Kris's body like this. Maybe they already have.

'Everyone.'

I stand up so fast my head spins, blood rushing in my ears as I see his figure silhouetted by the fire. Everybody gathers to him within seconds, some appearing as if from nowhere with tools and household implements in hand. It feels like forever since we all last met around the fire.

Tyra looks more pale and brittle than I've ever seen her, swaying in place before she kneels on the ground, and I want to ask if she's all right but the effort seems insurmountable.

'Hey,' Jake murmurs in my ear, and I fold into him in relief.

'Was wondering where you were.'

'Don't ask.'

He holds my hand tight as we sit down by the fire, looking at up at Don who seems smaller than I remember him, less certain. He's dressed entirely in black which gives him a spindly appearance, and I can't possibly be the only one reminded of Kris.

'Everyone. Thank you for being here.'

He speaks so quietly I have to crane forward to hear him, everyone shuffling inwards with bated breath. Every few words he pauses as though gathering breath or strength, his voice thin.

'This is... This is very difficult. I don't know how to begin, so please forgive me. I knew it was important that we all be together this evening, and I'm only sorry we couldn't be last night. I wasn't in much of a state to string a sentence together yesterday, and I know that many of you were recovering from what you'd been through out there.'

I try to make eye contact with him but his gaze is deliberately vague, addressing everyone rather than anyone. Does he know I was the one who found him?

'Kris.'

Don lets the word hang in the air for several minutes.

'Kris was an extraordinary person. Kris was one of the very first to join us here, and he shaped so much of the way that we do things. He didn't have any relatives left of his own, which I know he had come to regard as a blessing, and he was one of the first people who truly demonstrated to me the importance of a shared, consciously formed family. The principle that holds us all together here to this day.

'I first came to know Kris back in the city, where I ran free group therapy for military veterans. That endeavour was short-lived, but my relationship with Kris, happily, endured. And though I knew from the start that he was troubled – he wore it so plainly on his skin – I truly believed that I could help him. I think we all did.'

I risk a glance around the circle, but nobody is reacting at all, gazing unblinkingly at Don. Only Ruth's eyes are elsewhere, glazed, as though she isn't quite listening.

'Kris made great progress, for a very long time. He was on the right path, but as can happen to any of us, something changed. We all, unfortunately, saw his behaviour change, and I don't think there can be a person here who wasn't alarmed. But I'd be a liar if I pretended that I saw this coming.'

He looks down, white-knuckling the arms of his chair.

'Recency bias is a cruel thing. It's vital to me that those of you who have only known Kris for a short time don't remember him as he was this week. That was not the true Kris. That was Kris under the influence of a system that ultimately got the better of him, under the influence of the city and its rage and its toxicity. The Kris that arrived here from Manhattan was a different person to the one who left months ago. Kris was a good man, a good friend, and a good leader. This is how we should remember him.

'Here are some other things we should remember about Kris,' Don continues, his voice stronger now. 'Kris left. He left without any warning, without seeking guidance from me or from any of us here. He left against my wishes, and against his own better judgement, going back to the environment that made him sick in the first place. He went back to a world that did not want him, that did not welcome him back, that did not take care of him. There is only so much that I, or you, or anyone here can do for someone so bent on self-destruction.'

From his breast pocket Don takes out a wallet-sized photograph, flipping it over to hold up to us all. It's a picture of Kris, smiling faintly as though caught off guard by the camera, his torso slanted awkwardly away from the frame. His hair is longer and his face fuller.

'This was Kris just a month after he first arrived here. Full of possibility. Full of hope, despite his past, full of the will to connect, and escape, and detoxify. This is what he threw away when he left. Let him be a lesson to all of us.'

Don balls the photograph up and throws it into the fire, his aim savagely faultless. Jake shifts beside me, but when I turn his face is placid, almost bored.

'I have nothing else to say. If anybody else would like to speak on Kris, now is your chance.'

Everyone is silent, motionless. Watching the tiny glossy bundle burn away to ash. And I don't ask any of the things I know I should.

'Good, then. Well, I know you've all had a tough couple of days. I think at a later session we're going to need to get into the events of that night, and how traumatic it must have been for several of you. Rest assured that we will not allow this tragedy to poison our time together here.'

Finally he meets my eye, and I can feel the smile spreading across my face. It goes unreturned, his gaze flicking momentarily down to mine and Jake's intertwined hands. On reflex I try to let go, but Jake tightens his grip.

★

Later that night I'm walking back towards the house, but in place of the sloping lawn is a flat, fallow field, stretching out towards a long brick bungalow. A single watch tower sits at the building's centre, a figure just visible silhouetted against the evening sky. I'm walking along railway tracks, and this makes sudden sense to me. There are no cars here, only a single bus to Manhattan per day, so of course there are trains.

'This isn't where they found me,' Mary says.

'No?'

'Different tracks. In Queens.'

This place is familiar. It's a terrible place I visited only once, during a school trip to Poland in Year Nine, and have been trying to forget ever since. My dad had not wanted me to go, insisting I was too young and sensitive to cope, and for once he was right.

'Train tracks are the same everywhere,' I say, but Mary has walked ahead of me, and I ascend the winding steps to the watch tower as though floating, buoyed suddenly by certainty.

'Mummy?'

She has her back to me, looking out at the endless field, but when she turns around her face is warm and beaming, and as she opens her arms I fly into them.

'I didn't know you'd be here,' I say into her shoulder, warm too.

'Sorry, darling, I should have told you. I'm so forgetful these days.'

'No, it's me. I'm losing so much, Mum, I don't know what I'm doing here.'

'You've always known how to orient yourself.'

She's holding me gently around the shoulders now, still smiling gently, brushing my hair out of my eyes. It has grown long here, the ends splitting.

'I want to go home,' I tell her, and she looks sadly at me.

'They won't let you. You changed your name.'

There's a finality to this sentence that chills me. She never liked people shortening my name, despised even nicknames.

'No, I didn't change it, it's just Don. And the others...' They all call me Kate now, I realize, not just him. When did that start?

'A name is significant, Kate. It changes things.'

'Don't call me that, please.'

She's still stroking my hair, still gentle, still heartbroken, and I know she's trying to protect me from some greater truth. Outside the walls of the tower a siren begins, its sound awful and grinding in the air like metal.

And I wake up, and can hardly breathe.

CHAPTER SEVENTEEN

'I'm sorry it's taken so long for us to have this session.'
'So am I.'

'Have you missed it?'

'Your office? Not especially.'

'Our sessions.'

'Our sessions aren't an it. They're a them.'

'Are you angry, Kate?'

'That's not my name.'

'We discussed this. We agreed that Kate was more fitting to the new you than Caitlin.'

'Well, in our time off I've been reconsidering some things.'

'Would you like to talk about that?'

His impeccable calm is infuriating. It has been six days since I last saw him, when he threw Kris's photograph into the fire, and until my abrupt summons to his office this morning I'd begun to suspect I never would again.

But I'm back staring at the dark knots of wood on his table. Soon I'll be able to draw them from memory.

'How did the interruption to our sessions make you feel?'

'We were meant to have a session a week ago, the morning before Kris...'

'Yes, we were. But you disappeared into the forest after circle, and left nobody with any clue where you were or when you were coming back.'

'Of course I was coming back. What gave you the idea that I wasn't coming back?'

'You and Jake disappeared together. Into the forest.'

'He was upset. Surprisingly enough.'

'That's fine. But there are consequences to your actions, and your disappearing meant that I had to give your session to someone else. It was only fair.'

'Abandoned.'

'Sorry?'

'You asked how it made me feel, not having sessions. Abandoned. Not even a word, not an explanation, nothing.'

'You could have asked me.'

I stay silent, because this is true. But approaching him seems impossible, is designed to seem impossible.

'I am sorry, Katy. I am. Things have been... slipping, just these past few days. I'm finding it harder than I expected to get back on my feet.'

He looks very tired, his face more hollow than I remember it, and I feel a pang of regret for being so sulky.

'I understand.'

'I knew you would. I wasn't worried about you, which I suppose is part of the reason I overlooked the need for us to check in. That was wrong.'

A pack of Oreos was waiting on the table when I arrived,

and with the tension now slightly dispelled I can no longer resist the urge to break into them.

'I still don't really believe it happened,' I say, midway through nibbling the cream off my third Oreo. 'When I try to remember that night, it feels like trying to remember a dream right after waking up. When you know you should write it down or you'll forget it.'

'Maybe you should write down your memories of that night.'

'I'm not sure I want to remember it any more clearly.'

'I am sorry. That you had to go through that. I should have said it sooner – somebody told me it was you who found him.'

'It was Mary, I think. She led me.'

We sit in silence, my appetite abruptly gone. All I can think of are practical questions, the ones that have been circling in my mind unanswered for days, because I know too much not to wonder. Has anyone called the authorities, has anyone told his family that he's dead, where is the body?

'Kris didn't like me,' I say instead.

'What makes you think that?'

'I just know he didn't. He basically told me as much.'

'Why do you think that?'

There's something accusatory in his tone that stops me short.

'I think maybe because of Jake. Their relationship… there's a lot I don't understand there.'

'Jake,' Don says. 'Well. That's a thorny area for us to deal with now.'

'What do you mean?'

'I don't think it's appropriate for me to go into it with you.'

'To go into what?'

Don sighs, drawing himself up a little taller in his seat.

'Look, I suppose it can't be news to you that Jake and Kris were the only two who didn't take part in the hike that day. Nobody seemed sure why they chose to stay behind – neither of them warned Barb or Dale or anyone else that they weren't going. That's unusual in itself, even before what happened.'

'What are you saying?'

'Don't be dense.'

I keep expecting to close my eyes and wake up in bed, and realize that this session has been a vivid dream. Everything about it, about Don, feels off, and there's something like nausea in my gut that I don't think is down to the cookies.

'I would watch your step around Jake. I hate to say this, but I look at him now and I don't see the same kid I once did.'

'You're not seriously saying you think he did something to Kris? That's insane. Kris killed himself.'

'I have to be conscious of the feelings of the group, and right now there is a lot of unease about Jake. And by extension, anyone he's close to.'

The nausea churns.

'So, you're giving me a choice? Jake, or you and everyone else.'

'Don't be dramatic, you're better than that. I'm not saying anything of the sort. But things are not going to be easy for the next few weeks, while this is still reverberating, and you should think long and hard about whether you want to make things harder on yourself.'

'And what about Jake? Kris was his friend, probably more than anyone else, what kind of support is he meant to be getting? I thought the whole point of this place was supporting each other.'

'Jake will be getting all the support he needs. I'm just not convinced it should be from you. For your sake.'

'And I'm just not convinced this is any of your business.'

Minutes later I'm slamming through the forest with every footfall heavy and furious, trying to clear my head but succeeding only in clouding it. Don threw me out, and I'd seen it coming and still it stings. And now I have no idea where I'm going. I've arrived at my third dead end in as many minutes, and this simply shouldn't be possible.

This one is especially strange, too, the path that I swear used to be clear now blocked entirely by a ten-feet-tall tangle of thick branches and bramble. It looks like the living version of a child's angry pencil scrawl, all twisted spiralling tendrils reaching up from what might be a bundle of logs or a fallen tree.

Weirder still, as I look more closely, are the strands of what appear to be like long, black human hair. There's a little pile of them, stretched out long like spaghetti on the ground before the log pile.

Looking at it gives me an uncanny feeling in my chest, and as I turn around and begin retracing my footsteps I break into a jog almost involuntarily.

The ribbons have been moved yet again, and there's a lump of frustration rising in my throat now, the reality of what just happened with Don finally settling in.

I let the wind dry the few angry tears that fall, moving

fast enough that they don't stay on my cheeks for long, and at last I see a ribbon. It's tied around a tree that I'm sure was bare just two days ago, but I'm beginning to get my bearings again. The forest feels like it's morphing around me, deciding when and if to revert to its familiar form and allow me home.

'Hey.'

Jake is waiting, leaning casually against a tree almost as though we'd arranged to meet here. We didn't. Did we?

His smell is familiar now, the most familiar thing, and I hold on tight as he hugs me.

'Where have you been?'

'Where do you think?'

'You went to Don's.'

'You didn't think I was never going to go back. I told you I was.'

'What did he say about me?'

I must be staring at him like a deer in headlights.

'I know what they think. You don't have to protect me.'

'It's stupid. I don't even think he really believes you did anything, from what he was saying, it's just...'

'It's just "the Group",' he says, with verbal air quotes.

'I think everybody's just really upset, and looking for someone to blame. Bereavement does that.'

He doesn't reply, but takes my hand as we walk in despondent silence.

'I think it'll be okay, Jake. If you just explain, if we maybe held our own circle, an unofficial one, and just...'

'Bad idea. But I appreciate you trying,' he says, and draws me into his side, my ear pressed against his neck. Walking lopsided like this isn't comfortable, but I don't want to pull away.

'I still don't understand. If you won't explain it to them, at least...'

'What?'

'Why didn't you just come with us that day?'

He stiffens.

'You know I don't think you had anything to do with...'

'So what *do* you think?'

'I don't understand what you and Kris were to each other. Why you always seemed so tense, why he was so fixated on you, why you didn't come with us that day after he blew up at you.'

'It's... complicated.'

'I thought you said it was easier not to be hiding things all the time?'

'It's not some big mystery, it's just hard to explain.'

'Was he in love with you?' I finally say, a little breathless, not looking at him.

'What?'

But he doesn't sound surprised that I asked.

'It's not that neat,' he says, finally.

'What does that mean?'

'Kris never really... I never heard him talk that way about anyone. He never showed an interest. He didn't have parents, and I think he just wanted family. That's all. And I never saw him that day, I just figured he'd gone with the rest of you. I wish to God I had seen him,' he says, and as his voice wavers on this last part I hold on tighter to his hand.

'He didn't want to be helped.'

'Didn't he? So what was he doing here? Why didn't he just stay gone?'

I don't have an answer.

'How was it today, with Don?'

'Fine. It was great. Aside from the stuff about you, it was phenomenal.'

'Don't lie.'

'Is it that hard to believe that I had a good session? Or am I just too messed up for that to even be a possibility?'

'You are the sanest person here.' He grabs me by the shoulders and spins me around, looks hard into my eyes. 'Remember that. Okay? Remember that.'

Again, I'm speechless. Winded by how final this feels.

'Who moves the orange ribbons?' I blurt out finally.

'What?'

'The orange ribbons. On the trees around here. I assumed they were like path markers, to guide you, but they seem to move all the time.'

'They are path markers. They're for hiking, so you don't get lost, but they don't move.'

'Are you sure? Because I got lost on the way back from Don's cabin just now and that's just… I swear some of them aren't where they were.'

We're walking again now, his arm loose around my neck.

'There's no reason why they'd move. Unless somebody's playing a trick on you.'

'Wouldn't put it past you, soldier.'

★

There have been only two formal circles since Kris's death, three counting the one where Don threw the photograph into the fire, and they were anemic, numbing affairs, everyone glazed-eyed and struggling to string a sentence together.

Tonight is different. Something warm is in the air and everybody feels connected again, and even Tyra has the light back in her eyes. She hugged me spontaneously on the porch, whispering 'I missed you, girl' as though I'd been away, and in the moment it felt like I had.

Barb and Dale had been back in the kitchen, after a full week of famine where we'd all grazed off cold cuts and fruit, and the results were spectacular as ever. In the full, muzzy haze of apple and cinnamon, my session with Don began to feel like a bad dream, and I've had enough of those to know how to ignore them. He is here, and though he doesn't look at me this is nothing new, this is circle, he can't pick favourites, he can't acknowledge my apologetic gaze. But his steely presence is comforting, and I know things will be better soon. They have to be.

We had all sat at the fire and talked not about our pasts, but about our futures, Ruth asking each of us to name the thing we wanted most for ourselves ten years from now. Nobody had an answer, but it was generally agreed that we wanted to be here. Nowhere but here.

I'm carrying the mugs unsteadily back down the sloping lawn when, in the distance, I catch sight of black hair on white cotton, and this suddenly feels right. I haven't spoken to Mary, been near her even, since she held my hand in the forest and led me downhill. She's been a staple in my dreams, appearing again and again on the train tracks leading towards that watch tower. I think she was at circle, lying with her head in Ruth's lap as Ruth stroked her hair, maternal, but that image seems treacherous even as I recall it. Could Ruth be like a mother to anyone?

I half-jog across the lawn, goosebumps rising on my skin from the cold. She seems to be growing smaller the nearer I get but it's a trick of the light, perhaps, or otherwise I'm just drunk.

'Hey!' I shout clumsily, trying to pin her in place with my voice. 'Mary.'

Finally I catch up to her semi-hiding place in the bushes. She's sitting with knees drawn up to her chin, eyes almost closed, serene but for her clenched fists.

I lose all of the words I'd been planning to say, the endless questions I had falling away as I look instead at what's in her left fist. Several strands of gossamer black hair, held like a delicate string instrument as she makes a wrenching motion with her right hand and pulls out another.

Her hair.

On the forest floor.

My voice is loud and magnified, detached from my body as I say, 'Robin.'

She turns to look at me, calm, resigned.

'Robin. You're Robin. Don's patient, the one from Manhattan. They found you on the train tracks. Please tell me.'

But she will not tell me, and she doesn't need to.

CHAPTER EIGHTEEN

I wake up winded, and find I can't draw a deep breath. My sheets are drenched, the vest top I'm wearing ripe with sweat, nausea churning. I swing my legs over the side of the mattress and test the ground beneath my feet, its solidity suddenly ambiguous.

I have no concept of how long I've been asleep. The clementine sunlight through half-drawn shutters suggests early evening. I can hear food being prepared outside, the clink of pans and enamel, the rustle of corn being shucked.

I try to recall a single, definite event that has taken place in my recent life. What have I done, besides sleep? The last thing I remember is Jake. His skin on mine and the warmth of the fire, but what day was that? How long ago? There's an ache in my chest, and I don't know why.

I get up unsteadily, my head strangely heavy, and peel off everything. Wishing I could drop my skin to the floor beside my underwear.

Tyra's bed is cold again, impeccably made, and I know instinctively that she hasn't been back here, not for the time I've been asleep. Is this my room alone now? I'm not sure I like the idea of having my own room again.

As I shower, I hear whispering in the water, the words indistinct and restless.

Afterwards, I stand in front of my suitcase for a long time, frozen. Most of my clothes lie in a dusty pile waiting to be washed, and I can't remember how laundry works here. I only half-recognize my body. I look strong. There's definition in my stomach and my shoulders, and as I raise my arms I can see my ribs through the skin of my chest. The sunburn along my forehead and outer arms has begun to brown.

None of these thoughts quite sit right in my head, like I'm worrying about my appearance on autopilot. Everything seems far away, and in the end I put on a plain black dress which I have never liked, but now hangs better than I remember. I pull my damp hair back into a high ponytail, splash tepid water into my bone-dry eyes, and go outside.

It takes a strangely long time for me to see anyone I recognize, so long that I wonder if I've developed some kind of face blindness, though it's really the sun that is half-blinding me. Faces smile politely as I emerge onto the deck, down into the field where meat is being grilled. I feel like I'm watching myself move through an endless tracking shot.

As I walk under the shade of a tree I catch sight of Ruth, shucking a pile of corn, and before I can pretend not to see her she looks up.

'Kate.'

'Do you need a hand?'

'No, thank you. But come over here for a moment.'

I obey her.

'How are you?'

'Fine, I think. What day is it?'

'Thursday,' she answers, continuing her work without looking at her hands, eyes fixed on me.

'God. I must have been exhausted. I don't even remember the last time I slept past noon.' Even on Saturday mornings before all-night circle, when a lot of people stayed in bed past lunchtime, I never managed it.

'Do you know if Jake's around?'

'I don't.'

I wait, expecting some explanation for why she beckoned me over, but nothing is forthcoming. She's watching me calmly, curiously, and I back away feeling exposed, moving so far that I collide with Dale at the grill.

'Hey, girl,' he says over my mumbled apology. He smells like salt and timber, and I hold on for slightly too long as he one-arm-hugs me.

'How's tricks?'

'Weird. I feel really... really weird. I just slept for an entire day, I think.'

'You probably needed the rest. Your body's still adjusting to the new schedule, new demands.'

Sean doesn't even acknowledge my presence.

'Do you know where Jake is?'

'Nope, haven't seen him.'

His tone is light but his implication is not. And I turn my back on him without explanation, an ache in my chest because I need to see Jake so badly I feel tearful.

I check his room and find it empty, his belongings all gone. I check the bed, the sheets still unmade, and beneath the pillow is Jake's Swiss Army knife. All of his things gone, but he would never leave without this. I clutch it tight and slip it into my sleeve, because he'll need it back.

Outside again, Barb grabs at my arm with a strange smile. 'Somebody's asking for you.'

And I run full pelt down the steps and out onto the lawn where Barb is pointing, because of course he hasn't disappeared, of course he's asking for me.

But Don. Don is asking for me. He's standing, feet planted, jaw set, as I stop short in front of him feeling winded.

'Hi, Katy.'

I smile numbly at him, and follow as he beckons me towards the forest, obeying puppet-like though I'm desperate to continue my search. I should try Kris's old room, of course, why hadn't this occurred to me? He'll be there, trying to connect, maybe trying to understand, and I can find him. But instead I walk with Don.

'Do you know where Jake is? His stuff is gone, and I'm… I don't understand.'

He doesn't reply, lengthening his strides so that I have to almost jog to keep up.

To my surprise, we haven't even covered half the ground towards his cabin when Don stops abruptly, head cocked as though listening for something. He mutters something incomprehensible to himself, and I know better than to ask him to repeat it.

'I'm very sorry about our last session. I hate to see you upset.'

I don't want him to apologize. The very fact of it turns my stomach. I want him to be right. He looks so hesitant, suddenly, almost tremulous and I want to slap the strength back into him.

'I don't know where Jake is,' he continues. 'No one does. He hasn't been seen in over a day, not since our last circle. At first we all assumed the two of you had... gone off together again.'

'No, we didn't.' I don't think we did. Truthfully, I remember scarcely anything of that night, how I got to bed, how I came to sleep for so long. Snippets are bobbing behind my eyelids like apples underwater, but I don't want to fish them out yet. I need to focus on now.

Surely I would remember. If we had been together that night, I'd remember him.

'I know you didn't. He's gone, Kate. That's what I need to tell you.'

'No, he's not gone. What do you mean?'

I feel as though I should be sinking to the forest floor, my legs giving way beneath me. But I'm rigid. And Don looks shattered, bewildered, so I have to be strong.

'Let's go to your office,' I murmur. 'I don't want to be here.'

Inside the cabin, we both seem to be lacking a script. I've never been here this late in the day, with the afternoon sun low and half-molten across the lake's surface, and everything feels off-centre. If I closed my eyes and woke up in bed, I wouldn't be surprised. I try.

'Open your eyes.'

I obey, and we're both still here, though Don is sitting on

the sofa that I usually occupy. I perch on the broad leather arm of the sofa that I've come to think of as his.

'I am sorry about our last session.'

'You said that already. So am I.'

'Did I?' He rubs his eyes, shakes his head brusquely as though trying to judder dust loose. 'I let my concerns about Jake get in the way of our therapy, let them cloud my judgement in dealing with you. That is unforgivable.'

In my head, I'm back in the house and Jake is there, waiting. I'm so convinced now that he is in Kris's room that the conviction is like a physical weight. Don is mistaken, and it's not his fault.

'I hope you understand that I was trying to protect you.'

'From what? From Jake and his temper? You honestly still believe that?'

'No, I jumped to conclusions. I've become so attuned to the mentality of the group, the needs of the group, that I can be swayed by the hive mind. At a time like that, people look for someone to blame. I should have known better than to follow suit.' He shrugs. 'We're always learning. All of us.'

'Why did anyone think Jake would? I still don't get it.' But I do, I suppose, when I really think about what Jake told me that morning, the truths he whispered into my skin about why he left home. His head like a shell, nothing but sand and echoes inside.

'What's that?'

I don't realize I've spoken out loud.

'Nothing.'

Why am I wearing this dress? It's a paper-thin H&M

thing, maybe even designed as sunwear, and when I'd put it on it had looked like summer outside my window. But in fact, it has been autumn for weeks.

'Are you cold?'

I'm trying to rub the goosebumps out of my arms. Don stands, takes off his jacket and puts it over my shoulders, the inner lining silky and warm from him.

'Thanks.'

'Jake was a fool to give you up. Young men never know what they have when they have it.'

The goosebumps remain.

'Are you all right?'

'I need to go and find him.' But the words sound sad even to me, now. 'I think he might be in Kris's room.'

'You're holding on too tight. You've never been left before, have you?'

I've never had anyone for long enough to be left.

'He wouldn't just leave.'

Yes, he would. Men do this all the time, this could not be any more of a cliché. He got what he wanted, in the woods, and now he is gone. There's something else nagging at the corner of my mind, persisting despite the nausea that's settling like smog.

'Nobody here uses their real name. Do they?'

'What do you mean?'

'You call me Kate. Katy. Everybody has these neat, four-letter names, like Mary. And that's not her real name, is it?'

He blinks, like a spasm.

'That's not for me to say.'

'Why not?'

'Everybody here chooses who they want to be known as, going forward. That's a rebirth. We don't look back.'

'That's all we do. What's circle about, if it's not looking back? What are these sessions about?'

'We look at the past, to help us understand how it shaped our present. But we don't dwell on who we were before.'

If I simply listen to his voice and don't absorb the words too deeply, it's the most soothing thing I've ever heard.

'Who were you before?'

My voice comes out weak, half-croaking, and Don jumps to his feet as though gripped by an electrical current. He reaches out a hand to me, palm flat, sinews strong, and I grip it and pull myself up.

'I'd like you to lead circle this evening.'

'Really?'

'Really. I think you're ready. And I think it would mean a lot to everyone, after everything, after Jake… You're uniquely placed to bring us together in this moment.'

'Okay. Thank you.'

Somehow, word has already spread by the time I am back at the house, and Barb is there still with a smile ghosting around her eyes. I smile back, hard, matching her energy.

'You gonna lead us this evening?'

'I am. I'm ready.'

'You are ready, sweetheart.'

I barely resist flinching away from her hand on my cheek.

'You want to help Dale and me finish dishing up dinner?'

'Sure. Just one sec, I want to go down to the fire pit and get into the right headspace. I'll join you inside.'

But where I actually go is away. I keep walking, straight

down the lawn towards the forest, but instead of following the path I cut straight across the grass onto gravel, where I haven't been since Jake parked his car that very first day.

The house looks different, so much less vast than last time I saw it from this angle.

Tiny stones crunching beneath my feet with every step, I follow the driveway down, down, steadily down until it opens out, and then there is the road. Undulating down and around the house, and stretching out well beyond it. It has always been here, waiting for me, waiting for this moment.

And I start walking and don't look back.

CHAPTER NINETEEN

Monticello is not what I pictured. The name had put me in mind of a rustic haven carved into the side of mountains, populated by farmers and simple country folk with olive groves and sunflowers visible from every street. I realize now that this place I'm picturing is actually an Italian village I visited with my parents as a child. It had seemed so obvious to me that I would find Jake in Monticello, the town he told me about specifically as I sat in his passenger seat, the town that I've subconsciously pictured as a safe place. But now, looking at the single bleak road stretching out in front of me, the dirty buildings and the empty lots, it's unimaginable to me that he would choose to come here.

'MONTICELLO – 1 / NEW YORK – 87 / BINGHAMTON – 90', a sign promises, and a mile later it has grown almost completely dark and I'm shivering so hard that my jaw hurts. Even with the hoodie I had hastily grabbed from my room,

I might as well be naked for all the insulation my summer dress is providing. I take a turn onto a road dubiously named Broadway, power lines arcing overhead against the dying evening light. It feels as though I'm heading towards civilization, with lights twinkling in the mid-distance and cars passing me at a calmingly steady pace. But the shuttered store fronts still look as though they've seen better days, dusty even in the near darkness, and from the corner of my eye I become aware that I'm being watched. A group of four young men are huddled by the roadside, hoods up, eyes reaching, and I cross the road away from them, picking up my pace. Finally there is something with its lights on, a diner, one glowing letter broken so that its doorway reads 'P E N'.

'Anywhere you want,' the man behind the counter barks by way of a greeting.

I hover in the doorway, because of course I have no money. I can't so much as sit down or order a cup of coffee.

The place is almost empty, and the few customers there don't take much notice of me. I should leave now, before this gets awkward. But I'm drawn in, almost magnetized by the thrum of life. How long it's been.

'You need help?'

Why is he asking me this?

'No, I'm fine, I just… Is there a phone here that I could use?'

He regards me for a second, sizing me up.

'In the office, through there.'

I follow the arc of his arm, pointing me through a narrow corridor into a slightly less narrow office space, cosily decorated like an eccentric relative's living room. There are miniature knitted wall hangings, ceramic tiles spelling out cutesy slogans ('Home Is Where The Coffee Is!'), a collection of owl-shaped ornaments arranged in a wooden shelving unit that looks hand-made, carved into the shape of a tree.

The phone is there, too, but it takes me a moment to make sense of it. It's as though this particular region of my brain has rusted over, in all the time that's passed since I last laid eyes on a phone, much less made a phone call.

I remember learning about schemas in psychology, how the brain memorizes processes from everyday life so that we can access them unconsciously, with no effort. This is how we know how to behave in a restaurant, where no instructions are presented and yet none are required. But I barely remember how to make a phone call. My mind is rusting.

The receiver is solid in my hand, and muscle memory is a miraculous thing because I start dialling a number with no conscious effort. I don't think I know any numbers by heart, except my dad's landline, and even that I can't bring to mind now. In any case, it's not the number I'm dialling.

0 1 1. Exit code.

4 4. UK.

2 0. London.

My finger stalls.

7 4 9 4

3 6 5 4

'Hello, and welcome to the Prince Charles Cinema,' a deep male voice intones. And the sound of it winds me. Of course this is the one number I remember.

'The box office is manned between one-thirty p.m. and eight-thirty p.m. daily. To listen to what we are screening today, press one. To buy tickets, press two.'

There's something to be said for consistency. The Prince Charles Cinema's automated phone service is still the most human I've found, because the film times seem to be newly recorded each day by the same calm, deep-voiced man, and occasionally he will stumble over a word or pause for a deeper exhale, faltering just enough to remind you he is a real person.

This reliable automated service became a lifeline for me, when my mum was at her worst.

More times than I can now count, sometimes daily, I dialled this number and simply listened to the same young man list the film times. Usually I had no intention of going to any of them, but the solidity of knowing that these films would be shown, that no matter what happened in my house this is what would be happening at the Prince Charles, was intensely comforting.

I don't recognize any of the film titles he's now listing, and that's strange, because I usually know every one.

'Thank you for calling. Goodbye.'

The three beeps are brutal, and I had forgotten this. There is no option to press another number, or hear the listings again, or speak to an operator. You are simply disconnected.

Without realizing it I've hunched down onto the ground, knees drawn up to my chest, and my knuckles are hurting from clutching the phone so tight. The sound of another English voice alone is like an electric shock, my heart struggling to right its rhythms afterwards.

And I know with sudden, absolute certainty that I will never see the Prince Charles again. I will never see Soho or Chinatown again, and films will continue to show there without me because things and places outlast us. London is so long ago, and so far away, and I will never wake up back there no matter how hard I wish.

The certainty of this makes it easier, somehow, to stand up and support myself back out into the restaurant, my bones fortified by sheer longing.

'Everything okay?' the same man behind the counter asks. He's in his fifties, I guess, salt-and-pepper beard trimmed neat around a kindly chin. 'Did you make your call?'

'I did. Thanks.'

'Can I get you some coffee? On the house.'

I nod, mumbling a thank you, and sit up at the counter rather than peeling off to a booth alone. My toes and fingers feel numb, and I don't know any more if I'm cold.

Even the thickness of the white enamel mug in my hand feels foreign, in contrast to the brittle clay things we use at the house. I pour four tiny containers of half-and-half into my coffee, because who knows if I'll get the chance again. Not on the paleo plan.

'Is that an Australian accent?'

'English.'

'Spent some time over there myself. Whereabouts?'

I swallow hard, looking down into my coffee, and say London. He doesn't ask me anything else, and from the corner of my eye I can see he's distracted, serving a plate of pancakes to a hard-faced woman at the other end of the counter. He won't ask me anything further.

Do you need some help, I imagine him asking again, because I'd do it all differently this time.

'No. Someone's coming for me.'

I say this out loud, and it, too, is a certainty. It takes slightly longer than I expect.

The hand on my back is familiar. Dale stands silently beside me, looking expectantly at my half-finished cup of coffee.

'Time to go, girl.'

I ignore him for as long as I can.

'Katy.'

'I'm just going to finish my coffee.'

So he stands beside me, watching every deliberately slow sip I take. And I'm gripped by a sudden urge to run, because maybe I could do it, maybe I could outrun him. I know I could.

'Okay. I'm ready.'

I'm a coiled spring as we reach the doorway, ready to unleash, my legs practically twitching with pent energy. Until I realize that I am flanked on either side, Sean as silent and solemn as Dale, both of them looking straight ahead as they lay hard hands on my shoulders.

'This is not a great neighbourhood,' Dale is muttering, too close to my ear. 'You're lucky nothing happened to you.'

And I let them steer me into the car, numb again, my legs heavy. Nobody speaks on the drive back as I sit in the middle of the back seat, Dale and Sean's legs like vices encasing me on either side. Ruth is driving. It's a while since I've been in a car, not as long as since I used a phone, but close enough for this to feel novel.

Maybe Dale senses my tension, because he offers me a hip

flask without a word and I drink, knowing of course what it will be. The cider is stronger than usual, perhaps brewed for longer, and it does not mix well with the aftertaste of coffee. Still, I keep drinking. There is nothing else to be done. I can feel myself melting into this, giving in, resistance fading. And why not? The world is too sharp for me now, my skin too thin, my mind like an exposed nerve. Better not to be out in the elements. I know my limitations.

'We're going back,' I say, but looking around there is no indication that anyone has heard me.

The gravel crunches under my feet just like it had when I left, but everything is changed. My own head feels different as I gingerly get out of the car, lighter on my shoulders, and pins and needles flood through my body like fire. There's a fog descending, hoary hanging in the air like vapour, just enough to make the place seem charged and distant.

I have no concept of how many hours have passed, but I'm sure I have missed circle. The fire pit looks cold, untouched, and yet everybody is still awake, waiting on the slope in expectant clusters.

I'm reminded of the very first morning, when Jake's parents' house became something else. Everybody returned from the vision quest with their faces dirty and eyes blank, and they had looked like a different species to me. They didn't make eye contact with me then either.

I glide through them like a ghost, insubstantial. Only Mary meets my gaze, her eyes boring directly into mine through the smoke that's growing thicker around me, and I begin to move over to her but am held back by Dale.

'Come on, this way.'

And he leads me to my room, where Tyra's bed is still cold and untouched, and closes the door behind me. I never knew that there was a lock on the door until I hear it slide around and click into place. There did not used to be a lock.

'Dale?'

But he is gone.

My heartbeat is too loud, as though two new pulse points have opened inside my eardrums. I try the door, and understand suddenly that the lock sliding into place translates to the door being immoveable. I'm locked in.

Why didn't I run? I could have kept walking on past the diner, up and up and up that endless strobe of tarmac until I hit the freeway, and maybe the bus would have been waiting for me there.

You really think you're capable of going back to the world now? You don't think everything that's out there will chew you into mulch and leave you hollow? You're an idiot. To think you could survive now.

The pins and needles is getting worse, my skin crawling with it as I try to shake out my limbs, thrusting them back and forth to the tune of my thoughts. Idiot. Should have run. Should have stayed. Should have known. Finally the weight of it drags me down, exhausted onto my back, making it only halfway onto my mattress.

You can still come with me, says Jake from somewhere close by, but I can't see him. My head too heavy to lift, I close my eyes and let the fog descend.

CHAPTER TWENTY

I am trying to sleep, but it's too loud.

Dale and Tyra and Sean are talking nearby, and I want to ask them to keep it down but no, be cool, be fun, don't be that person. It's nice that they're here.

In my room.

They've been talking about me, not to me, for so long that I can no longer make out who is saying what.

'Is she asleep yet?'

'She'll probably never sleep again.'

'Once your head starts twisting it never really stops, you know?'

Twisting. Everything is twisted but still I'm here, and I can feel the mattress beneath me. And Tyra is back, though I don't remember seeing her face. They're shapes and voices rather than faces, and when I try to look around the room it's hopeless. My eyes are fog.

'Did you hear what she did?'

'Ugh, can we just not? She's not worth it.'

'I know, but how does she just keep getting away with this stuff? It's nuts.'

'She's Don's pet, is how she gets away with it. His little rag doll pet.'

'Yeah, well, not for too much longer I'll bet.'

'I'd love to know what got into Jake. But, well, I guess he's pretty messed up in the head too. Was. He's not much of anything any more.'

What do you mean?

My voice won't work. When I try to speak I hear a sound like a horn in the distance, an echo.

'I knew she was crazy. That first day, her eyes were weird and I just knew, some people are born with it in their blood. You know her mom was, right?'

'Yeah. She drank battery acid or something.'

Bleach, not battery acid. That was only once, and I had to believe her when she told me it was an accident, that she wasn't trying to kill herself. Or damage the lining of her oesophagus so badly that she couldn't eat solid food for months.

'She should kill herself too.'

'Oh, it's coming, you just wait. You just wait, girl.'

'How do you think she'll do it?'

Their voices are louder and closer now, and when I press my hands hard into my ears it makes no difference.

'That lake would be a pretty place to drown, right?'

'She'd have to weight her boots with sand.'

'Put stones where her eyes are so she'd stay dead.'

They are voices, only voices, no shapes at all any more,

and they sound nothing like Tyra or Dale or Sean. They're all one voice, low and flat and creaking at the edges.

My eyes are gone.

The blood comes as a surprise to me, as I come back to myself and see chipped white paint on wood, tiny specks of red scattered across one panel. Kneeling in front of the bedroom door, my fist still half-raised and knuckles torn, I have no memory of getting here. If I close my eyes and open them again, I could easily be back in bed.

But my throat is hoarse too, and it takes another slow beat to realize that the screeching white noise around me is coming from within. I feel nothing, watching myself from above, and it's a pitiful sight. Scraped knees and summer dress, wailing like an overgrown child sent to bed without dinner.

There's light coming in through the window now, but this could mean anything. I could have been here for an hour or a week, and there's nobody in the world to miss me so what's the difference? Abruptly the bolt slams backwards, and I stagger aside just in time to avoid being hit by the door as it's thrown open.

'Come here,' Tyra hisses, dragging me to my feet as my back collides with the wall. 'How could you? After everything we've done for you, you just left?'

'I wasn't trying to run away, I was just... I wanted some air. And to make a phone call.'

'You don't make phone calls. You don't reach back out to the world, you know that. There's nothing out there for us.'

'I know. I know. I get it now.'

Her grip on me tightens, and I'm holding onto her wrists drawing circles with my thumbs, trying to soothe. I've never seen her like this, and maybe it's a dream.

'Were you here earlier?'

'What?'

'Were you here last night? Or... I don't know, maybe not last night, I don't know when. In the room? With Dale, and Sean?'

'What are you talking about?'

'Forget it.' I know better than to ask this. They were not here. My mind is in pieces, but it will be better soon if I try.

'You're bleeding.'

'Yes.'

She pulls my knuckles towards her for a closer look, scrubbing at the blood hard enough to draw more fresh from the wounds.

'They'll heal on their own.'

'I want to see Don.'

'He's busy.'

'No he isn't. He's not too busy to see me.'

'You are not the centre of his universe.'

She adjusts her grip just enough for me to shove her aside, and as she spirals backwards I bolt through the door and run blindly, breathlessly out of the carriage house towards the forest.

The wood of Don's cabin door feels like certainty against my hand, and I pound and pound and pound and keep pounding even after the door has gone and he grips onto my wrists, gently, firmly, anchors me inside.

'Hey, hey, hey—'

And I cling onto him and sob, my whole body shuddering painfully as he strokes my hair and says ssssh.

'Come inside, come on, it's all right,' he murmurs into my ear and I hold on harder, feeling less steady than ever.

'Katy, I'm worried about you.'

And I don't want to hear this, press hands against my ears because this is what I dread.

'Why did you lock me in?' I ask, voice muffled against his shoulder. 'I've been in there for days, and I couldn't sleep because everyone was too loud and they were talking about me, and all I wanted was to make a phone call.'

He tugs my hands gently down to my sides, and I force myself to stand back from him.

'Katy, we locked you in for your own safety. All right? Your own and other people's. Do you remember what happened, the night we brought you back from the diner?'

I think, and remember flickers. The foreign taste of cream stirred into coffee. The dial tone. Dale and Sean's hands like rivets on my shoulders.

'I came back with Dale and Sean. In the car. I don't really remember… I was tired.'

'You were psychotic.'

A shiver.

'Psychotic?'

'You were hallucinating. Talking to people who weren't there, telling them that you were being poisoned, that your thoughts were being tracked.'

I have to laugh then, because he has taken this verbatim from our sessions, from what I've told him about my mum.

'This is really sick, what you're doing.'

'Katy, this is serious. I know what psychosis looks like, and this was severe. And violent. You gave Dale a black eye when he tried to restrain you.'

'No, I don't… That didn't happen.'

But the feeling of bones crunching under my knuckle comes back to me, more vivid than a dream, too vivid.

'Why would I do that?'

'You kept saying you just wanted to go home. You were saying the water here was poisoned, that it wasn't safe, and you wanted to go home.'

My mother used to say precisely this. She refused to drink water for months, either from the tap or from a bottle, convinced that it was laced with chemicals that were making her ill. She knocked a full glass out of my hand once, shouting at me, and then tried to pick up the shards until her hands bled. I froze, that day. I should have stopped her from picking up the glass.

'Do you still want to go home now?'

'No. No, I don't— I don't understand what's happening.'

'Don't you remember anything else at all from the night you came back? Just try to relax, and breathe, and see what comes up.'

The fog is what comes up. Thick and hanging, obscuring everything, settled heavy in my brain since that moment. I try to explain it to Don and my words come out jumbled, and as I look desperately up at him it's clear he's trying to hide his concern.

'I had another… thing. A fog. Like I wasn't there, like I was watching myself from above and everything was too loud and looming down on me. All I can remember is that, the fog. I can see myself walking from the car back towards the carriage house, just caked in it. And that's all.'

Don sighs, heavily, not meeting my eyes now.

'I was hoping I could keep this from you for longer.'

Nausea rises in my chest, and I sink onto his sofa with hands gripped hard around my knees, bone on bone my only stability.

'The night you told me about in Manhattan. There was more to the story, wasn't there?'

'What?'

'You didn't just leave the bar, when the fog came down. There was an incident. You were hallucinating, there were witnesses, the police were almost called.'

'No. That didn't happen.'

'And Jake saw it. It's why he tracked you down. You were wondering why you, what he saw in you – this was it. Given his own history, he felt that he could help you, bring you out here before your episodes got any worse.'

'I don't have episodes. Nothing happened in the bar, I just left. I remember.'

'Katy, I need you to open yourself up to the fact that your memory is faulty. I need you to trust me more than you trust yourself, because I don't know how else to help you. This is why Jake left.'

The pit in my stomach contains multitudes. It's vast and vacuum enough to prevent me from ever speaking again, and when I do my voice is barely a croak.

'What do you mean?'

'He saw how this was going. How all he was doing was

making you worse. The two of you were poisoning each other.'

'We were good for each other.'

I know this. This is more or less the only thing I still feel sure of, deep in my gut even when I was so angry with Jake. How long ago that was. How long ago was that?

I try to remember what the Prince Charles Cinema recording had said about the date. They always lead with the day and date, and why didn't I pay attention to this?

'What happened to Kris's body?' I ask, and I know I have asked before. Have I ever known the answer?

'Don't get distracted, Kate. Focus on yourself.'

'How long have I been here?'

'You don't know the answer?'

'I'm not... I'm not sure. I lost track somewhere.'

I can tell this is yet another source of concern, and my stomach knots at the look on his face.

'Well, you arrived in July. And now it's January.'

'January? That's impossible.'

'What do you mean?'

'It's not... There hasn't been Christmas. I haven't been here for six months.'

His frown deepens, and he grips me gently around both shoulders.

'Katy, how long do you think you've been here for?'

'I don't know,' I cry, because how ridiculous that I'm arguing this point when I truly have no evidence to the contrary. Six months. How have six months fallen through my hands like sand? The weather is winter and here I am still in my summer clothes like a lunatic.

My mum never knew what the season was. Even when she was better, she struggled with this. One of her many medications gave her near-constant hot flushes so that regardless of the month she was always overheated, convinced it was the height of summer. For days on end one November she wore the same black Marks & Spencer bikini, now two sizes too small for her, wore it around the house and to put the bins out and once even to Sainsbury's Local, where two of my classmates spotted her. That was a fun month at school.

'I knew this was going to happen.'

'Nothing has happened yet. You're going to be okay.'

'No I'm not.' And I love him, fiercely, for saying it, though we both know it's a lie.

'You are. Listen to me. You are in the right place to get better. You are going to come back here every day for the time being, you and I are going to have daily sessions, and you are going to get your feet back on the ground.'

He's beside me on the sofa now, holding both my hands in his right palm, stroking my hair with the left.

'But if you don't surrender completely to the process – and that means no more unscheduled trips to town, no more violent outbursts, no more skipping out on sessions – then I cannot help you. And if I cannot help you, nobody can help you.'

'I know that.'

'If you don't surrender to this, you will not get better. Do you want to get better?'

Yes.

'Please. I have to get better. I can't be like this.'

'You will get better. I promise you that. Do you promise me you'll trust me?'

'Yes. I trust you.'

I close my eyes, my skin humming, and focus on his touch.

CHAPTER TWENTY-ONE

'Your thoughts have no more power than you allow them. You can stop them in their tracks, if you don't like what they're saying, and I want you to try. I want you to focus your attention first on your breath—'

And he puts one palm flat against my sternum and the other against my lower back, a silent encouragement to push back against his grip, and I do. My breath expands. 'And focus on the phrase "I am curable".'

'I am curable.'

'Don't say it out loud. Repeat it in your mind, slowly, one hundred times over. And when other thoughts try to intrude, or distract you, I want you to issue the command "Stop".'

The statement to be repeated changes daily. The first day was 'I am damaged'. The second day was 'I am diseased'. The third, 'I am dangerous'. Today's is the most positive yet, and yet somehow the most exhausting, to the point where I can scarcely think anything but stop stop stop stop stop.

'Have I done this before?' I'd asked Don in our first session after my breakthrough, my fingers clutched in my lap like a cat's cradle. 'How long have I had these episodes for?'

'That's impossible for me to say, and irresponsible for me to estimate. But I can help you to figure it out, if you'll let me.'

Of course I'll let him. I'm a hostage of my own diseased brain, have been living in blissful ignorance of the chaos I'm wreaking, deaf and dumb like a feral animal. I said the last part out loud.

'I don't ever want to hear you talk about yourself that way again,' Don replied sharply. 'You understand? You are a beautiful, special, frankly miraculous girl, Katy, and you are exactly where you're supposed to be. Rather than feeling sadness or rage, feel grateful that the universe has led you to this place.'

But it wasn't the universe that brought me here, and this remains a sore subject between us. It doesn't stop me from bringing him up.

'I still don't understand. He's the only part that just doesn't make any sense to me,' I had said a day later, and watched Don's mouth harden into a line.

'I don't understand why this is so confusing for you.'

'Of course it's confusing. He just left.'

'Well, I know that you don't have much experience with men. If you did, Jake's actions wouldn't seem so alien to you.'

Did I hide how much this stung? I can no longer judge my own facial expression with any degree of accuracy, the muscles there becoming periodically numb as though I have been anaesthetized.

'I need you to stop this. This Jake business,' he continues.

'Why?'

'Because it kills me. To see a girl like you, taken in again and again by someone like him, buying his snake oil. It's a pattern, a compulsion, and you can't even see it.'

And maybe he's right, because Jake was lying to me from the first moment we ever met and I forgave him because of how I felt when he smiled at me. I say nothing.

'So. Have Dale and Tyra got you back on the fitness regimen?'

'Yeah. We went this morning. It was awful.'

'Why was it awful?'

'Because they all hate me.'

'That is not true.'

But it is, and he's trying to be kind. Like when a teacher tells a group of children to stop picking on an outcast – well intentioned but with no understanding at all of how the dynamics work, making it worse by intervening. Don, at least, has not tried to intervene.

Nobody will look me in the eye. Sean woke me by shaking me hard, then waited outside my room as I dressed, and led me outside to the front lawn in silence. Dale and Abby stopped talking the moment they saw us coming, didn't say a word except to mutter instructions. I hadn't tried to speak, either. We ran six miles and did our lunges and push-ups and deadlifts in perfect quiet, so perfect that I could close my eyes and pretend I was alone.

'It is true. Tyra didn't even come.'

'Tyra's been a little sick this week. Needing a lot of rest. It's nothing to do with you.'

I knew she had looked sickly. I haven't seen her in our

room for days, though at this point I assume she's moved to different quarters. And who can blame her? I wouldn't want to share with me either.

'You need some air,' Don murmurs. 'Let's take this outside.'

This is unusual. We never take this outside, a crucial line drawn between session and circle, though it's possible this divide matters only in my mind. And when we're outside, the frosty morning air making my eyes water, I realize that it's not the first time.

'We were here last night. Outside. Weren't we?' We were. I remember the feeling of this frost-bitten ground under my palms, the outline of the little jetty on the water, the cold. I remember looking up at the night sky for a very, very long time.

'Yes,' Don says.

'Why?'

'Are you losing time again? Blackouts? Katy, you need to let me know if that's happening.'

Is that what's happening?

'I remember last night. I remember more.' And I hear him sigh.

'I was hoping you might have forgotten. This is very natural, by the way, there's no reason to be ashamed of it and I tried to tell you that. It's called erotic transference.'

His mouth on mine. His weight on me. Did I want this? Have I wanted him? Maybe.

'I'm afraid I may not have handled it well,' Don continues. 'I just had to put a stop to it. I know that I upset you. But it's the therapist's responsibility to protect the patient, and although transference is absolutely normal, it isn't appropriate. We can discuss it more in a later session, but now I'd like you to focus.'

I'm lying on the ground now, for no clear reason other than that it seems secure, trying to press as many inches of myself as possible against the earth. Everything around me feels too mobile and Don paces overhead, beside, around me, his footfalls a ragged rhythm.

'Why do you think you're angry?'

'I don't think I'm angry.'

'Katy, do I have to remind you what you've done? The fact that you have no memory of the episode does not mean that it didn't happen. I've been a psychotherapist for a very many years, and I can tell you that I have never known anyone to lash out like that without cause. Probably a trauma.'

I try, yet again, to remember violence. The feeling of bones under my knuckles, Dale's bones, I can still recall. But the sensation alone, no sounds, no sights. If my brain could have failed to store information so vital, then anything is possible.

'So this is what I mean by detective work. I need you to think back, throughout your whole life right back into your childhood, and tell me why you think you are angry.'

'Do you think I've had episodes before? I would have known, someone would have told me.'

'What do you think?'

'I don't think I had them before. Not before this year.'

'Last year, Katy. It's January now, you remember?'

January. All my lost time. My dad has spent Christmas alone.

'Last year. Yes. When I came here. I wasn't myself. Kept feeling like things around me weren't real.'

'Stress is often a trigger for these kinds of breaks. And you are in the right age bracket for a first episode.'

'I know.' All those hours at the library taught me well enough; psychosis first occurs most commonly in the teens and twenties. Slightly later for girls than for boys.

'You look sad.'

'I've been thinking about him a lot. My dad. Keep having dreams about him.'

It's true, though they aren't quite dreams so much as static visions, my dad's face fixed behind my eyelids with an expression I can't read but instinctively fear. His eyes dark. Other times he looks impossibly sad, and I have woken up crying.

'I think I was too hard on him,' I continue. 'I was very... shut down. I didn't let him in. Not that he was trying to get in, but after she died I just went back to university, I didn't go back home until Christmas. He was rattling around alone inside that house, drinking, having to sort through her things. And now he's alone again.'

'Was your father ever physically abusive?'

Déjà vu. He has asked me this before, I know, but when? And what did I say?

'No. Never.'

'Are you sure?'

'Yes. Why?'

'Because to be frank, your behaviour is consistent with physical abuse.'

He looks at me with nothing in his eyes, and how can he possibly know that this is precisely the expression my father wore for months, this and only this.

'Stop it.'

'What do you see, Katy?'

My eyes squeezed shut now, I ignore the question. He does not need to know everything, not when he's changing his face like that with no warning.

'I don't know what you want me to say.'

'You were angry with your father the night you left home. Tell me why.'

'Because he was drinking. Because I didn't want to watch him die. I told you.'

'Go deeper.'

'Because he was lying, again, the same lie he'd told so many times, and I didn't want to listen any more. Because I knew that house was going to kill me.'

I'm not even sure that I'm speaking out loud any more, but Don looks as though he can hear every word.

'And because you were afraid of him.'

And he is right, of course he's right, and why would I question him? He's never been wrong about me once. I think now that he is the one person in the world who has ever truly known me, and the feeling of it swells so large in my chest that I ache. Don.

I want to tell him so, but my tongue stalls and instead I say, 'How can you know these things?'

'You know that I can see inside your mind. More or less. There's nothing I know about you that you don't know yourself.'

'I only know myself when I'm with you. When I'm not, it's... all a fuzz. I'm indistinct.'

'You don't need to be distinct.'

'I still hear things sometimes. Things that I'm not sure are real.' I can't say the word 'hallucinations', will never be able to speak it aloud.

'I know. That's all right.'

'I keep thinking about my mum. How she started.'

He shushes me, and I bite back the tears in my throat.

'So long as you stay here with us, and you keep doing your work with me, you will be safe. And when you hear something like that, something that you don't believe is real, or when you have a thought that doesn't feel right to you, I want you to take hold of that sound, or that thought, and say: stop. Just that. Stop. You have the power to stop those unreal things.'

'Stop.' The word feels foreign suddenly in my mouth, like a sound I've never heard before. The way my tongue moves to create the delicate 'st' and round 'p' seems alien. 'Stop.'

'Good. And when you have thoughts of your father, anything like the thoughts you described to me earlier, thoughts of guilt or sympathy or love for him, I want you to do the same. Stop.'

'Stop.'

'Good.'

'Please don't let me go crazy.'

'You're going to be just fine.'

His arm encircles me as I sit up eyes closed and mind wandering aimlessly out into the wilderness where white wolves gather in the branches, ears pricked and eyes gentle, their tails and limbs interlocking like a daisy chain.

'Why does everybody here have four-letter names?'

'What's that?'

I feel half-asleep, the sentence rising up from me like free association, something I had no idea I'd been wondering. But I have asked him this before, haven't I?

'Everyone has four-letter names. Nobody's is longer, and nobody's is shorter. Except yours.'

'Yours is seven. Caitlin.'

'You never call me that. Nobody calls me that here. Nobody uses their real name.'

A long pause, so long I wonder if he has heard me.

'I don't believe that your birth name has to define you. But there is a pattern to the way we do things here, and how we address one another. Four letters just has a symmetry to it, don't you think?'

I do think. Katy is so much more my name than Caitlin ever was, and I'm actually laughing out loud with the euphoria of having realized this.

'I don't believe that your birth has to define you,' he murmurs into my ear. 'You are not your parents. You are not your past.'

I am curable. My past is gone.

'You are doomed, of course.'

He says this so effortlessly, and when I look up he shows no sign of having spoken.

'What did you say?'

He looks startled. 'Nothing. I haven't said anything for a couple of minutes.'

And I take this moment and fold it in upon itself so many times that it becomes small, and do not think of it again. Stop.

CHAPTER TWENTY-TWO

'Do you still want to escape?'
The words strike me like a shudder. I can't now imagine how I ever tried to leave, can barely conceive of the outside world as anything more than a theoretical concept. What was I thinking?

Barb is watching me cautiously, trying to pretend that she isn't, chopping carrots without looking down at her hands. I'm afraid she's going to draw blood.

'No. I don't.'

'I'm glad. We were real worried about you there, for a while.'

'I was worried about me too. Still am.'

I've been scraping this same potato for too long, well past its skin and into its flesh, but there's something too soothing about its weight in my hand and the motion of the paring knife to stop.

'You know nobody blames you for what happened. You weren't yourself.'

My breath catches. Nobody but Don has spoken of this to me, not even Dale himself, his bruises now healed completely. Some part of me had clung onto believing that it never happened at all, because nobody spoke of it, though I know better than that. I am damaged, diseased, dangerous.

'You mean when I attacked Dale.'

She winces, and I can see that it truly hurts her to remember.

'I did attack Dale. Didn't I?'

'Yeah, honey. You did.'

'Why?'

'I wish I knew, sweetheart. I know that your heart's in the right place, and I think you just got a little mixed up. It happens to people.'

My head throbs, like it has for hours. I keep wondering whether I'm coming down with whatever Tyra had – my brain is fuzzy, and light is almost unbearable, so much so that I squinted my way through the forest to Don's cabin this morning. And I have the feeling, sticky and creeping, that I have forgotten something.

Our sessions have continued in the same intense vein – exercises in regression, Don steering my mind into half-forgotten places it refuses to go smoothly or quietly, memories stored behind a glass pane breakable only by force. If it's not exactly force that Don exerts, maybe it's closer to pressure, a psychological grip equal to the weight of his hands on either side of my ribcage.

I have never been thinner. Undressing last night I froze in mid-air, my arms raised, transfixed by the sight of my own chest, at the visible ribs through tracing-paper skin.

My own smallness, my insubstantiality, is dizzying, all the more so when Don makes note of it. But my body no longer feels strong, muscles robbed of the new definition I'd noticed so recently, though I can't truly remember how long it has been since that night I startled myself in front of the mirror, the night Jake disappeared.

My own body feels mysterious to me, and I have lost all grip on my mind. My thoughts have become treacherous, double agents whose loyalties remain a permanent mystery, and though I'm sleeping better my dreams feel invaded. I'm drinking Apfelwein again, despite Don's reluctance – alcohol could disrupt my mental rhythms, he said, but I'd been craving it desperately for days and now in the kitchen the drink's rich warmth is coating my jangled nerves, calming them by force.

'Where did I go?'

'What's that?'

'When I left, that day – where did I go?'

It's a blank in my mind now, that day. All I remember is skin under my nails, and someone holding my arms behind my back, and the taste of coffee. I've tried and tried to get it back and with every try the details seem to fade more. My best current memory, the one I go back to and pray not to lose, is running with Tyra. After weeks of not speaking, not seeing each other, I'd scarcely believed it when she strode up to me with something of her old energy, looking determined.

'Girl, I don't know about you, but I am feeling way out of shape. When was the last time we hit the trail?'

I wanted to hug her, to hold onto her and the memory of what we both used to be, but I settled for smiling and saying too long, it's been too long. I could have kept on running forever that day. The two of us perfectly in sync, moving alongside each other through the sun-dappled woods, so light on our feet we bounced off the forest floor.

The exertion seems unthinkable now. I feel weak, fuzzy, as though I'm coming down with something, my brain compressed in my skull. Over the past few days I've found light increasingly unbearable, the morning sunlight exploding grotesquely into my eyes when I stepped out of the carriage house this morning.

At least, I think it was this morning. It could have been more or less any morning.

I think it was also this morning that I woke up with Jake's name on my tongue, and his broken body behind my eyelids. It was the kind of dream that is so indistinguishable from reality that you can't trust your surroundings after you wake up, because if one world could disintegrate then there is nothing to stop this one from doing the same.

I've had this dream before, I think. I'm in the woods, all of us are, walking down a slope so steep it's almost vertical, and we should be tipping over and tumbling into darkness but somehow we stay upright. The darkness has texture, weight, and grows heavier the deeper we go, like air growing thinner at the summit of a mountain, and by the time we reach the bottom my breathing is shallow. And there he is, Jake, snapped in half like a wooden puppet, draped over a tree branch that looks too thin to support his deadweight.

The dream goes on much longer, but his silhouette is the final thing I remember, when I wake up exhausted and reach for him. The worst part is that it takes me a long time, a very, very long time, to remember who it was that actually died in the woods. If someone told me now that Kris never existed, I'm not sure that I could convince myself otherwise.

Circle that night passes in a haze, histories and stories blurring into one another so that I can no longer remember if it was Abby or Sean or Dale talking about how flesh and blood doesn't mean family, and how their own family never understood them. I can't focus, my mind slipping into cracks, and I concentrate on smiling benignly as they speak. It's all the same story. How is it possible that everyone here has the same story to tell? Everyone's family abandoned them. Everyone's story becomes the same. Everyone's name becomes four letters. We are all here for each other, and we are nothing without each other.

We are nothing without each other. This has never struck me before as sinister, and as Don looks at me I don't feel held so much as clutched. And I remember his hands on me then, the moonlight gleaming on the lake through the window as I pushed him away. Did I push him away? Did I lose consciousness? Was any of this real?

Everything is dark now. It takes a while for me to realize my eyes are open, and it's the middle of the night, and I'm in my room, or at least what looks like my room. Everything around me has taken on the feeling of a dream, and I blink hard several times and wave my arms before me because as a child, this was how I woke myself up from dreams.

Nothing around me dissolves, and I can see the room now through the dark. It is my room, without doubt. And it's at this point, as I gingerly raise myself upright, that my head explodes. It's pain like I've never felt before, lightning bolts ripping upwards through my skull and I'm on my knees with the humbling force of it, pressing my forehead to the ground and praying, praying, praying for it to stop.

What time is it? I thought night-time from the dark outside my windows, but I can hear voices outside and there's at least a fifty per cent chance they're not in my head. My brain is a queasy shattered clock-face, its numbers all odd and its hands no longer pointing straight. It could be any time at all, and I could have been here for an hour or a day or a week.

The only thing I know is the memory of Don's weight on me, pressing me down into the earth. Into the couch. And I find Jake's knife beneath my pillow and now I am sure of two things.

'Katy?'

Tightening my grip, I try to focus on the door as it swings slowly open, pain still humming around the base of my skull.

'You all right, hun?'

It's Tyra, crouching beside me with her face scrunched up in concern.

'What time is it?'

'Just coming up to eight. I tried to wake you for dinner, but you were dead to the world. You've been sleeping all day.'

Again. I don't sleep all day, not ever, but here I seem to do nothing else.

'There's something wrong with me.'

My eyes refuse to focus but I try to hold her gaze, because I need her to understand and I think she does, I think she must. There's something wrong with us.

'I know,' she murmurs soothingly, but I can tell from her

tone that she's missing the point. 'When I came by earlier you said you got sick during your session. Had to leave early.'

Is that what happened?

'Why did you move out of here?' I ask, as I uncoil from the foetal position.

'It was just time. Been wanting my own space for a while, truth be told.'

'But your things were still here. For days, you weren't here at night but you left everything. You said you slept at Don's once.'

'At Don's?' She laughs, too hard. 'When the heck did I say that? That'd be something. No, I guess whatever I left here was just stuff I didn't need. I'm sorry, though, I should've said something to you instead of just vanishing.'

'You looked ill. Sick. For weeks, soon after you stopped sleeping here.'

'It's you I'm worried about right now,' she frowns, pressing a hand against my forehead. 'You think you're coming down with something?'

'Something. I don't know how I got here.'

But I know where I need to go, and she can't come with me. I tell her I have a session this evening and though it makes no sense, though I clearly don't know what time of day it is let alone where I'm due to be, she doesn't argue.

The forest feels changed as I walk through it, trying hard to move in a straight line, bundled in a hoodie two sizes too large. I see Mary in the trees, I think, but when I blink and look back she is gone, and the cold is too complete to be sure of anything, dulling my senses. I tried asking Sean what month it was once, and he looked at me with a kind of impatient pity, as though I'd asked for his star sign. At circle now we bundle up in layers and warm our hands around the fire, and I keep wondering when there will be snow.

When I arrive at Don's cabin, a temporary wave of adrenalin propels me over the threshold and keeps me on my feet, my dreams giving me a story to tell.

'I think Jake is dead.'

His frown is compulsive, like a twitch.

'Why would you think that?'

'I just had a feeling. This morning, and a few mornings before. Him not being here, disappearing like that, there is no explanation that makes sense if he's alive. I think he's been dead for a long time.'

'Sit down. You look feverish.'

I feel feverish. Shaky and unsteady, close to delirious, and maybe I never did wake up this morning. If I close my eyes now, I could wake up in bed and be only mildly surprised, and it's tempting because the light is unbearable here. Don pushes me gently down onto the couch, sits beside me with a hand pressed on my shoulder. I should not be here. But I have to know for sure, and this is the only way.

'You know that Jake isn't dead. There is no evidence to suggest that. This is your paranoia talking, and that's worrying to me because I thought we were making progress.'

Were we? Nothing about my mind now feels like progress. Maybe I do have a fever, and maybe I'm wrong about Don. Please let me be wrong.

'People leaving you and people dying are not one and the same, Katy. You have to learn that.'

'Maybe.'

'Let me make you some tea.'

'I'm fine.'

'No, you're not. You need to put something in your stomach.'

I'm not sure that tea counts as putting something in your stomach. I'm imagining Earl Grey, almost salivating at the thought, the bergamot sharpness so vivid in my mind that I can smell it, but what Don brings me is different, black and almost bitter, with an edge of something like cinnamon. It feels heavy in my mouth as I swallow it, but everything feels strange to me nowadays, and this at least is warm. I should not be drinking this tea, just as I should not have been drinking the cider or probably eating the food, but am I paranoid? Just like my mum with the chemicals in the water.

'You should eat,' Don says, gesturing towards the obligatory Oreos perched on his table, and I pick one up obligingly. Finding it hard to imagine how I once desired them.

'No appetite.'

'Maybe you are coming down with something.'

He presses a hand against my forehead, pushes my hair back.

'I used to love being ill. So much that I used to pretend sometimes, when I was young.'

'Why?'

His voice seems both far away and too close, like an echo inside my skull. My head is pillowed on his thigh, though it's too sinewy to really be a pillow, more of a headstone.

'My mum was always great when I was ill. Even if she was in one of her bad times, if I was ill, she would rally and be there to take care of me. She was amazing.'

'No child should have to feign illness just to get the attention of their parents. Your mother did a real number on you.'

I feel treacherous, now, because that's not what I meant at all and somehow I feel my mum can hear this. She was always there, and my being ill only made it easier to notice. I want to explain all of this, but I don't have the words, and I don't think Don would listen.

My eyes are closed and I'm walking through ivory-pale slender trees. What I'm looking for are the train tracks, and I know that if I can only find the train tracks then I can pull myself along them like a length of rope in water, and gradually they will lead me out of here. But I can't find them, and now there's music in my ears, low and staccato like a schlock-horror soundtrack.

'Why didn't you tell me about Mary?'

I can barely hear myself over the music, but he hears me. His hand in my hair goes still, rigid.

'What about Mary?'

'That she was your patient before,' I whisper, the words feeling thick and mealy in my mouth. 'The one who walked along the train tracks, she had a name like a bird, I think. Did they give her shock treatment? Did you touch her?'

'Sssh. You're not making any sense, Katy. Just close your eyes and rest.'

But this is what I've been forgetting. One of many things, I suppose, and already I'm losing track of why it matters, or when I last saw Mary. Stay awake. I have to know for sure.

'Just rest.'

His fingers are feather-light as he pushes my eyelids closed.

CHAPTER TWENTY-THREE

The floor beneath me feels slanted, like I could roll over and keep rolling until I fall right off the edge of everything. I can't steady myself, even as I raise my head and try to find equilibrium, everything tilted back and forth like a funhouse mirror. Don's cabin seems tiny and far away, a doll's house version of itself with me peering monstrously through the doorway, but here I am, on the wooden floor, and there is the sofa, there are the bookshelves, and there is the blood.

Blood on the wall, half in handprints, and on the floor, red leaking between the floorboards like rotted grout, red turning black against the dark wood and none of it mine. I know without looking that I am not bleeding, but there's something sticking my hair to my neck, half-dried now. It was so easy in the moment, the choice between his body and mine, and even with the handle in my hand I never truly expected this to work. He held me down but he didn't bank on the knife, didn't imagine for a moment that I could have something up my sleeve that cut his throat like fish flesh.

I'm shaking too hard to get up, and I don't know how I got on the ground or how long I've been unconscious, but there's daylight now, and I need to know if I really did this. The floor is inarguable beneath my hands as I push myself over to him, and everything in me wants to recoil but I have to touch him to know.

I can't find the pulse in his neck but there's too much blood there for me to be sure, my fingers slick with it, and I'm breathing too fast and too loud and still not getting any air. He's not cold, and neither is his blood, and for the first time in weeks I don't feel even slightly like I'm dreaming. When I finally find the pulse on his wrist I choke in a real breath because still I can't bear the thought of him dead, and God, how did any of this happen?

But of course this happened. He couldn't keep me from going crazy and he was never trying to, and maybe this was what he wanted, the final proof that I really am diseased and dangerous and now deadly. I have to get out. Now I can leave, really leave and go back to that diner because I know the way and this time I'll do it right. I'll tell the man there that I need help, that I need to know what day and month and year it is and that there are people here who are not safe, that there is something in the tea and the cider and maybe the food. I am not paranoid. In this moment, everything makes perfect sense and I wish I could capture it like a photograph before my mind loses its grip again. But then. How do I explain this scene?

'You should change your shirt first.'

I turn in what feels like slow motion, everything heavy.
'What?'

'Your clothes. The others can't see that,' Ruth says. 'I was never convinced by you, but you've turned out to be quite the self-fulfilling prophecy.'

I watch as she kneels beside Don, Barb hovering behind her, neither of them looking at me, neither of them flinching at any of this.

'Just unconscious,' Ruth murmurs to Barb. 'Hit his head, losing blood from the jugular, and let's leave him that way for now.'

'Figured we'd give you your shot,' says Barb.

'My shot?'

'Well, sure. He had it coming.'

He did. I close my eyes and open them and Ruth and Barb are still there, and the blood in my ears is making it impossible for me to hear what they're saying. I should run now, but if they call the police my DNA is everywhere, on the knife and on Don and on the room, and would they believe me if I told them why? I should run.

'I had to.'

'It's not up to us to intervene in Don's relationships with his patients. They're sacred,' says Barb, but there's an edge in her voice I've never heard before, something like sarcasm. 'None of our business, just like it's none of our business if he finally bites off more than he can chew.'

'He's been pushing things for months. Taking liberties, prioritizing his baser drives over the needs of us all,' Ruth says, and I'm not sure whether she's talking to me or to Barb. 'Giving him free rein was a mistake from the start, and things have been out of joint for too long already. We should never have allowed it to go this far.'

'What do you mean, free rein?' My mind is spinning with too many questions. 'Don's in charge.'

'I see why you got that impression,' Ruth says, with a chilly smile. 'He thinks so too. It's been easier that way. This house, this land, the money behind it all – that's Don, and that's essential. That's his role in all of this, but of course he has to think he's calling the shots. All men do.'

If Don reanimated right at this moment, wiped the blood from his throat and temple and told me this was all an elaborate lesson, designed to illustrate for me that reality is fluid or that authority extends only as far as the group allows, I'd barely be surprised. I'm struggling to focus on what Ruth is saying in part because it makes no sense, and in part because Don's body, not his corpse but his body for now, is looming in my peripheral vision.

'Katy?'

Barb has a hand on my shoulder.

'This is probably a lot to take in.'

'That's what he said,' I whisper.

'Don?'

'The first time we met, here. I'd been reading Freud, and he woke me up, and he said that.' He seemed so safe to me that day.

'Don pushed too hard,' says Ruth. 'He often does, but this time...'

She and Ruth share a long glance that I can't begin to decode.

'He told me you were his patients. Both of you, that you followed him out here from Manhattan.' But did he tell me this? Or did I just assume that Don was the sun and everyone else revolved in his orbit? It's been so long since my thoughts seemed clearly founded and supported by evidence.

'We were never his patients,' Ruth replies. 'I was his colleague, for a time. Don has always needed to believe that he's a leader. His sessions here, these one-on-ones, allow him to pretend to himself that he's still a doctor, that he still has authority. He needs that. But the reality is… well.'

'Did he tell you he gave up his practice in Manhattan because he was just too idealistic for the profession?' Barb asks. 'Couldn't make a real difference, wanted to help people on his own terms?'

'Yes.'

'Yep. Truth is, the profession pushed him out, not the other way around. Lost his licence to practise. You can only fool around with so many patients before one fights back. Well, I don't need to tell you that.'

And this makes a horrible kind of sense. Don has been an abstract concept because I let him be, as distinct as a silhouette, an amalgamation of so many half-truths I didn't question because I needed to let someone else steer me.

'It's done,' Ruth says, her voice sharp enough to cut through my fogged brain. 'She needs to change before the others return.'

'I'll take her,' Barb nods, ushering me towards the door. 'Come on.'

The carriage house is empty, and Barb explains that last night was a vision quest from which she and Ruth returned early. 'Felt like we needed to be here,' is her only explanation, and maybe they knew all of this was coming.

She waits outside the bathroom door as I shower, and I look down only once at the water running pink into the drain, rinsing his blood from me. There's less of it than I imagined, dried in streaks on my neck and into the ends of my hair, and outside the carriage house I had watched as Barb struck a match to my stained hoodie, but there's something else.

'The knife,' I tell Barb through the bathroom door. 'I left it there, in the cabin.'

'Don't worry about that.'

And I don't, but once I'm dressed and my hair is drying in the freezing winter air outside, I ask her more because Barb has always been steadfast, and surely talking to her will make all of this fall into place. What comes out of my mouth is so much angrier than I plan, and so much less articulate.

'How?'

'How what?'

'How could you just... let him do this?' She regards me in silence, and I press on. 'You of all people, after what you went through—'

'Oh, honey. That story. I swear, the number of times Don made me tell that same old sob story about poor little me, the pathetic battered wife. Again and again and again, he never got sick of it, even long after the rest of us did. Well, but he always did like his women to be needy. I came up with it to get him off my back, because he wants everybody to fit his narrative, but hell if I didn't regret it after the first five times.'

'It wasn't true?'

She sighs. 'Worked on you too. I guess it's not just Don that likes the victim thing. It fits, right? Seems like something that'd happen to a person like me. That whole backstory, Don's big on that, wants everybody to remember what brought them here, whether it's a fact or not.'

'It wasn't true. None of it?'

'Every lie's got a little kernel of truth,' Barb says. 'But you had to know it was a cliché, no? Smart girl like you, I'd have figured you'd be calling bullshit.'

'Is anybody's story true?' Everybody's stories are too similar, but Barb is the last person I would ever have imagined to be lying about hers.

'Oh, sure,' Barb hastens to reply. 'Some of 'em more than others. But you tell a story enough times, it's gonna change. That's the whole beauty of circle, it lets you define your own truth, tell whatever version of your story you need to tell. Don just likes to hear a certain kind of truth, is all.'

'Is he going to die?'

'Do you want him to?'

No. But I don't want the choice to be mine, and so I ask, 'What would happen if he did?'

'We'll go on. Just like we always have. It'll complicate things for a while, but in the long run...' She trails off with a shrug. 'I mean, you must have noticed he doesn't really have much to do with the day-to-day stuff here. Him and his cabin, what happens there, it's like a whole other world. Ruth's the one with the vision.'

And it's true, yet one more thing that makes such perfect sense when I hear it that I can't imagine how I was blind to it before. The practicalities of daily life, the things that have filled my hours not spent in the cabin by the lake, the diet and the workouts and the sleepless all-night circles, the vision quests and the shared pasts of the group, all of these are things from which Don has been separate. His agenda has always been something else, something removed from the core of the group, and I had assumed that he was the superior, rather than the outlier.

'Don likes young people,' Barb continues. 'And they tend to like him. The rest of us... well, we can go pretty much unnoticed.'

I want to ask if he does this to everyone, if only to ascertain how naive I was to believe even a single word he said. The hours and days are mounting in my memory, all the sessions where he'd looked at me and I'd felt so viscerally understood, so contained, and now it seems I was never more than prey to him. Easy prey, at that.

'He can go to hell, and so can you,' I say in a savage whisper. 'You smiled and went unnoticed and let him do it, and not just to me. To Tyra, and to Mary, and—' I cut myself off, hearing her name. Don lost his licence to practise therapy because he fooled around with one patient too many, one who fought back.

'What happened to her?' I ask slowly, with a shiver. But it feels horribly clear to me already, slotting fully formed into my brain like a memory from my own past. Barb has her eyes locked on me, barely reacting.

'To Mary?'

'To Robin. Before she was Mary.'

'So you know.'

'Don told me she was his patient, that she used to pull her

hair out, that she left therapy with him and ended up in a psych ward, catatonic. But that's not true.'

'It's more true than I'd have expected,' Barb says. 'Sounds like Don overplayed his hand a little, trying to get your defences down.'

She ended up here, catatonic, not in an institution, and though the latter sounded nightmarish to me when Don described it, how much better off would she have been?

'Why is she like this?'

'That's enough questions for now,' Barb replies, and directs me back through the woods towards the house, through the gathering fog. But instead of turning at the usual place she steers me onto a path I don't recognize, down a steep slope into a ravine where Ruth is waiting, a gentle smile on her face and a spade in each hand.

CHAPTER TWENTY-FOUR

'What is this?'

The fog is growing heavier, obscuring the ground so that I have no idea where I'm walking, my legs shaking as I descend the slope towards Ruth. My voice sounds reedy as she pushes a spade into my hand, nausea lodging in my gut.

'We need to start digging now, before nightfall. There's going to be a frost overnight, and the ground is already harder than I'd like.'

'Many hands make light work,' Barb chips in. 'Between the three of us, shouldn't take more than a few hours to get a hole big enough.'

And though the instinct to ask 'what for?' rises, I know that this isn't a question, and what I ask instead is, 'He's dead?'

'He will be soon,' Ruth replies.

'You're just going to let him die?'

She blinks.

'I assumed you'd be amenable to that eventuality. You are the one who started this.'

'But—' But what? What did I think was going to happen when I cut his throat, if not this? I do not want him dead and this is so much bigger than him now, because Ruth and Barb's nonchalance is setting my blood cold. This is what happened to Kris's body, and I cast my eyes around wildly as though there will be a marker somewhere here, a patch of freshly turned earth, something to confirm. How many other people are buried here, people who I never met?

'I'd noticed that you had started volunteering for more yard work,' Ruth says, 'in exchange for skipping the mind. That's fine, by the way – not everyone is cut out for the mind room, and I could tell that you were resistant in the sessions we had. There's time for us to work on that, but yard work is no less important to our cause.'

I'm frozen, looking dumbly back at her, and finally she sighs, putting down her spade and placing both hands on my shoulders.

'Listen to me. I know that you're struggling. But we have work to do. First, we clean up your actions, then we can clean up your thoughts. You're more familiar with thought-stopping by now, I assume? Don at least taught you that much?'

I nod.

'Good. Then you'll know that within time, you won't ever need to think about this again. You will not remember his blood on your hands, or his hands on your body. You will remember his death as an accident. I guarantee you that.'

I nod again, numb, and let her nudge me forward towards

the spot we are to dig. Something is telling me to keep her talking, keep both of them talking, long enough to get my thoughts straight and find my way out. I have to leave, but the rules have changed now and I know if I simply run they will bring me back like before. I'll never find my way in this fog, either.

'Your cause,' I say, echoing her words. 'What is it?'

'I suppose you might call it something like survivalism,' Ruth replies, pausing with her shovel buried handle-deep in the earth. 'Taking only what we need, living off the land as far as possible, and of course you're familiar with the paleolithic ethos by now. It's just a more pure way of living. But more to the point, it will soon be the only way of living. You've spent enough time in the outer world to realize that it can't survive for long in its current form, and I want everyone here to be as prepared as we can be.'

'Prepared for...' I have to stifle a hysterical giggle, biting down hard on my lip as I choke out, 'for what, the end of the world? Doomsday?'

'That's a touch dramatic. It won't be anything like I suspect you're imagining. There will simply come a point when the world can no longer provide its citizens with enough resources to live on. This isn't a secret, it's out there for anyone who chooses not to live in denial. Our country is more divided than it's ever been. Our government is run by a man with no diplomacy, no experience and no interest in maintaining stability. Society has been on the brink of entropy for a very long time. But we're the lucky ones, out here. We will abide.'

My body feels light and I can barely see the ground at all,

blindly shovelling. Behind us Barb stands guard, arms crossed like a sentry. When my eyes close I can see all three of us as though from above, and our conversation seems impossible, a ludicrous abstraction, one that should never have included me. I could float away in this moment and disappear altogether. It's raining now, though I can't feel the drops on my skin.

'You're ready in body now, at least,' Ruth continues, 'but your mind still needs work, as you know. Don wasn't wrong about that. It's not your fault, by the way – you come from a world so polluted that it's almost unavoidable. London, yes?' She says the word like a curse. 'And you fled from there to New York, going from bad to worse. People living on top of one another, consuming everything, producing nothing, their minds fogged by artificial desires and artificial struggles, obstacles created and perpetuated by their environment. There's so little hope, out there.'

'Don said the city could drive you mad. Psychosis is more common in urban environments than rural ones,' I parrot.

'I'm glad not all of your time at the cabin was wasted. Yes. The city is toxic, and you're not to blame. But I know that you think you can get back there, that you're longing to see it all again, now that Don's out of the way. You're planning to leave again.'

Digging is easier now, the ground beginning to soften with the weight of rainwater, soil turning to mud. The proximity of Don's prone body has begun to weigh on me. He will wake up at any moment, I still feel certain, and he can't be buried alive because I won't let him. I used to dream of being buried alive, a recurring nightmare in which my childhood best friend Felicity poured soil over my face as I stared mutely up at her, paralysed in the playground earth. Not that ending. Not even for him.

'If you try to leave, we will come after you. We will find you, and we will bring you back, because even if you don't understand it now, you are infinitely better off here than you could ever be out in the world. I know that you're young, and you don't understand yet what's coming.'

'I don't want to escape. I have nowhere else to go. You're right.'

'You don't need to humour me like you did him,' she says, grimacing as she hits something solid with her shovel. 'Or flatter me, for that matter. If there's one thing we can all learn from Don, it's that the male ego is a fragile thing. Your choice of words betrays you – you said "escape"', because you still see being here as an imprisonment. Soon enough, you'll realize that coming here in the first place was your escape.'

The darkness is beginning to settle, the twilight turning to yellow and it'll be gone soon, and once this day is over I will have no choice but to consign it to my memory, a reality, something that happened. It happened to someone, but perhaps not to me, because the fog is still hanging heavy and I can't see Don at all now, and none of this feels solid. I try to remember the feeling of the knife handle, the resistance of Don's sinew against the blade, but my hands are numb and I can't even feel the shovel in them now.

'Who else has died here?' I ask, though I know this is treacherous.

'You know the answer to that.'

'Did Kris really kill himself?'

'To the best of my knowledge, yes,' Ruth replies. 'There's very little reason to think otherwise. He was fragile, in the end.'

He was, and specifically coming back here to die makes as much sense as anything else I know about Kris. But if he was killed, killed for daring to leave or for daring to return, Ruth would still say exactly this. I have no idea at all what these people have done.

'It's time, then,' says Ruth. 'That's deep enough.' The spade is taken from my hand, and when I try to look down my head is spinning so hard that I lose my footing entirely, my knees hitting the ground hard, and the hole opens up like a void beneath us. I can't see the bottom of it, and there is no way we've dug this deep in so short a time, but then I have no idea how long we've been digging for.

There's movement behind me, noise, but I don't turn around, my eyes fixed on the hole we have dug, until I hear Barb say, 'Whenever you're ready, hun.'

'What?'

'You can do the honours.'

And when I finally turn, I see Don's body clearly beside me, blood dried on him now, his lips tinged blue and his skin translucent, frost gathered on his collar and his hairline. He has died, during the time that we've been here digging, and maybe he knew what was happening, maybe he felt it.

'What—' I say again, even as I'm scrambling backwards away from him, feeling numbly around for purchase on the ground, trying to stand.

'You can do the honours,' Barb repeats, nudging Don's

body with her foot, looking expectantly at me. They want me to bury him. Finish what I started.

'No,' I say, 'no,' and then I'm running, my legs numb and my eyes almost useless in the fog. The slope is so much steeper than I knew but if I can just get to the top then I'll be away. I can make it to the road like last time and I know that the fog is not real, that if I can get my head straight it will disappear, and all I need is time to think without anyone else reaching into my head.

I make it to the top, just barely, before a hand closes over my mouth and something sharp pricks into my arm, Ruth's face blurring in my peripheral vision as the outlines of trees all blur into one dark whole.

I can't remember the last time I woke up un-disoriented. This is the thought that hangs lowest when I come to on another hardwood floor, along with the awareness that 'un-disoriented' is not a word. Oriented? Can you simply be oriented? Orientated? This is bad, now, my thoughts are moving in concentric circles and I need to focus.

Think back. A pinprick in my arm, like a needle. Raising my arm is impossible, my entire body heavy and stiff, but finally I tilt my head enough to focus and there, in the inner crook of my elbow, is a small piece of gauze taped in place. I try to rip it off but find I can't get a grip on it, no strength at all in my fingers.

My muscles feel charged, energy squirming inside them and yet I can barely move at all. I'm sick of waking up like this, in varying states of mental and physical paralysis, and it stops here. I will stop this. I will not lose consciousness again, even with my eyelids this heavy. I am awake. Inside a room I don't recognize, with bright white walls and no windows, lit by a single flickering strip bulb.

I lie there, perfectly still, playing mental exercises to keep myself alert. Recite London street names in alphabetical order. Recite every station on the Northern Line. Name twenty actors who have played Sherlock Holmes on screen. I used to do this effortlessly, but now my mind is blank after the most obvious four: Rathbone, Brett, Downey Jr, Cumberbatch. My once-extensive pop culture knowledge might not be the worst thing to lose, but it stings nonetheless, the tangible proof of just how far I've strayed from myself. If this were a Sherlock Holmes story, this would be around the point where Holmes would make his deduction and explain precisely what compound is in the cider and the tea that we've all been drinking, what mind-altering substance I've been blithely slurping down for months, and the chemical process by which it twisted itself into my brain and mimicked all of the symptoms that I've always feared the most.

Whatever was in that needle was different, though. I've never felt this kind of bone-deep, paralysing exhaustion before, my muscles twitchy but my body so heavy I can't even move my head to further examine the room around me. I have to remember how to move, because I won't be alone here forever.

'What was in the needle?' I ask out loud.

'Thorazine.'

Yes. The voice comes from somewhere nearby, and it may even be real.

'Mary?'

She's watching me, and has been all along, seated with her back against the wall and legs drawn up to her chest.

'Thorazine,' I echo, the word mealy in my mouth. 'That's what Don told me they gave you, at the psych ward. He said that it made you worse.'

'It's bad stuff,' she says. 'Makes you stiff and slow.'

'I can feel that.'

I brace a hand against the floor, try bending my arm and putting weight on it, and though it feels close to impossible I eventually manage to lever myself upwards, just enough so that I'm leaning against the wall next to her. There's something beside her that looks like a shadow, until I look closer and realize that it's a small pile of her hair. She has one hand tangled near her scalp, fist clenching and unclenching around a handful of strands.

'They use Thorazine here? On us?'

'Not always,' she replies. 'Only some of us, only sometimes.'

She pulls, and I look away feeling nauseous.

'Don told me he didn't believe in medication. Said it was one of the failings of the healthcare system, medicating patients up to their eyeballs.'

'He told me that too.'

'This is insane,' I say, trying to make the edges of my words sharp and not slurred. 'How does this happen? How is this place allowed to exist?'

She looks at me with mild curiosity.

'Anything is allowed to exist.'

'No. All of this, it only works because we all go along

with it. If we stopped, if we said no, then the whole thing would crumble. I saw you out in the woods, so many times, and nobody was watching you, not really – you could have escaped. Any time.'

'Why?'

I stare at her.

'What do you mean, why? You could have got out of here, if you knew what was happening – you could have found help, got better.'

'Nobody gets better.'

'You mean here. Nobody gets better *here*.'

'Nobody gets better,' she repeats, full stop implicit.

'That's not true. Don wants everyone to think they're crazy and that he's the only person who can keep them sane, but—' I stop. Don is dead. Past tense, and she doesn't know this. 'It's a lie. You had a life before this, right? Your name was Robin, and you went to NYU, and…' I'm struggling to remember any more details from the story that Don told me, but maybe it doesn't matter because maybe none of it was true. To my surprise, she starts talking, and keeps talking, toying with another strand of hair at the base of her scalp. Her voice is odd, still, a kind of singsong like she's reciting all of this by rote, and her gaze is unfocused but her words are sharp.

'I never liked Robin. It never felt like my name, and Don let me choose a new one. I'd been to therapists before and none of them had ever asked to call me by a different name, but once he said it, it made sense. Therapy is about changing the narrative, he said. Telling yourself a new story until it becomes true. I liked that. I needed to change something, because at college things had been getting worse, not better. New York was violent. Everything felt too much, too loud, too dirty, too angry. I was walking around with a layer of skin missing all the time, exposed, getting infected. And then I found him, and I felt shielded.'

'How long were you his patient, in New York?'

'A long time.'

'Did he tell you that you were special?'

Of course he did. Just like he also told her that she would be fine so long as she trusted him entirely, opened herself up to him entirely. He would keep her from going crazy.

'Did he have sex with you?'

I know I'm badgering her with questions and she's beginning to shut down, but I can't stop now that I've started asking. She doesn't respond.

'That's why he left the city. Because he was having sex with his patients. Ruth told me that.'

Still no response, and I suppose I don't need one.

'Why do you do that?' I ask as her hand comes away from her scalp with another two separated strands. It looks unimaginably painful but she seems to feel nothing.

'It makes me calm. Anything that hurts will work, but this is easiest, less messy. I stay away from blades now, nothing sharp, nothing hot. That was one of his conditions. He told me that I tried to kill myself, and he was bringing me out here to get better, to get away from everything and detoxify. He saved me.'

'When? How long have you been here?'

She shakes her head, because of course she doesn't know. Maybe doesn't care. They wouldn't tell her, even if she asked.

'I did think I could leave, once. I tried to leave. I walked into the woods and I kept on walking, around the lake and through the trees until I hit a road, and I walked until I found a town. I stayed there, for a time, on the streets, and it was bad.'

'Bad how?'

'Bad. There were bad people there. Desperate people. People so poisoned they were willing to do anything.'

'You keep saying poisoned like it means something,' I tell her. 'But we're literally being poisoned. Here. There's something in that cider, something that makes you crazy. Maybe in the food, too, I don't know.' Yes, I sound paranoid, I realize this and it doesn't matter because, for once, I know what is true.

'I can't drink the cider,' she replies.

'Did they tell you that you did things? Things that don't feel true? They told me that I attacked someone, and I don't think that was true, I don't think I ever touched him. Don told me that I had some kind of episode at a bar in New York, that the police almost came, and that's just—' I'm laughing again, because this sounds truly ludicrous now that I'm saying it out loud. 'It never happened.'

Her eyes slide to a point somewhere near me, but she's looking through me, not at me.

'You remind me of someone,' I tell her then.

I stop just short of adding that she reminds me of my mother, when she was taken away and I finally saw her again and she was so medicated she barely recognized me, her eyes vacant and her skin strangely chalky to the touch. Was she on Thorazine? I used to know the names of every drug she had ever been prescribed, along with dates and dosage and resulting effects, because I had to know, and now I don't. But yes, Thorazine, the name feels familiar in a way that I think is real.

Robin doesn't react, and in any case I have remembered the thing that I really need to ask her about, the thing that feels so obvious I can't believe I've waited this long.

'The night that Kris died. You led me to him. You did, didn't you? That really happened, I didn't imagine you?'

She nods.

'Why? Why me, why didn't you go and get Don, or Ruth, or someone?'

'You needed to know, because you were thinking of leaving. Kris left. He left us and he went back to the city, and he stayed there for too long. By the time he came back here it was too late. He was poisoned.'

'I don't think that's what happened,' I say, my voice a whisper. 'I think you've got it backwards.'

We fall into silence, for a while. It seems to me as though the ceiling bulb is getting brighter, until I realize that there is greyish daylight coming in through a narrow skylight, so tiny that I missed it earlier, and there's a faint drumming sound overhead. When I look closely, I can see raindrops blurring against the glass.

'Why are you here?'

'I don't know,' I answer. 'They... I woke up here. Did you see who brought me here?' Why would they lock me in with Robin?

'Why are you here?'

I look at her to make sure she has really spoken again,

and she looks expectantly back at me. Because my parents are crazy. But no, that's flip. My mum is dead and my dad will drink himself to death soon, and I needed to take control, which is ridiculous because being here is the opposite of being in control.

'I don't know.'

I don't know how I got here. How I came to this. I wonder how I would ever explain this to my dad, how I let myself get so lost, and there's a lump in my throat because I know I will probably never have the chance to try. I'm lying down again, the rain falling straight towards me, and it strikes me that we all see roughly the same sky and maybe my dad is seeing rain now too through the skylight in his study. And maybe somehow, he will know that I'm sorry.

CHAPTER TWENTY-FIVE

I'm not sure what has woken me, until I hear it again. A car engine, a sound so alien it takes me a while to identify it, muffled as it is by the storm. The rain has grown heavier in the time I've been asleep, so violent now that I think it may be hailstones hammering the skylight. But there it is again, in the distance, and when I raise my head I find that my body moves normally again.

The room feels unsteady around me as I stand, but as the door swims into focus I realize that there is no lock. I can't hear anyone else, but we're too far up to know for sure, and I can't stay in this room any longer no matter what.

'Mary?' I grip her by the shoulders, shaking, trying to force focus. 'Robin? You have to come with me.'

She looks directly at me, finally.

'I'm going to stay here.'

'Please, just come with me. I know you think that you're safer here but you're not, this is not safety. This is prison.'

I know it's hopeless, but I keep trying in spite of myself, trying different combinations of words to convince her as though there exists one single sentence that will unlock her mind. I played this game with my mum so many times, against the advice of doctors who told me it was hopeless to use logic in the face of delusion.

'Robin, listen. Don is dead. Don is dead, and Ruth and Barb let him die, and they're in charge now and I don't know what they're planning but it's nothing good. Do you understand what I'm saying? Don is gone.'

I'm holding her tightly now by both shoulders, and she seems truly adrift, further away than ever.

'We have to go,' I almost yell at her, my voice cracking, her bones so sharp beneath my hands. 'Please.'

'I can't. Maybe you can.'

And I let go of her, my throat closing up with tears and I blink my eyes hard to keep them dry, moving as quietly as I can through the door and down the corridor without looking back. There is nobody on the first floor of the house, and nobody in the kitchen to stop me and I keep my eyes forward, forward, forward, until I'm out and running in the direction that I know in my bones is away.

'Hey!'

I jolt to a standstill as a lasso lands around my torso, but with a twist of my head I realize it's Barb's arms holding onto me, and I run my elbow as hard as I can into her face and don't stop to watch her stagger backwards. My muscles are still stiff and my legs heavy, blood struggling to pump like it should as I sprint down the sloping lawn and into the trees, still not looking back for fear that I will see them following me. The rain is coming hard and thick, the heavy, gummy drops that soak you to the bone within seconds, the sodden ground sinking beneath me with every step.

I'm going to die if they catch me. The thought comes to me fully formed as numb disbelief settles in and I just keep running, all of my training with Tyra coming back to me as I make low, light-footed strides, focusing on landing on the ball of my foot first. God, Tyra. I'm leaving them all. The thought has no weight, there's no room in my chest for anything but fear and yet their faces are all in my head, because how long have they all been here really? If I don't get out now I will die here. If I don't get out now I will die here. If I don't get out now I will die here.

Suddenly there is no more path, nothing but trees and no clear way through them, and every step I take is strangled by roots and tangled branches. I slip on leaves and fall hard, and for a second I'm completely frozen in place as my brain tries to function in a fog, my thoughts on a loop. If I don't get out now I will die here.

And then, flat on the ground, I hear it. The undergrowth is alive under my cheek. I'm blind, almost, the woods around me damp and endless and I pray they'll keep me safe.

'Caitlin!'

The voice is so close but I still can't recognize it, can't identify it as male or female even, and when I listen hard I can't hear it at all. I'm imagining it, but what if I'm not? If I'm wrong, if I show myself now, they will crush me and literally trample me into the dirt after all this. There's soil in my lungs, inhaled as I breathed too hard, and the cough spasms inside me as I press both hands against my mouth. I can't breathe. My ears ring.

'Caitlin!'

I cough, hard, and start running again blindly away from that voice, its presence now my only sense of direction, but I can hear trampling in the undergrowth behind me, footsteps much too close. When the lasso lands around my torso again I scream, and thrash, and try to twist in its grip but it's so much tighter now, pinning my arms to my sides.

'Caitlin,' he says, his breath warm against my ear and his voice so close. 'It's okay. It's okay. It's me.'

I freeze.

'Let me go.'

He does, slowly, and I try to steady myself. Close my eyes, tightly, and open them again to see whether he vanishes. He's still there, hair plastered against his forehead, his skin paler than I remember but his eyes just as warm, and I'm shaking.

'What are you doing here?' I try to scream at him, but it barely comes out a whisper. 'Where have you been?'

'I'm sorry I left. Everything's going to be okay now.'

'You have no idea. You have no idea what's been happening.'

'Tell me,' Jake says urgently, stepping closer to me and pressing his hands against my cheeks, cradling my face. So I tell him.

'Don tried to rape me while I was barely conscious, and I cut his throat with your knife. Sharper than I expected for such a small blade. Ruth and Barb know about it, they don't care, they seem thrilled at the chance to take over. Ruth apparently thinks Doomsday is coming soon. They injected me with Thorazine when I tried to run. That's an antipsychotic. My mum was on it once. And they made me dig a grave and I think Don is buried in it now, somewhere over there.'

The hysterical laughter that's been building in me for hours now finally comes out, and I can barely breathe I'm laughing so hard, in jagged shrill bursts that I can't stop. I push my face into Jake's chest when he pulls me in, holding onto him despite myself.

'What month is it?' I ask him.

'October. Today is October twenty-third.'

'Don told me it was January. I knew that was... I knew I hadn't been here six months.' But I didn't know. It took so little effort for him to convince me I was wrong. Damaged, diseased, dangerous.

'The police are here,' Jake says into my hair.

'*What?*'

'That's where I went. I knew things here weren't right, and I had it all planned out. I was gonna leave, go straight to the nearest town and tell the sheriff's department everything, get them to come out here. I knew I didn't have much solid to tell them, but I had Kris, I had some details about him, I could tell them that he died out here and they buried him like a dog and never told the authorities. I knew that would be enough, at least to get the place investigated. But when I got out there, on my own, it took me a while to get my head straight. It was like I was withdrawing.'

'You were,' I say, voice still muffled against him. 'The cider, I think it's drugged. Maybe the food, I don't know, but it's something that makes you ecstatic or makes you hallucinate, makes you believe you're losing your mind. I don't know why—'

'Just to keep you off-balance. Easy to control. That's what it's all about, here. That's what I liked, having all my decisions made. But wait, Caitlin—' Jake tugs my head gently upwards to face him. 'Don's dead?'

I nod, swallowing down bile.

'And he tried to—'

He can't bring himself to say it.

'Yes. He's done it to other people. Mary. Tyra, I think. Anyone he could.' A cliché comes to mind then, *everything is about sex, except sex – sex is about power.* 'You?'

'No,' Jake replies immediately, looking sick. 'I don't think he… No.'

He looks as though he's struggling with something else he wants to say, but pauses, glancing over his shoulder back towards the house. A second later, I hear it. Raised voices, one of them unmistakably Barb's.

'Come on,' Jake urges, and I follow him back through the woods, back towards whatever is waiting. I'm calm now, and this no longer feels like a nightmare in which I've killed someone and am trying to evade being found out. I will tell the police that I killed Don, that it was self-defence, and whatever comes next is out of my control. I rehearse the words in my head as we walk, trying to imagine how to describe any of this, how to say that I believe I've been drugged without sounding paranoid. Maybe they can test my blood and know for sure.

'I'm sorry,' Jake says, when we're almost through the woods. 'That I didn't take you with me. Everyone was watching you, is the thing, but I never would have left you here if I'd...'

He trails off, and I let him. This isn't a conversation I can have right now, not with everything else pressing in on us.

'What did you tell the police?' I ask, but before he has time to answer we're through the trees and I'm trying to comprehend the scene there.

Tyra, Dale, Sean, Abby and Otis are lined up on the porch, stiff and small-looking, motionless at least from a distance. A uniformed officer stands next to them, not talking to them but staring outwards across the lawn, his arms crossed as though waiting for instructions, and his presence seems impossible. An unfamiliar face, in a place where I've known only the same ten day in, day out. Fewer days than I thought, because I know that I arrived here in July, soon after the Independence Day weekend, and now it's October. It took only three months for me to get this far from myself.

'Jake Rush?'

We both turn as another officer emerges from the woods behind us, Ruth and Barb both trailing him with placid smiles.

'Yes, sir,' Jake responds.

'I'm Officer McGillivray, with the Monticello PD. You were the one who called this in? Asked for us to take a look around the place?'

'Yes, sir. I made a statement to Officer Morrow at the station.'

The officer nods, squinting against the rain.

'In your statement, you didn't make any reference to a new body.'

I look at Jake out of the corner of my eye. He's impassive.

'Body?'

'We found a freshly turned dirt hole, just out there in the clearing. Mostly filled in, won't be touched until we can get forensics here, but it looks to me like a grave.'

'Officer, with all due respect, this is absurd,' says Ruth. 'We grow all of our own vegetables here, the earth is regularly turned—'

'Ma'am, Mr Rush has given us reason to believe that you all have buried bodies off the books before,' McGillivray replies. 'You are aware that it's illegal to dispose of a body without registering the death with the county coroner? You need a burial permit, you need a death certificate. You can't just be burying your people out in the woods with no oversight.'

'Of course not. I used to work as a nurse, I'm aware of the requirements in case of a death, but I can assure you that nobody has been buried here.'

'Yes, they have,' Jake interrupts.

'Jake, you don't know what you're saying,' Ruth replies sharply, her eyes fixed on McGillivray. 'This young man is unwell, he has a history of paranoia, anger management issues. Whatever he told you about us, all that has ever happened here is people trying to help each other. We're a family.'

'Blood family?' asks the second officer, who's moved over to join his colleague, everyone else trailing behind him. Tyra is holding onto Dale as though her own legs won't hold her, one arm outstretched aimlessly at her side.

'What's going on?' Abby asks quietly. 'Where's Don?'

'No,' Barb says, addressing the officer. 'Not blood family.

Better than. Everybody here came of their own free will, came to make a better life for themselves than the ones they were handed by birth.'

'Some of these kids barely look old enough to vote,' McGillivray says, writing something brief in a crumpled notebook. The second officer murmurs something to him, their conversation inaudible for a minute or two, and I avoid looking at Tyra or Dale or any of the others as I finally find my voice.

'There is a body in that hole. In the woods. You need to dig it up. His name was Don, I never knew his last name, and he was in charge here. Or I thought he was. He's dead.'

I hear Tyra crying but it's a blur to me, they're all a blur as I try to keep talking, try to make sense. 'Bad things have happened here, not just that. It's been bad, for a long time. But he is dead, Don, and it was me.'

'Caitlin, wait.'

I turn in surprise to look at Jake.

'Stop protecting me,' he tells me, pressing a hand into my shoulder as he steps forward towards McGillivray. 'I need to take responsibility for this. It wasn't her. I killed him. The murder weapon was my knife, it has my initials on it, you can check.'

'Jake—' I start, but he talks right over me.

'I came back here last night, like I told you I was going to, and I went right to Don's cabin by the lake, the place where he holds the therapy sessions that I talked about in my statement. I expected to find him there alone, but Caitlin was there with him, unconscious, half-dressed, and he was...' Jake trails off for a second, shaking his head.

'And I had the knife. And that was it. He fought me, and I had the knife, and I killed him. I didn't mean to, but that's what happened.'

McGillivray looks at me expectantly.

'Is this true? That you were assaulted?'

My vocal cords feel frozen, and I wish Jake would look at me.

'He tried to,' I say eventually. 'Yes. I was out of it, but I... yes.'

'And then I buried him, and they helped me do it,' Jake says, gesturing to Ruth and Barb. 'They wanted him gone, so they could be in charge. I think maybe they'd always wanted that.'

Ruth is shaking her head in silence, exchanging a glance with Barb who is also silent. They know better than to say more now. Jake finally turns to look at me properly, his eyes boring into me like he's daring me to contradict his story, and if I were a braver and a better person, a person less desperate to see my home again, I probably would.

The downpour is still coming, all around us like gossamer curtains. It rained last night, so hard, long before Don was put in the ground. Hard enough to wash his body clean, blood and skin and DNA all rinsed slowly into the earth until, now, there is not a shred of me left on him.

CHAPTER TWENTY-SIX

I'm in the backseat of a police car with Tyra and she's crying, silently and violently, her body curled inwards with the force of it, and I want to take her hand but I'm too afraid. On her other side, Sean is staring straight forward with his eyes focused on nothing, not moving at all except for the restless, rhythmic twitching in his right leg. We've been driving for hours, it seems, though perhaps only minutes. I have lost consciousness twice during this drive, and though I know this is not normal I can't find it in myself to be worried.

Later, I come round in a bed with papery sheets, looking through a window with a view of a brick wall. There are wires in me, and I try to reach an arm to my head to see if there are wires there too, but I can't move.

'You're in a hospital, you're fine,' they say. And when I try to ask why, they just tell me to rest.

I'm in the hospital for three days, I find out later when

I finally wake up and manage to stay that way. Three days in which I lapsed in and out of consciousness, my dreams strange half-formed things in which the room around me was always present, but changed, swallowed up by shadows and silence, overrun by insects that crawled along the floor and up the walls and I closed my eyes before they could reach the ceiling and drop onto me. I dreamed the hospital was abandoned and I had been left here to die, and later I dreamed that Don was in a bed three feet from mine watching me with dark thirst in his eyes, and I wished for nothing more than to be abandoned again.

When morning finally comes, they tell me that I'm malnourished, and that I'm fighting off a fever, and that I have been drugged.

'Were you taking any medication?'

I shake my head.

'Any recreational drug use?'

'Never.'

'No pills for depression, nothing like that?'

'Nothing. That I know of.'

The dark-eyed nurse nods, as though my answer has confirmed something for her.

The first time I hear the word, later that day as I'm steeling myself to get out of bed, it's by accident. The nurse pauses in the doorway to my room with a uniformed man I don't recognize, and I feign sleep to hear their conversation.

'... DMT with MAOI, it helps it to cross the blood–brain barrier. They make it into a tea, usually, or sometimes a brewed alcohol.'

'You've seen this before?'

'We had a case over in Albany, actually two cases. Cult activity.'

They move away before I can hear any more. When the nurse fills me in later, she tells me what I already know.

'We found a drug called DMT in your system – that's a very potent psychedelic – and a couple of other traces. Thorazine, a first-generation antipsychotic, which is not a drug you want to be taking under the best of circumstances and definitely not one you want to be mixing with DMT. That combo could have killed you.'

'It wasn't voluntary.'

'Was everybody taking the same stuff? All of you at the house?'

'We were all drinking the cider and I think it was spiked, but I don't know. And they injected me with the Thorazine. Is there a girl called Robin here? Or Mary?'

She frowns.

'Dark hair,' I prompt. 'Long, dark hair, very pale, doesn't talk very much.'

'Yes. That poor girl. She's been moved to the psychiatric ward.'

There's a hollow tightening in my chest, because when I first awoke here and saw the wires and the strip lights, I felt certain that's where I was, committed just like my mother before me. I think there is a part of me now that will never stop believing I lost my mind for good, somewhere in between those woods and that room, and that everything Don led me to believe was true.

Jake was taken in a separate car, along with Ruth and Barb, and in my memory he was handcuffed though I can't be sure. When McGillivray arrives to take a statement from me I ask him, and he tells me that they're under arrest: second-degree murder, assault, something about fraud that I don't fully take in.

'What about everyone else?'

'Gone, mostly. Made their statements – they'll have to give depositions down the line, but we didn't have any reason to hold them for now.'

'Gone where?'

This feels impossible, anticlimactic. After so long together this is how it ends, no closure, no chance to ask each other how we got like this.

'Some of these kids, they'd been missing. Their parents had filed reports.'

Because their stories were not true, or maybe parts of them were true but not the unifying theme, the idea that all of us have been cast out by our families and we are orphans taken in by a benevolent new home. These are children with parents who missed them, and searched for them, and maybe mourned for them. This was kidnapping.

I tell McGillivray everything that I can remember, though it comes in ragged non-linear bursts and I can tell he's growing frustrated. He lets me talk, though, making notes and recording our conversation on an old-fashioned cassette machine that I find comforting. He asks me questions, specific ones about how I got here and what I was doing before this, and these I find easier to manage.

And when it comes to it, when he finally sets his pen down slowly and looks at me with fingertips tented into a prayer, and asks me what happened the night Don died,

I lie effortlessly. It helps that vagueness is built into the premise of my story: I was drugged, I was barely conscious, I remember more or less only what Jake told me.

'I don't even know where he got a knife,' I lie.

'Had you known Mr Rush to be violent before? Ever seen him lose his temper?' It takes me a moment to realize that he means Jake. Surnames are strange to me now.

'No, never. He's never been anything but sweet to me.' But then, since there's no need to lie unnecessarily, I add: 'He did tell me he had trouble readjusting, after he was discharged from the army. Some PTSD.'

'Train young men to kill, then let 'em back into the world and expect them to assimilate,' McGillivray mutters. 'It happens.'

'I really don't think he meant to kill Don. That place messed all of us up, and Jake was protecting me. If he hadn't intervened, I would have been raped. I know that for a fact. So just... Don't forget who the victims are here.'

McGillivray is silent then, making a few final notes before closing his notebook with a snap. 'This is just an initial statement – you'll need to give a deposition if this goes to trial.'

Before he leaves, he tells me that he's sending someone else to speak to me this afternoon, and I don't realize until she arrives that he did not mean another police officer. Her name is Louise, a woman in her mid-forties with dark skin and wide, gentle eyes, and she calls herself a specialist in 'exit counselling'.

She asks me if I know what month it is, as though she knows there's a part of my brain that still believes

I've been gone for months, maybe years. Before long I'm almost stumbling over my words in an effort to answer her questions, about Jake and about Don and about how lost I became, how I believed I was losing my mind in all the ways I always feared. And I know that my sentences are not clear and sometimes turn into fragments, but she seems to understand, she seems unfazed. This happens. I am a known quantity.

She explains to me that time distortion is a mind control tactic, that the goal was to disorient me just like the sleep deprivation and the restrictive diet and the drugs. 'Did you ever try to leave?' she asks me, after I explain how Jake led me there, and the moment I realized this was not his family's home.

'I wanted to leave straight away, but there was only one bus back to Manhattan and I'd already missed it for that day. So I agreed to stay just for the night, and—'

'Are you sure?'

'What do you mean?'

'That there was only one bus back to Manhattan.' She looks almost apologetic. 'There are actually about a dozen buses, from Monticello to Port Authority. Every day. They run from eight a.m. through till about eleven at night.'

'Are you sure?'

'I used to take that bus three days a week. This might seem like a small detail,' she acknowledges, 'but I want you to understand the extent to which you were being manipulated from the beginning. Lied to about your environment, made to feel more isolated and dependent on the group than you really were.'

Ditto the mysteriously moving ribbons on the trees, though that remains a logistical mystery to me because surely people other than me needed to use those ribbons for navigation. Was everyone in on the plan to disorient me? Or had everyone else already long given up on their environment making sense? The term for this is gaslighting, Louise explains, named after a 1940s film in which a man attempts to torment his wife into losing her mind by periodically dimming the lights outside her house, all while telling her that she's imagining things. She recommends that I do not watch it, at least for now, as though whatever's in that film could haunt me more than what's already in my head.

'Sometimes it helps to talk about the future, when the past is overwhelming,' she says next, breaking several minutes' worth of silence. 'Have you thought at all about what you'd like to do next?'

No. I can barely think past the walls of this room, and she doesn't push. She leaves her card on the way out, telling me that the first session is free and that she operates a sliding scale fee if I don't have insurance. I know that I won't see her again, but I will keep her card for a very long time nonetheless.

When McGillivray comes back the following day, bringing with him a few of my belongings and clothes from the house, I'm ready.

'I need to see Jake.'

'He's in custody. Bail's set at a hundred thousand dollars, which he can't post.'

'I can.'

He looks at me sceptically.

'You can.'

'Yes. But I need to make a call.'

And before I discharge myself as they'd told me I could this afternoon, there is one other thing I need to do.

There is no actual psychiatric ward at this hospital, as it turns out. There are three rooms, unmarked, at the end of a corridor leading to something called the Behavioural Health Unit, and in one of these rooms I find Mary. Her eyes are open but empty, cloudy as though a film has formed over them, and she doesn't acknowledge my presence at all.

'She's been catatonic since she was admitted,' a white-coated man told me quietly before I came in. 'Don't be too alarmed if she doesn't respond to you. We have her on some medication that I'm hopeful will improve her condition within a week or so.'

But looking at her, I'm not hopeful at all, and the heaviness in my throat has finally given way to tears. I curl into the plastic chair beside the bed and try to cry silently because the last thing she probably needs to hear is this, and I hold her hand just below the stark yellow band around her wrist that warns 'FALL RISK'.

'It's over,' I tell her, once I'm confident that my voice will not shake as I speak. 'You're safe now.' Even if she can hear me, I'm unconvinced this will comfort her, but I keep saying it because nothing else is coming to me.

'Does she have any family coming?' I ask, when the doctor returns to usher me out.

'We haven't been able to ID her. Hasn't said a word, all we've got to go on is Mary.'

'That's not her name. Her name is Robin, and she was

a student at NYU.' I rack my brain for anything else, but it's a blank. 'Don was her therapist, in Manhattan. I don't know when, exactly, but if you tell that to the police I'm sure they'll have enough to go on.'

As I'm almost to the door, I turn, hauled back by the fear that they won't.

'If they can't find her family, can you let me know? Or even if they do, could you still let me know?'

'Sure. Leave your number and your name, we'll put you into the system as her emergency contact for now.'

But I don't have a number, of course. I take the pen and the overturned business card, and I hold onto it trying not to think about how long it has been since I wrote anything down. When finally, miraculously, I remember my own email address, I write it down praying that Gmail doesn't automatically purge unused accounts.

In the hospital hallway, I finally make the call. It comes as a surprise to me that I still remember his number.

'Hello?'

He sounds normal, casual even, though I don't know what I expected. Perhaps that my absence would leave a hole in him deep enough to hear.

'Dad, hi. It's me.'

There's a long silence.

'My God.' Rustling, as though he's moving between rooms or more likely sitting. I can see him sinking into that armchair, the cordless phone in one hand, probably already with a drink in the other. 'Are you all right?'

'Yeah, I'm fine.' A white lie worth telling, no need to overwhelm him. 'I'm fine, but—'

'Where are you? Where have you been?'

'In America. I've been in New York, since I left.'

'I'm coming there to get you,' he says immediately.

'No, no, don't do that. Do not do that. There is something I need— It's going to sound crazy, but please trust me and I'll explain everything when there's time. I need you to transfer a hundred thousand dollars into my bank account. Whatever the pound equivalent of that is. There's plenty of money in the trust.'

That trust, left for me by my mother, is under the supervision of solicitors until I turn twenty-five. A withdrawal of this size is sure to raise some red flags, but with my dad's say-so it can be done.

'A hundred thousand dollars,' he repeats. 'Is this a joke?'

'Do I sound like I'm joking?' Not the time to be snappy. I take a breath, press my lips together hard, and try again. 'I know this sounds like one of those internet scams where a relative calls you from abroad and begs for money. But you know that I'm responsible with money. I'm in some trouble, but everything is going to be fine, and I'll get the money back. I can't come home unless I pay it.'

Manipulative, this last part, I know it. Another long, almost endless pause follows.

'I will do this,' he says, finally, 'on two conditions. First of all, you tell me where the money is going and I'll pay it myself, no transferring it into your account. Secondly, I will book you a flight to London, and you will promise me that you'll get on that plane.'

I don't tell him that all I've ever wanted from him is this. Boundaries. Structure. Parenting.

'That seems fair.' And when I tell him where the money needs to be paid, assuring him in the same breath that I'm not under arrest, he has the immense restraint not to ask any more. He's always been willing to throw money at a problem, and maybe I take after him.

'Have you been drinking?' I ask him before I lose my nerve.

'No. No, I haven't touched a drop in—' He pauses, as though counting. 'Sixty-one days. And I'm sticking with it this time, darling. You were right.'

And I choose to believe him, I make the illogical leap of faith and force myself not to question it. Not now.

CHAPTER TWENTY-SEVEN

It takes two days for the money to be wired across the Atlantic, two days that I spend in constant motion: first walking the streets, later pacing the carpet of my hotel room, the TV on as background noise turned down to its lowest setting. I find the rhythms of it almost unbearable, the relentless aggression of voices, the way pundits and hosts and anchors talk over one another and through one another making me doubt whether I'll ever be able to hold a conversation in the world again. But this room is on a high floor, too high to hear the street noise, and silence is the most unbearable. In the silence, I begin to hear things I know aren't there, whispers that make me doubt myself.

I am back in Manhattan, because returning to the city was the only thing that made sense, but it feels nothing like I left it. Stepping off the bus at Port Authority, the dozen-times-a-day bus that I could have taken all along, I walked as though in a trance through the grid, trying to find my way to something familiar, hoping to end up back downtown. But finally I realized I had been walking in the wrong direction, when the streets opened out and the light seemed so much vaster than anywhere else in the city, and street signs confirmed I was now uptown. I checked into a room at the first hotel I came across, a faceless corporate chain near Central Park offering deep discounts for the off-season. My room is identikit, the sheets almost clinically white, the dimensions comedically too large for me and my scant possessions, and this was a bad choice. The sheer size of the room is overwhelming, so much that I have to pull the covers all the way over my head and wait for the two pills to kick in before I can fall asleep. And when I get there I realize that I'm back in Don's cabin and have never left, moonlight gleaming off the surface of the lake outside, and he is sitting across from me on the couch asking me a question I can't hear properly. I ask him to repeat it, because I know that it's important to keep him talking and keep him happy until I can get out of here, but his words still don't make any sense, and as he comes into focus through the darkness I realize that something is very wrong, his face a blank slate of skin with no features, eyes and mouth and nose all replaced by scar tissue. You never escaped.

I wake up paralysed, my voice stolen from me by sheer dread and it takes me several minutes to remember anything, or to recognize the room around me. Those three words linger in the air as if someone has really spoken them, clear as day: you never escaped. Just a dream, I tell myself, or maybe I really did say the words out loud. Maybe it's the first really honest thing I've said in days. I reach a hand out to the bedside table next to me, focusing on the physical solidity of it until morning comes, anchoring myself to the world, willing myself not to fall back into that dream. I walk for miles that day, all the way down to the lowest tip of Manhattan, across the Brooklyn Bridge and into Prospect Park, time and mileage a blur, and it occurs to me later that I remember almost nothing from that entire walk.

'The drugs you were on will have after-effects,' the doctor told me after my psych evaluation concluded. 'Fatigue, brain fog, maybe difficulty recalling words. Try not to worry too much. I'm going to prescribe you a mild sedative to help you sleep, ease any anxiety symptoms, until you're back to normal.'

At the time, I'd stared at him incredulously. The last thing I need is more sedatives. But now that unfilled prescription is a constant presence in my mind, hovering in my peripheral vision as I try to sleep. I am not back to normal.

On the morning of the third day, I wake up and take a detour to avoid the fluorescent thrum of Times Square, cutting through Hell's Kitchen back towards the bus station where I told him I would be waiting.

'A hundred thousand dollars?' he says, by way of greeting, and to my astonishment he's smiling, almost laughing, though he looks rumpled and pale and as tired as I feel. 'You just had this kind of money lying around? I'm a gold-digger and I don't even know it?'

'Believe me, I had to suffer for it,' I tell him, and I'm laughing too. 'That was not exactly the way I'd planned on making contact with my dad again.'

'Wait, you called your dad and told him you needed a hundred grand to bail your boyfriend out of jail?'

'Pretty much.'

'Damn.'

I'm aware that there was a time, not very long ago, when his use of the word 'boyfriend' would have undone me, and now I have to remind myself to notice. Everything that happened by the lake has deadened something inside me, maybe the part that craved, or the part that allowed me to feel fragile.

As we walk uptown through the park, warming our hands on cups of takeout coffee, he tells me that Ruth and Barb are out too, released on bail before he was.

'I'm pretty sure they'll just blame Don for everything, deny all knowledge. Claim he masterminded everything and they were just going along with it. They were already doing that in the car over to the station.'

'Is that... good for you? That's good, right? Scapegoating Don?'

'I don't know.'

'Jake, look, I've been thinking. It was self-defence. If I tell them the truth, they're not going to prosecute me – it's my word against his, and he doesn't get a word any more.'

'I'm not taking that chance. Don comes from a pretty powerful family. Old money, real estate moguls. That's why he got to leave the city quietly when he lost his licence instead of going to jail.'

I look away, trying not to think about Don. Trying not to think about him takes up more of my thoughts than anything else.

'This isn't me taking the fall for you,' Jake continues. 'This is me taking the fall for what I did.'

'When we first met, all I wanted was for you to save me. I didn't expect it to happen this way.'

'I've never saved you. Not one time. I did the opposite of save you. At least in my story, I get to ride in and be the hero.'

'That's really screwed up.'

'Yeah, well.' He shrugs, as if to say *that's me*. And I curl myself around him and press my lips to his jawline, pushing closer until finally he turns and kisses me, his warmth everything I remember. But it does feel like a memory, this kiss, not like a present reality, and I have to force myself to focus on the feeling of his skin, his hair under my fingers and his tongue against mine: be here, be here, be here. This may be the last time you see him.

'My dad booked me a plane ticket back to London.'

His arm tightens around my torso.

'When for?'

'Three days from now.'

'And I guess you have to go, now that he put up all that cash.'

'Yeah.' But this isn't why I'm going, and I don't want to pretend to him. 'I can't stay lost forever, is the thing. My only plan, coming here in the first place, was to get lost. And I got so much more lost than I thought was possible.'

He doesn't say anything. Looking at him feels like a countdown to something awful, like this entire evening has just been borrowed time, and for one insane second I want to tell him to come with me.

'It was a cult,' I say instead, breaking the silence. 'Where we were. That's the word for it. And you were there so much longer than I was. What they did to us, the drugs, the mind games, starving us, depriving us of sleep— I didn't see it, any of it, but no wonder we're messed up. It's not your fault, any more than mine.'

His body stiffens, everything suddenly rigid as though I've spooked him. And in that moment, I revise my mental inventory of things that I can say. I don't tell him that I think I saw Ruth in SoHo yesterday, gazing straight at me from the centre of a crowd on Broome Street as I turned a corner, her hair silver-white and almost gleaming in the cold November light, her eyes as black as I remember them from that first morning at the house. I don't tell him how my entire body jangled with dread as I turned back with a blink and Ruth was gone, nowhere to be seen, and I had spent the rest of the day trying to convince myself that of course I was imagining it, because the alternative was impossible. I don't tell him that there's a part of me that will never believe I'm safe.

'I keep thinking about the others,' I say instead, carefully. 'How I never got to… I mean, most of them were just kids. My age or a bit older, and some of them had been there since they were teenagers. They didn't stand a chance.'

I don't tell him about Mary, lost inside herself in that eternal cold room, and how easily I could have been her.

'What are they going to do now?' I push.

'Don't.'

'Jake— We should talk about this. I *need* to talk to someone about this.' My voice is unsteady. 'I feel like I'm going to lose my mind.'

'I can't. Talk about it.'

And he suddenly seems further away than I can comprehend.

CHAPTER TWENTY-EIGHT

Suspended in the air, enveloped in the white noise of the plane's engine as it settles into a rhythm at altitude, I'm remembering why I told Don this was the last place I felt safe. Limbo. Far enough from the ground that nothing matters.

I am not back to normal, whatever that means. Everything in the world seems slightly too loud, and standing in the concourse at JFK I came close to what must have been a panic attack, my lungs tightening like drawstrings as I tried to make sense of the departures board. Jake drove me to the airport, saw me off at the security line with a lingering hug like we were a loving couple parting ways before a business trip. But we have not recovered, in truth, since that moment I realized he was not going to provide me with the closure I needed. Understanding the past four months of my life is not a privilege to which I am entitled, and maybe that's the lesson I have to learn from Jake.

'Take care of yourself,' he whispered into my forehead, lips brushing against my temple just before he pulled back, and I nodded without speaking, knowing I would cry if I tried and not be able to stop. I've been crying more, lately, and for longer, and it's been harder to stop. But I didn't cry on him as we parted ways, at least not enough that he would notice, and I didn't tell him anything that I now regret.

I think I told him that I love him last night, but I had drunk a lot of cheap wine that wasn't mixing well with my mental state, and I can't be sure what I said once his hands were in my hair. Sleeping with him again last night of all nights, when I felt further from him than ever and every touch felt like an ending, was not the best decision I could have made. But it's not the worst decision I've made of late either, and though it might have started as desperate scrambling I wouldn't take back what it turned into, the way he consumed me so fully that for a few moments I knew perfect safety. I wouldn't take back a second with him, in the end, even the ones that may have ruined my life.

There is a risk that I will not be able to come back to the United States. I have overstayed my visa waiver, which Google tells me should be used for a maximum of three months, and it's unclear whether joining a cult is adequate grounds for leniency. This is one of many hurdles I need to confront, once I'm back on solid ground.

The flight is far from full, the two seats next to me empty, and now that I'm drifting in and out of sleep I am suddenly very aware of the plane's velocity, the sheer speed with which we're hurtling through the air. I've never feared flying, and though the possibility of a crash now feels larger and more detailed in my mind than it ever has before, I'm not on edge or even worried. Possibly this is the anti-anxiety pill kicking in because yes, of course I filled the prescription, was this ever truly in doubt? *Just in case*, I told myself as I stood in line at the pharmacy last night, because an American prescription will be useless back home and it's better to be safe than sorry, just keep them in your back pocket for a rainy day, why not? That rainy day came just a few hours later, after Jake had fallen asleep and I remained impossibly awake, eyes so bone-dry that my eyelids seemed to creak with every blink, trying to focus on my own breathing to drown out the whispers I know are not real. Will this ever stop?

I keep repeating to myself again and again the doctor's words as I left hospital, but the memory seems less and less solid every time I return to it, like a photograph exposed to the light too many times. Did he simply say *anxiety symptoms* were normal, or did he mention lingering hallucinations, paranoia, a sense of detachment from things? I should have told him about the fog, the strange episodes that Don called dissociative, because they pre-date everything else and I know I didn't mention them because I was too afraid to.

I don't feel as though I've been asleep, but the flight time passes in a bewildering rush, with the cabin lights dimmed and the blinds drawn low to eliminate any clues. My sense of time is not back to normal either, as becomes clear when the flight attendant taps me on the shoulder and pushes a breakfast box into my lap, offering tea or coffee, telling the passenger across the aisle that we'll be landing in forty-five minutes.

Walking through the automatic doors that swing outwards like a flourish onto the arrivals concourse, I realize I have never been met at the airport before, have never looked out for an eager face in the crowd as I emerge. I can't see my dad, though I'm trying hard to pick him out amidst the anxious mothers and the suited men holding up iPads with surnames on them. It's been days since we spoke to confirm my flight number and arrival time, and now it strikes me that he may not show up at all, may have drunk himself into a sleep so deep that he missed his alarm. This has happened before, many times, most memorably after a school trip when I sat and watched everyone else's parents appear one after another, until finally a substitute teacher gently suggested that she call home for me. Humiliating, more than anything else.

He is here, though, standing stiffly at the very end of the barrier, and he seems as startled by my appearance as I am by his.

'Darling,' he says quietly, and doesn't hug me because this is not something he has ever done. I kiss him on the cheek and he squeezes my arm as I draw back, taking the rucksack from my shoulder and asking me how my flight was.

'It was fine. Went quite quickly.'

As we sit across from each other a few minutes later in Costa Coffee, he seems suffocated by the weight of all the things he wants to ask me, though maybe this is me projecting. He looks so much older and thinner, his eyes too large for his head, and I pretend not to notice his hand shaking as he stirs too much sugar into his coffee.

'I tried to ring you,' he says, 'on your mobile. Just rang and rang. I thought maybe you'd left it behind.'

'I lost it.' Close enough to true.

'Thought you might have. I bought you a replacement one, just in case you need it. Kept the receipt, because I wasn't sure what sort you'd want.'

I don't know what to say. He's always found it easiest to show affection through things, spending money effortlessly while keeping his emotional costs consistently low. But for him to have thought deeply enough about my return to realize that I might need a phone, to have tried to decide what model of phone I would like, this feels new.

'Thank you. That's... yeah, I'll definitely need a phone.'

'What happened to you?' he asks then, finally.

'Nothing. I mean... it's going to take a while before I can explain it. But I'm fine.'

'Are you in trouble with the law?'

'No.' I pause, taking a long sip of my extra-shot Americano, though it's still really too hot to drink. 'But I might have to go back to New York, to testify in a trial. I met someone, and he took me somewhere that was... not a good place. And I didn't know that until it was too late.' I'm suddenly very conscious of my own hammering heartbeat, a strange rushing sensation rising in my eardrums. 'Can we not talk about it now?'

And the thought occurs that maybe he doesn't really want to know where I was, because he knows the answer is more than he can contain. I know for a fact that he doesn't want to have the conversation about why I left, doesn't want to revisit our last meeting any more than I do.

'Your room is still the same,' he says eventually. 'I haven't touched it. I wasn't sure what your plans were, but if you want...'

I'm not sure either. Coming back to England has been such an abstract, surreal concept in my head for so long that I never stopped for a second to consider where I would live when I was back. What were my plans, before I left?

'You said you might get a flat with Sophie,' he prompts. 'Before.'

'Yeah.' That's right. It comes back to me when he says it, the perfect ripeness of the spring air that afternoon we'd walked along the South Bank all the way from Waterloo to North Greenwich, Sophie's arm in mine, and how clear it was to us both that we would live together, start our post-university lives together. I can barely remember her voice.

'I'll stay for a while, if that's okay,' I say. 'At home. Until I get my bearings.'

In truth, the idea of returning to my childhood bedroom and the silent tree-lined street outside makes me twitch. I need to be central. Rent a room somewhere that's never deserted, somewhere with crowded streets to walk and noise to fall asleep to and more noise to pull me out of my worst dreams. I intend to bury myself in the city, wrap myself up in its thrum and noise and humanity, enclosed on every side so that I will always be safe.

'How are you, though?' I ask him, trying not to let my gaze linger on his still-unsteady hand. 'Really.'

'Don't worry about me. You should just look after yourself, for now.'

And I almost laugh, because if only he knew how easily I put myself first. How easily I left them all behind, in the end.

'We are here for each other, and we are nothing without each other.'

'What's that?'

I don't explain. I couldn't, even if I wanted to.